A NEW DAY

A NEW DAY

Beryl Matthews

This first world edition published 2012
in Great Britain and in the USA by
SEVERN HOUSE PUBLISHERS LTD of
9–15 High Street, Sutton, Surrey, England, SM1 1DF.
Trade paperback edition first published
in Great Britain and the USA 2012 by
SEVERN HOUSE PUBLISHERS LTD

British Library Cataloguing in Publication Data

Matthews, Beryl.
  A new day.
  1. Brothers and sisters–Fiction. 2. Orphans–Fiction.
  I. Title
  823.9'2–dc23

ISBN-13: 978-0-7278-8182-3 (cased)
ISBN-13: 978-1-84751-436-3 (trade paper)

All Severn House titles are printed on acid-free paper.

Severn House Publishers support The Forest Stewardship Council [FSC],
the leading international forest certification organisation. All our titles that
are printed on Greenpeace-approved FSC-certified paper carry the FSC logo.

MIX
Paper from
responsible sources
FSC
www.fsc.org FSC® C018575

Typeset by Palimpsest Book Production Ltd.,
Falkirk, Stirlingshire, Scotland.
Printed and bound in Great Britain by
MPG Books Ltd., Bodmin, Cornwall.

One

Lambeth, London, 1938

'I didn't know what to do!' Jack Foster's head was bowed, looking at the papers he was clutching tightly in his hands, and when his head came up, his cut lip and bruised eye made Hanna wince. 'I don't want to leave you, but if I stay I could do something terrible to that man.'

Stooping down she gripped her young brother's arms. 'I'll be all right, Jack. You're fifteen now and old enough to make your own decisions. You must think of yourself and leave. I'll do anything to support you, so tell me again what you've planned.'

Hope flared in his dark brown eyes. 'Well, Talbot's gone out and won't be back until this afternoon, so when his wife sent me on an errand I jumped on a bus and went to the docks. You know how I like to watch the ships coming and going. I saw this notice pinned on the gates advertising for crew in a hurry. They are sailing tomorrow and were short handed. I didn't even think about it, I just walked into the office and volunteered. I told them I was eighteen, and they believed me when I said I didn't have a birth certificate because I was an orphan. They said they needed a deck apprentice and I could have the job. I agreed to join the ship, and I signed the papers there and then. I know I should have talked it over with you first, but I was desperate, and it's something I always wanted to do. I had to make my mind up in a hurry or I would have missed the chance.' He gazed at her anxiously. 'Are you angry with me, Hanna?'

'Of course not.' She smiled although her heart was aching. 'You have to get away from that man, and you're doing the right thing. And I guess from those papers you are mangling in your hands that they're the ones you signed.'

'Er . . . yes.' He held them out to her. 'You keep these safe for me, Hanna. I don't want that brute to find them.'

She took them from him and popped them in her bag. This was so sudden and it was going to be painful to see him sail away, but it had to be done – for his sake. She had only been eight when their parents had died in a train accident. With no other family to take them in they had been put in the orphanage. Jack had been terrified, and she had looked after her five-year-old brother, refusing to let them be separated. No one had wanted to take the two of them so they had remained in the orphanage, but as the years slipped by it worried her in case she had deprived Jack of finding a real home and a family to love him. Then a year ago a couple had wanted Jack, and after discussing it with him, he had decided to go with them. What a mistake that had been! The man had only wanted a strong lad to help him with his greengrocer's business. Jack was worked from dawn to dusk and thrashed often. Now the Talbots were talking about legally adopting him and he had to get away. All of her efforts, letters to those in authority and complaints had been ignored. She had seriously considered them running away together, but where would they go? They had no friends, nowhere to go and no money. They would have ended up on the streets, and that was far too dangerous. There had to be another way, but she just hadn't been able to find one. Now her young brother had settled that question.

Jack still looked worried. 'I'm leaving you with an awful mess to clear up. When I've gone that brute will come looking for me. He'll hurt you, Hanna.'

'No, he won't, because I won't be here. I've only stayed at the orphanage to be near you, but I'm just a skivvy, doing all the rotten jobs. I'll get myself a job and save hard so I can make a home for the both of us. When you sail back into port there will be somewhere for you to come back to.'

'Oh, it would be lovely to have a place of our own, and if anyone can do it, you can,' he told her confidently, more relaxed now he had his sister's support. 'And I'll save some of my pay to help.'

'Don't you worry about that. When you go to other countries you'll want to have fun. You enjoy yourself. Promise?'

'All right.' He smiled as much as his sore lip would allow. 'What kind of a job are you going to get?'

'I'll have to go into service first. That will give me food and a roof over my head. In fact, I've already been offered something. A group of people came to look round the orphanage last week and one of them said she needed to employ a girl to help with her children. She asked if I would consider taking the job, but I wasn't sure, and she gave me a couple of weeks to think it over.'

'You must take it!' Jack was on his feet, brimming with excitement. 'Why didn't you tell me?'

'It would have meant moving away, and you know I wouldn't go too far from you when you need help so much. They live in Kensington.' She shook her head sadly. 'I feel so guilty about not trying to persuade you to refuse the Talbots, but I felt you were now old enough to make your own decisions. I'm so sorry, Jack.'

'Hanna, you haven't got anything to be sorry about. I made up my own mind, and it was the wrong thing to do, we can see that now, and I know how hard you've worked to try and get me away from them. You've always put me first, and I love you for that, but it's time you got out of here. You're good at looking after kids. That's why this place hasn't let you go although you're eighteen now. Go and see this lady today and tell her you'll take the job. Please! If I know you're away from here I won't worry quite so much.'

'I'll go this afternoon. What time do you have to be at the ship tomorrow?'

'I've got to be there by six o'clock in the morning, so I'll have to creep out around four o'clock, while he's getting the van ready to go to market. I've been told that if we can get to the main road by four thirty there's a lorry coming around that time who picks up any who need to get to the docks early.'

'We must make sure we catch that then, Jack. I'll wait for you at the end of the road then, but don't pack a bag. Put your clothes on in layers and shove anything else into your pockets. But you must only walk out of that house with the things you went there with, and then he won't be able to accuse you of stealing. It would be easy to make a mistake, so be careful, Jack.'

'I won't even take a pair of socks they gave me. Don't worry; I don't want anything from them. I'll be very careful.'

'We'll go to the docks together and I'll stay there until your ship is safely at sea. If anyone comes and tries to stop you then I'll fight them off!' They grinned at each other as she hid her tears, determined to stay bright and positive. This was a big decision for him and he needed her support.

'Thanks.' He clasped her hand, his eyes shining with love and amusement. 'I know no one will get near me with you there on guard. But seriously, Hanna, I'll only be able to go with an easy mind if I know you're leaving that place as well. Promise me you'll go and see about that job today.'

'I promise.' She managed a smile. 'Now, you had better get back before Mr Talbot gets suspicious.'

She watched him hurry away, so proud of him. He had grown into a fine boy, tall, strong and courageous. He was determined to make a better life for himself, and she must do the same.

She spent the next two hours at the beck and call of everyone, as it had been for years, but not for much longer. Once Jack had sailed away then she would have to get away from here, so she was determined to make this her last day in this place. The realization that she would soon be leaving the orphanage filled her with excitement, happy not only for herself but for her brother as well. They were finally going to take charge of their own lives. The address of the lady she was going to see was in her pocket and she touched it, making sure it was still safe. She would go there this afternoon in her free time.

The house was nearly as big as the orphanage, but there the similarity ended. The orphanage had a grim neglected look about it, but this was beautiful! Oh, she hoped Mrs Harcourt still needed a nanny. What if she had found someone else already? Suppose she wasn't at home?

Pushing the doubts aside she hurried up the long driveway, her heart beating uncomfortably. So much depended on this job. She wanted Jack to be able to leave knowing she was settled in a good post. As soon as she reached the front door she knocked firmly, composing herself. She must look calm and competent.

The door opened almost immediately by a maid in a pristine uniform. 'Mrs Harcourt asked me to call,' she said quickly. 'My name is Hanna Foster.'

'Come in, Miss Foster. I'll tell Mrs Harcourt you're here.' The maid gave her a friendly smile and ushered her into a small side room. 'Wait here, please.'

There had been many disappointments and heartaches in Hanna's life so she had learnt not to take things for granted. It had made her strong and able to bend like a willow in a storm. If this position was no longer available then Mrs Harcourt might be able to tell her of another one. She would ask.

The maid was soon back, still smiling. 'This way please. Good luck,' she whispered as she opened a door for Hanna.

Smiling her thanks she stepped into a lovely sitting room, the beauty of it nearly taking her breath away. This was how she had always imagined a family home would be like. The decor was in pale apricot, giving a glowing warmth to the room, tidy, but not too tidy. Daily newspapers were thrown on to a small side table, books on one of the chairs, and a toy train sticking out from behind the long window curtains. So one of the children was a boy.

'Thank you for coming, Miss Foster.'

She turned her attention to Mrs Harcourt, returning the lady's smile. She spoke clearly. 'You told me you needed a nanny, Mrs Harcourt, and if the position is still available I would like to be considered.'

'I do still need a nanny.' She gave a wry smile. 'I have interviewed many girls, but did not feel that any could cope with my boys, until I saw you handling all those children with such ease and kindness. Sit down and we will have tea while we talk.'

Surprised at being offered tea, Hanna sat in the nearest chair, sinking into its comfort. In these lovely surroundings she was very aware that her clothes were shabby, but they were clean and well pressed.

Mrs Harcourt rang a bell and ordered refreshments, then turned her full attention to Hanna. 'We talked a little when we met, but I had the impression that you didn't like to say too much. Am I right?'

'Yes, Mrs Harcourt.'

'I understand. Would you tell me about yourself now, and how you came to be at the orphanage?'

The tea arrived, and when they were alone again, Hanna talked freely about what had happened to her and Jack and how determined they were now to make a new life for themselves. There wasn't the slightest hint of self-pity as she talked, and the only emotion she showed was when she told Mrs Harcourt about the treatment her brother was receiving.

She sipped her tea to compose herself, and then looked up. 'You see, Mrs Harcourt, I've looked after my brother since he was five years old, and all the time we were in the orphanage I could protect him, but now he is with these people,' she couldn't bear to say their name, 'and I have been unable to watch over him. But he's a sensible and brave boy and has joined the Merchant Navy. Now I can move away and make a home for us so he'll have somewhere to stay when he comes back from a voyage.'

'I understand, and if you agree to come and work for us I will expect you to have a room in the house, but there is an annex for the servants and your brother can stay there when he is home.'

'Oh, that is kind of you!' Relief showed in her smile. 'We will pay for the room, of course.'

'You will not,' Jane Harcourt told her firmly, and then laughed. 'You will take it as a reward for looking after the boys. So, are you going to take on the task?'

'I'd like that very much.'

'Thank you, Hanna, that's a brave decision without even seeing them.' Her smile was full of amusement. 'When can you start?'

'Tomorrow afternoon. Jack's ship sails early in the morning, then I can come straight here.'

'Don't you have to give the orphanage some notice?'

'No, they have never formally employed me. I've only stayed on to be near my brother. For the work I do I get a room, food and two shillings a week. I am on call day and night.'

'That is outrageous! They have been taking advantage of you.'

'I know, but I had no choice, Mrs Harcourt, and it suited

me to stay there. It became even more important when that brute of a man pretended that he and his wife wanted an older boy instead of a baby. I was suspicious then, but the orphanage seemed satisfied and I didn't want to deny Jack the chance to have a proper family. It soon became clear that he only wanted a strong boy to work as a slave and vent his violent streak on. No wonder his wife is a timid woman, afraid to open her mouth.'

Hanna's eyes misted with tears. It hurt to talk about it, but Mrs Harcourt should have the complete story. She lifted her head again. 'But Jack's had the courage to do something about it, and I'm so proud of him.'

'You are both strong and brave, and we will be delighted to have you care for our boys.' Jane Harcourt tipped her head to one side and listened to the sound of excited voices. 'Ah, here they come.'

The door opened and two children erupted into the room, rushing over to their mother, both talking at the same time about the deer they had seen in Richmond Park. They were about three years old, Hanna guessed, fair hair tousled from the wind, and faces flushed with excitement.

'Children!' Their mother laughed. 'You can tell me later. There's someone here for you to meet.'

Their heads turned and Hanna was looking into two pairs of the bluest eyes she had ever seen, and it wasn't only their eyes that were identical. She gasped and her smile spread in delight. Twins!

A deep laugh came from the doorway and she looked at the tall man standing just inside the room. There was no doubt that he was their father. He had an air of authority about him and she got to her feet.

'They come as quite a shock when you first see them.'

'Yes, sir.'

'Darling, this is the young girl I told you about, Hanna Foster, and she has agreed to be the boys' nanny.'

'Splendid.' He strode over and shook her hand. 'My wife needs your help as I'm away quite a lot. Please sit down.'

While the introduction had been going on the boys had edged closer to her, and one of them said proudly, 'Our father is captain of a big ship, and we've been on it.'

'How exciting!' She couldn't take her eyes off the twins, gazing from one to the other, looking for any physical difference. She couldn't find anything, but she was already in love with them. 'My brother is sailing on a ship tomorrow morning.'

'Have you seen it?'

'Not yet, but in the morning I will watch it until it's out of sight.' She smiled as they stepped closer, interested in what she was saying. These were happy, secure children, not poor frightened ones needing comfort.

'Our father drives a battleship with lots of guns. Do you know what your brother's ship is like?'

'It will be quite different.' She glanced at Captain Harcourt. 'Royal Navy, sir?' And when he nodded she began to explain the difference between the two services. The boys listened with rapt attention until she had finished.

'Thank you,' they both said together, and then ran back to their mother, wanting to tell her about the things Hanna had told them.

She glanced up and saw Captain Harcourt studying her intently. 'Is your brother the only family you have?'

'Yes, sir.'

'You are going to miss him, but he can make a good life for himself if he is willing to work hard.'

She nodded. 'It's the first time we have been parted, but Jack will be free. He isn't afraid of hard work and loves ships. We've spent hours at the docks watching them sail in and out.' Her smile spread as she remembered. 'When he was little he was always begging me to take him to see the boats.'

'He's younger than you, then.'

'A little, sir,' she said cautiously, not wanting to give away Jack's age.

The man sitting opposite her wasn't fooled, and said gently, 'Don't worry, I ran away to sea when I was only fifteen, and as soon as I was old enough I joined the Royal Navy. I fully understand your brother's desire to go to sea.'

'I'm sure you do, sir,' she replied with relief.

He stood up. 'Do you boys want to help me pack my bag?' When the twins yelped with delight and ran to his side, he said, 'Say goodbye to Hanna and thank her for agreeing to come and look after you.'

Two heads swivelled round and when their gorgeous eyes fixed on her she couldn't help smiling. Now they appeared to be violet, not blue. How extraordinary.

'Thank you,' they said in unison. 'When are you coming to live with us?'

'Tomorrow afternoon.'

One of the boys stepped closer. 'That's good because our father is going back to his ship in the morning so we'll all be feeling sad.'

'My brother is leaving then as well, so we'll be able to cheer each other up.'

They nodded, smiling again, and she was surprised when the one who had spoken reached out and touched her hand.

'Do you know lots of stories?' he asked.

'Hundreds.' She tipped her head to one side, studying them for a moment. 'I expect you like stories of knights on brave adventures.'

'Yes, yes!' Their faces were glowing now in anticipation of all the tales they were going to hear.

'Come on, boys, you can talk to Hanna tomorrow.'

Rushing over to their father they left the room, their excited chatter fading as they climbed the stairs.

There was silence for a few moments before Hanna asked Mrs Harcourt, 'How do you tell them apart?'

'Physically it's almost impossible, but their personalities are different. Andrew is the quieter of the two, more thoughtful and shows his emotions. He's the one who came close to you just now. David is always on the go, wanting to see and do everything. He will plague you with requests for adventure, and –' she smiled wryly – 'you won't get any hugs from him when they get to know you.'

'It sounds as if David has his father's sense of adventure.'

'That is so, but it seems as if my husband's character has been shared by the two boys – one all action, the other kind and loving. Andrew tries to keep his brother in check. They are a handful, Hanna, but when I saw you with the children at the orphanage I was sure you would be able to handle them.

And from what I've seen so far I believe I was right. The boys have already taken to you.'

'I will love looking after them, Mrs Harcourt, and thank you for offering me the job. It has come at just the right time.' She stood up. 'If you will excuse me, please, I must get back.'

'Of course.' Jane Harcourt stood as well, her expression serious. 'If you have any trouble leaving the orphanage so soon, then tell them to contact me.'

'Thank you, I'll do that.'

Hanna hardly remembered the journey back to Lambeth; her mind was in a whirl with everything she had to do. The first stop was at the greengrocer's shop to see Jack. She was selecting apples from a box outside when her brother came out of the shop. He handed her a paper bag, and as she put the choice pieces of fruit in the bag, she whispered, 'I've got the job, Jack, and I start tomorrow afternoon.'

'Wonderful!' He sighed with relief.

'What you doing here?'

'Buying some of your beautiful apples, Mr Talbot,' she said politely, not wanting to do anything to raise this man's suspicions. 'You've got the best ones I've seen, and I thought I'd give the youngest children at the orphanage a treat.'

'Humph, well don't stand here gossiping. Jack ain't got time to waste. Weigh them for her and then get back to shifting those crates. And you make sure you charge her full price.'

'Yes, sir.' Jack put them on the scales with his hand underneath so they wouldn't register properly, then he took one coin from Hanna. He stepped close and whispered in her ear. 'The mean old devil; these are only a penny to you. See you tomorrow, like we said.'

'Tomorrow,' she replied, putting the rest of her money back in her pocket. She needed every bit she could scrape together to give Jack in the morning.

Two

Although it was the beginning of July, Hanna shivered as she waited at the end of the road for Jack in the early hours of the morning. She had managed to slip out of the orphanage without anyone noticing, but would her brother be able to get away unseen? He had to! She would give him a little longer, and if he didn't come she would darn well go and get him. Nothing must stop him. This was his chance for a new life, a chance to do something he had always dreamed about, and she was damned if that brute of a man was going to stop him.

A movement further down the road caught her attention, and she watched anxiously. When she could make out the figure of her brother, she nearly cried out with relief. Without a word he grabbed her arm and they ran as fast as they could, not stopping until they were well away from the Talbot shop.

'I was afraid you weren't going to get away,' she gasped.

'It wasn't easy. I felt as if he was watching my every move this morning, but I wasn't going to let anything or anyone stop me.' They had reached the main road to the docks, and Jack was looking anxiously around.

'I hope we haven't missed that lorry,' she said.

'A man told me he comes every day without fail.' Jack put his head to one side, listening, and stepped into the road, waving to catch the driver's attention. 'Ah, this could be him.'

'If you're going to the docks then hop in,' the man said as he pulled up.

They settled in the back of the truck, and by the time they reached the docks he had picked up about a dozen men. Hanna was glad to get out because she had been teased all the way, and it had been a new experience for her. They thought it highly amusing that a girl should be sharing their lift to the docks.

When they reached the ship Jack was going to sail on he

stood gazing at it, a smile on his face. 'She's a general cargo ship. Isn't she beautiful! *North Star*, she's called.'

Hanna thought she was big and ugly, but she agreed with her brother, not wanting to spoil his excitement. This was a huge step for him to take, and her heart beat with pride for the courage he was showing. She was determined to be just as brave, even though her heart was aching at the thought of saying goodbye to him for a while. They had never been apart in their lives before.

'Hello, I saw you in the office yesterday, didn't I? You're Jack Foster, aren't you?'

'Yes, sir,' he said to the man who had approached them.

'You don't need to call me sir. Frank's my name and I'm the cook.' He gave Hanna a curious look. 'And who is this? Your girl?'

'No,' Jack laughed. 'This is my sister, Hanna. She's come to see me off.'

'Pleased to meet you, Hanna. Don't you worry about Jack, because we'll take good care of him.'

'Thank you.' She returned his smile.

'We'd better get on board, Jack. Say goodbye to your sister. We're on our way to New Zealand, but we'll be back in time for Christmas.'

Jack hugged her, suddenly looking apprehensive and a little tearful now the moment of parting had arrived.

'Write when you can – and good luck.' It was a struggle to keep her own tears at bay, but she managed it. 'Have a good, safe voyage, and when you get back we'll make it the best darned Christmas we've ever had.'

While they had been standing on the dock the sky had begun to brighten as the sun peeped over the horizon. 'Look, Jack, a new day.'

He nodded. 'A new day, and a new beginning for both of us.'

Without another word he turned and walked away with Frank. She watched as he boarded the ship, and then settled herself on an old crate to wait for them to sail.

It was two hours before the ship began to move away and she scanned the rail hoping to see Jack and give him a last wave, but there was no sign of him. She didn't turn away until the ship was almost out of sight, and only then did she make her way back to the orphanage. Jack was safely away from Talbot, and now it was time to cut her ties with the orphanage and begin her new life.

A voice she knew only too well could be clearly heard when she walked in the door. Talbot was demanding to know where Jack was. Knowing this moment had to be faced, she braced herself and walked into the office.

Talbot spun round to face her, his face bright red with anger. 'Where is he?'

'Somewhere you can't get at him.' She had no intention of telling him where Jack really was.

'You'll tell me where he is, girl!'

She didn't flinch or move away when he came close to her, even though his hands were clenched into fists. She knew he wanted to beat the information out of her, but if he did she would lash out as well. It didn't matter now. Jack was out of his way, and she would be as well soon. 'No! You'll never find him.'

'He's mine and you'll bloody well tell me where you've hidden him!' He gripped her shoulders painfully and shook her.

'Take your hands off me! You're a bully. Are you really surprised that my brother wanted to get away from you?'

When his fingers bit into her thin shoulders she turned her head and looked at the woman who was in charge of the orphanage. 'Call the police, Mrs Buxton, this man is attacking me.'

'There's no need for that,' he snarled, stepping away from her and looking at Mrs Buxton. 'You order this girl to tell me where the boy is. He can't run away because we've adopted him. He's mine and I want him back!'

'You haven't legally adopted him yet and he has every right to leave if he wants to.'

'Hanna, you must tell us where Jack is. He's too young to be out on his own, and he might not be safe.' Mrs Buxton looked flustered.

'He isn't on his own, and he is safer than he was with Mr Talbot.'

'I can't force Hanna to tell us where he is, Mr Talbot. I'm so sorry.'

'You haven't heard the last of this, Mrs Buxton. If he doesn't come back then you will owe me!' he stated with menace. He stormed out and slammed the door with such force that the old building almost rocked on its foundations.

Taking a deep breath Hanna faced the woman she had always considered quite incompetent to be in charge of so many vulnerable children. 'How could you have let that odious man keep my brother? I told you time and time again that he was beating Jack, but you did nothing. You're not fit to be in charge of children, and I'm going to do my best to see that you are removed from this job!'

That brought a reaction. 'Who do you think you're talking to? Where is your brother?'

'None of your business! And as soon as I've collected my bag I'm leaving as well. You won't see either of us again.'

How Hanna climbed the stairs to her room she didn't know. Her legs were shaking and her shoulders hurt where Talbot had gripped her, but she wouldn't show any sign of weakness because Mrs Buxton was following her. Her bag was already packed, and she picked it up.

'Where do you think you're going?' the woman demanded. 'You are both being very foolish. If you think you can survive on your own then you are mistaken. You are only used to the institution, and will not be able to cope outside. That is why we persuaded you to let your brother go to Mr and Mrs Talbot.'

'Yes, I did agree, thinking it would be right for my brother, but it was a terrible mistake. At least while he was here I could protect him, but there was little I could do to stop him being thrashed while he was in their house.' She glared at the woman in charge. 'And you did nothing!'

'It was out of my hands. Jack made no effort to fit in with the Talbots.'

'What absolute rubbish! No one would fit in with them. Talbot is a bully and a coward! You could have reported him and had Jack taken from him, but that was too much trouble for you, wasn't it? Get out of my way.'

'You won't last long. You'll soon be back begging me to take you in again.'

Shaking her head in disbelief, Hanna stormed out and walked quickly towards the bus stop. That wasn't the way she had intended to leave. A polite, dignified exit had been planned, but there hadn't been anything dignified about her outburst. She had always held her tongue in an effort to protect both of them from any unpleasantness, but that was no longer neces- sary, and her anger had spilled out. Well, that couldn't be helped now. What was done was done, and couldn't be changed. The past was behind them and they had a future to build.

The twins rushed to meet her as soon as she arrived at the house. 'Did you see your brother's ship?' they asked.

'Yes. And I watched it sail out to sea. The sun was shining on the water, and it was a beautiful sight.'

'Father has gone, as well, and mother is visiting Grandma. She'll be back soon, and she told us to look after you.'

Hanna studied the children, but could not tell them apart yet. She looked at the maid. 'Do you know who is David and who is Andrew?'

'No idea,' she laughed. 'Every time I think I've worked it out they play little tricks, and I'm confused again. They enjoy fooling people. It's a huge joke to them.'

The twins were grinning.

'Oh, I'll sort you two out in no time,' she teased.

They thought that was very funny, obviously sure she didn't have a chance, and the two girls joined in with the laughter.

'I'm Mary, by the way,' the maid told her. 'And I'm very glad you're here. Come on, boys, let's show Hanna her room.'

'You're next to us.' Andrew and David spoke together.

'You'll get used to that,' Mary explained as they climbed the stairs. 'They seem to know what the other is thinking and often say the same thing at the same time. But it's when they're talking to each other you will have trouble. None of us can understand a word they say then. They seem to have a language of their own. Here we are.' She threw open a door. 'This is yours.'

When Hanna walked into the room she couldn't believe her

eyes. It was huge, and very beautiful. The decor of cream and pale pink took her breath away. 'This can't be right, Mary?'

'This is your room.' One of the boys caught hold of her hand and pulled her towards a door, while the other twin opened it. 'We're in here. You're next to us in case we need anything in the night.'

'But we never do,' the other one told her. 'Or not often. We're very good.'

'I'm sure you are, but I won't mind you calling me in the night if you need to.'

The boys gave each other a knowing glance.

'Now they've got you where they want you,' Mary whispered in her ear, trying not to laugh out loud.

The rest of the day flew by. Mrs Harcourt arrived home at four o'clock, and insisted that they all have afternoon tea together. By the time the twins were fast asleep, Hanna was drained. It had been an emotional day and she was relieved to climb into her own bed, sinking into the luxurious comfort.

Tired as she was, sleep didn't come at once. This was the first quiet moment she had had to herself, and her thoughts naturally turned to her brother. He would be well out to sea now, and she prayed that he was going to be all right on the ship. That man, Frank, had seemed nice enough, and she hoped he meant it when he'd said they would keep an eye on Jack for her.

For ten years she had looked after him, protected and worried about him. Now he was on his own in a man's world. She didn't try to stop the tears flowing, knowing she was going to miss him so much. It had been hard to let him go, but it had been the right thing to do.

'Be happy, Jack,' she murmured as she fell into an exhausted sleep.

Three

'Whoops!' Jack slid along as the ship pitched, landing on his backside. Strong hands lifted him up, and he grinned at the sailor, wondering how he was managing to stay on his feet without holding on to anything. 'Thanks. I've been told to get some grub. But that's easier said than done. How do you stay upright?'

'You'll get the hang of it. Come and walk with me and I'll give you a few tips.'

At that moment the floor fell away from under his feet and Jack was saved from falling again. He burst out laughing, finding the whole thing hilarious. 'I certainly need some tips.'

The sailor grinned at him while holding him steady. 'What's your name, lad?'

'Jack.'

'Welcome aboard, Jack. I'm Bill. Do you feel all right?'

'I'm skidding about all over the place and keep getting lost, but apart from that I'm all right. This ship is like a maze.'

Bill nodded and took a firm grip of Jack's arm. 'You'll soon find out where everything is. Let's get some food.'

The mess was nearly empty when they arrived. There were only two men sitting at the table clutching mugs of steaming tea and looking very sorry for themselves.

'I hope you two want something to eat,' Frank, the cook, said.

'What you got?' Bill asked, sitting Jack on a seat. 'Stay there, lad, I'll get your food.'

'You've got pie and mash,' Frank told them. 'And you're lucky to get that in this weather.'

'Lovely.' Jack rubbed his hands together in anticipation. 'I'm starving.'

The two sailors already at the table looked at him in disbelief, and one groaned before saying, 'Not another one with a cast-iron stomach?'

Bill put a plate of food in front of Jack. 'Hold on to that or it'll end up in your lap.'

'Thanks, I'm ravenous. Must be the sea air.'

Frank burst into laughter. 'I knew he was a born sailor the moment I set eyes on him.'

The other two men dragged themselves to their feet and staggered out of the mess. Then Frank joined them at the table with his own plate of food.

'Smashing pie,' Jack said, tackling his food with gusto.

'You can have as much as you like. I'm not going to get many customers tonight.'

'Why?' Jack asked. 'This pie is the best I've ever tasted.'

'Quite a few of them won't start eating until we're through the Bay of Biscay, then they won't feel sick any more.'

'I didn't think sailors got sick.'

Bill chuckled. 'Some throw up every time they set sail, and bad weather lays out a few more. Admiral Nelson suffered with sea sickness all the time.'

'Did he? Gosh, I didn't know that.'

'Looks as if you're going to be like the two of us. The motion of the ship never bothers us.' Frank picked up Jack's empty plate. 'Manage another helping?'

'Yes, please, Frank. I haven't had anything to eat since break-fast, and that was a long time ago.'

'I'll have some too.' Bill held out his plate. 'Shame to let it go to waste. How's the tea pot?'

'Been standing around a bit, so I'll make us a fresh pot.'

'What made you join the merchant navy?' Bill asked, while they waited for their second helpings.

'I've always watched the ships and wanted to sail in them.'

'Your sister's a pretty girl. Has she got a boyfriend?' Frank asked as he served them the food and tea.

'No.' Jack shook his head. 'She's never had time to enjoy herself. We were sent to the orphanage when I was five, and she looked after me, refusing to let us be separated.'

'She sounds like a good person.'

'Oh, she is, Bill. I don't know what would have happened to me if she hadn't protected me. Now I'm going to be a sailor she can think of herself for a change. She's got a nice job to go to today. This is a new day for both of us.'

'You're glad to be getting away from the orphanage, then?'

'Very!' Jack finished his tea and waited while Frank refilled his mug. 'Er . . . I know we're heading for New Zealand and this is going to be a long voyage, but do you know the other places we'll be going to? I didn't ask when I signed on.'

Bill gave him a studied look. 'You were that desperate to get away from whoever was beating you? The bruises still show.'

Grimacing, Jack merely nodded.

Not probing any further, Bill changed the subject. 'We'll be going through the Suez Canal, on to India, Ceylon and Singapore.'

Jack gasped. 'I've only ever seen those places on a map. Have you been to New Zealand before?'

'We've been there a few times, and it's a beautiful country. We usually have a couple of days' leave when we arrive, so we'll show you around.'

'Will you?' Jack couldn't hide his excitement. 'I've never been outside of London before. I must write to Hanna. Is there some way to send letters back home?'

'We'll be able to collect our post from the Port Agent when we stop, and we can post letters then.' Bill stood up. 'I'm on watch in twenty minutes, and you must get some sleep, lad. It will be a busy day tomorrow. Come on, I'll see you safely to your bunk.'

Jack stood up with the help of the experienced sailor, still holding on to the table that was screwed to the floor. At that moment the ship dipped and then rolled from side to side, and if it hadn't been for the two sailors he would have been the other side of the mess on his backside again.

'Don't fight the motion of the ship,' Bill advised. 'Widen your stance and go with the roll.'

Concentrating hard, Jack let go of the table and took a couple of cautious steps. He grinned for a moment and then yelped as the ship gave a huge lurch, and Bill stopped him again from crashing into the bulkhead. Laughing, he straightened up and insisted on trying to stand on his own. He planted his feet wide apart as Bill had told him, and managed to stand unaided, albeit with difficulty.

Nodding his approval, Bill slapped him on the back. 'We'll make a sailor of you in no time at all, lad. Come on, time you had some sleep.'

It was only when Jack climbed into his bunk that he realized just how tired he was. The day had been long, but very
exciting, and the men were friendly. There appeared to be a
comradeship between them, and he had been quickly included.
Bill was a leading seaman with twenty years' service, and Jack
knew he couldn't ask for a better man to give him advice.
There was so much to learn, and he couldn't wait to tell Hanna
all about it, but writing a letter tonight was out of the question. The ship was pitching and rolling too much. He'd start
a letter as soon as he could and have it ready to post at the
first port of call.

'Hope your day has been as good as mine, Hanna,' he
murmured, before falling into a deep sleep.

'Jack! Wake up, lad.'

'What?' He shot up, banging his head on the bunk above
him, wondering where the devil he was for a moment. 'Ouch!'

The small space was full of sailors preparing for the day
ahead, and as he slid out of the bunk he was slightly disori-
entated after sleeping heavily. 'What time is it, Bill?'

'Five. Get dressed quickly. We'll have breakfast and then I'll
take you to the officer on watch. He'll tell you what your
assignments are for the day.'

'Right.' Jack reached for his clothes, and then stopped
suddenly, a wide grin spreading across his face. 'Hey, I can
stand up!'

Bill laughed. 'The storm has blown itself out. Move it, lad,
or you won't have time to eat. You must never be late for duty.'

After a quick slosh with water, Jack was ready in ten minutes.
Thank goodness he didn't have to shave yet. If Bill noticed his
lack of morning whiskers he didn't say anything, but he was
certain the sailor knew he was under age. That was probably
why he had taken him under his wing straight away, and for
that he was very grateful.

No more than half an hour later he had received his duties
for the day. The ship was huge, but everyone was very friendly
and helpful as he tried to negotiate himself from one job to
another. Every part of the ship he was sent to he bombarded
the men with questions. The knowledge he gained was

meticulously recorded in a notebook he had in his pocket. He was determined to be a good sailor.

It was late afternoon before he had a moment to himself, and after grabbing a cup of tea he headed for the deck. The sea was calm now and he leant on the rail, gazing at the huge expanse of water.

'Like what you see?' Bill joined him.

'Oh, yes,' he sighed. 'Look at the sun glistening on the water. I always thought the sea was either blue or grey, but it isn't, is it? There are so many colours. It's breathtaking.'

'I never get tired of looking at it. Not only does it have many colours, but also many moods. Sometimes, like now, it's gentle, other times it's boisterous, and sometimes violent and cruel. The sea is ever changing, Jack. Love it, respect it, but never trust it. Have you finished your tasks?'

'Yes, I'm free now until tomorrow morning. I haven't actually done much today, I've just been told to watch and learn, but I hope they let me start working soon.'

'You'll be doing jobs on your own from tomorrow, I've no doubt. I'm free for the rest of the day, so let's get some food.' He glanced at Jack's too-thin body. 'We need to get you fattened up a bit. You look as if you haven't had a decent meal for ages.'

Jack grimaced. 'That brute ran me ragged, and he wasn't very generous when it came to feeding me.'

Bill's mouth set in a grim line. 'We'll soon put that right.'

The scene in the galley was very different from the previous night. It was crowded. Men were eating, talking, and there was a serious game of cards going on. Bill and Jack squeezed in at the end of the long table.

'Hey, lad, want to join us?' one of the card players asked.

'No, thanks. I don't know how.' He looked at the pile of coins on the table and shook his head. 'I haven't got enough money anyway.'

'We'll show you, and we'll take markers until you get paid.'

'No, I don't gamble.'

'That's sensible.' Bill gave the men a stern glance. 'This boy's got more sense than to let you take his money.'

'He might win. Beginners are often lucky.'

Bill gave a dry laugh. 'Not against you lot they're not. Biggest load of cheats I've come across in twenty years at sea.'

Jack grinned at the roars of protest and good-humoured banter. Everyone was laughing by the time Jack and Bill had plates of sausage and mash in front of them.

'Don't let them entice you into playing cards with them,' Bill warned.

'No fear. I'm going to save my money for my sister. She's going to make sure we have a place of our own.' A wistful look crossed his face. 'I was only a nipper when we were sent to the orphanage, and I don't remember what it was like to have a proper home. Hanna told me to enjoy the voyage and spend my money, but I'm going to save some because I'm not going to let her do this on her own. I'm older now and it's time she had some help.'

'In that case you've got something worth saving for.'

'Oh, yes. It's our dream and we'll make it come true. I must start my letter to her tonight. I've got so much to tell her.' He frowned and sighed. 'I feel guilty about being so happy. I hope she's all right.'

'I'm sure she will be. She sounds a sensible girl.'

'Of course she will, but I can't help worrying.' Jack cleared his plate and pulled a face. 'Silly of me. We're both away from the orphanage now, and that's what we always wanted. If the job she's got doesn't work out she'll get something else. My Hanna's strong and determined.'

'I'd like to meet her one day.' Bill slapped Jack on the back, and called to Frank, 'What's for pudding?'

'Spotted dick with syrup.'

'Oh, smashing.' The smile was back on Jack's face.

Four

Movement on her bed woke Hanna up, and in the gloom she saw a small boy sitting beside her. 'Is something wrong?' she asked, pulling herself upright.

'I'm hungry. Is it breakfast time yet?'

After switching on the bedside lamp, she looked at the clock and shook her head. 'It's only four o'clock. Would you like me to go and get you a glass of milk?'

'No.' He wriggled until he was sitting comfortably beside her, then he gave her an engaging grin. 'Will you tell me a story?'

There was a patter of little feet as the other twin came into her room, climbed on to the bed and settled the other side of her, then leaned across to his brother. 'What are you doing here? We told Hanna we were good at night.'

'It isn't night! It's nearly morning. Look.' He pointed to the clock on the bedside table. 'It's four!'

'You can't tell the time.'

'Yes I can. See the big hand is there and the little hand down there. That means it's four o'clock!'

Hanna watched in amusement as the twins argued about how to tell the time, and decided that was something she would start to teach them. One child was holding the small clock, and the other stretched across her legs to get a good look. Their mother had said that the twins were very different in nature, and she was beginning to see that for the first time. She decided to put it to the test.

'Put the clock down, David, and I'll tell you a short story. But then you must go back to bed.'

Two pairs of eyes fixed on her, and she knew from their expressions that she had been right.

David put the clock back and said, 'I'm Andrew.'

'No, you're David.'

Andrew giggled and pushed a lock of hair away from his eyes. 'How did you know?'

'Aha, that's my secret.' She reached out for the book on her bedside table, and knew that she was going to have to gain their trust and affection quite quickly, or these two little imps were going to have her running around in circles. They were very bright, and more than that, it was clear that this little episode in the early morning was a way of testing her. They were trying to find out just what they would be able to get away with. Well, they would soon find out that their innocent looks didn't fool her one bit.

'Told you she was smart,' Andrew said, sitting back and looking at her expectantly, waiting for the promised story.

Later that day, when the boys were tucked up for their afternoon nap, Mrs Harcourt sent for Hanna.

She knocked on the sitting-room door and walked in, a smile on her face. The smile vanished in an instant when she saw who else was in the room, and her heart raced in alarm. Her gaze was unwavering as she looked at them, knowing that she must stay calm and not show the slightest hint of fear. They couldn't touch Jack. She glanced at Mrs Harcourt, who gave her an encouraging smile, coming to stand beside the policeman, showing her support for Hanna.

'I told this officer that you would soon be able to clear up any misunderstanding, Hanna,' Mrs Harcourt said. 'I know you haven't done anything wrong.'

Talbot looked smug. 'Didn't think I'd find you, did you? It was easy. I followed you when you left the orphanage. I've come for your brother, and this officer is here to see you tell us where you've hidden him.'

The odious man was about to say more, but the policeman stopped him. 'I'll handle this, sir. Now, Miss Foster, will you tell me where your brother is and why he ran away from Mr and Mrs Talbot?'

'He ran away because Mr Talbot is a bully and beat him regularly.' She spoke clearly, looking the policeman straight in the eyes.

'Lies!'

'No, it's the truth, as anyone who knows him will tell you, and my brother said that he hits his wife as well. That's why she's so frightened of him. You might want to look into that, as well, Officer.'

'Don't listen to her! She'll say anything to protect her brother.'

Hanna immediately picked up on the word 'protect'. 'You're right. I would do anything to *protect* Jack, but I don't need to lie because you can't touch him now.'

'Officer! Arrest her. She's done something bad to that boy!'

'I told you I'd handle this, Mr Talbot.' The policeman silenced the irate man, and turned his attention to Hanna. 'You had better tell us what you mean by that, Miss Foster. Mr Talbot has reported his disappearance, and it is our duty to find him. He obviously isn't with you, and as a minor, we must make sure he is safe.'

'Minor?' Hanna frowned.

'Yes, at twelve years old he is considered as such.'

If the situation hadn't been so frightening, Hanna would have laughed. 'Is that what he told you? Who is telling lies now, Mr Talbot? My brother will be sixteen on the second of November.'

'Can you prove that, Miss Foster?'

'Yes, if you will allow me to go to my room?'

The policeman nodded, and Hanna sped up the stairs, opened the wardrobe and retrieved an old battered tin box, then hurried back to the sitting room. She opened the box in front of the policeman and handed him Jack's birth certificate.

After studying it for a moment, he turned to the man beside him. 'It seems you were mistaken about the boy's age, sir.'

The smug look had gone from Talbot's face. 'It don't matter how old he is. I want him back and it's your job to find him.'

'Mr Talbot is right, Miss Foster.' The policeman gave her an apologetic smile. 'I do need to know where your brother is. I can see that you love him too much to have caused him harm, but I have to file a report.'

'I understand.' She took some more papers out of the box and handed them over, watching the corners of the policeman's mouth twitch as he read.

When he looked up there was a gleam of laughter in his eyes, and she couldn't help smiling broadly at him. Now she looked closely he had a nice face and eyes with a touch of green in them. She immediately felt comfortable with him, and knew this was a man she could trust. All her worry and apprehension disappeared.

'What's going on? What you got there?' Talbot made a snatch at the papers, but the policeman moved them out of his way and handed them back to Hanna.

'We owe these ladies an apology for taking up their time with something which is not a police matter.' He turned to Mrs Harcourt first. 'Thank you for allowing us into your home, Mrs Harcourt. I know you told me that the boy was safe, but I had to talk to Miss Foster to be certain of that.'

'I understand. I knew Hanna would as well, and that is why I agreed to this interview.'

He turned to Hanna. 'I apologize for subjecting you to this ordeal, Miss Foster. No law has been broken here.'

'What do you mean? Where's the kid?'

'Jack Foster is now in the merchant navy and on his way to New Zealand.'

'But he can't be!' Talbot spluttered. 'He's too young.'

'It isn't unusual for boys to go to sea at an early age, and by the time he returns he will be past his sixteenth birthday. You have not adopted him legally, so you have no claim on the boy, sir.'

Talbot glared at Hanna, but she ignored him. The policeman was satisfied. The law was on their side, and Talbot now knew that he couldn't do anything about Jack leaving. The relief was enormous, but years at the orphanage had taught her to keep her deeper feelings to herself.

The policeman wrote in his notebook, tore out the page and handed it to Hanna. 'I want you to contact me should you have any future problems, Miss Foster, but you shouldn't hear any more about this matter.' He looked pointedly at Talbot. 'Will she, sir?'

'This is a bloody disgrace!' Talbot was red in the face with rage.

'Watch your language, sir. There are ladies present. Now, you will need to accompany me to the station.'

'Oh, I'll do that all right! And I'll have a word with your superiors about your handling of my complaint.'

'That is your right, sir.' He smiled at Mrs Harcourt and Hanna. 'Thank you again for your patience.'

The maid was waiting outside the door to show the two men out, and when they were alone, Hanna let out a ragged breath. 'I do hope that young policeman doesn't get into any trouble over this. Mr Talbot is a very unpleasant man.'

'He won't. He handled everything quite properly, and I shall write to the chief of police telling him so.' Mrs Harcourt gave a wry smile. 'He happens to be a good friend of ours.'

The last vestige of worry left Hanna, and she laughed freely. 'Oh, Mrs Harcourt, I bless the day you came to the orphanage. For the first time in my life I feel as if there might be a guardian angel looking out for us. I've been wondering if Mr Talbot would try and make trouble, but he can't now. Can he?'

'No, Hanna. If he comes anywhere near you we will be able to get him arrested, and he knows that. The policeman made it clear to him that he had no claim on your brother. Talbot is absolutely furious, but there isn't a thing he can do about it. You and your brother should now be free from this unpleasant business.'

'It's a relief to know it's all over and Jack is safe from his brutality.'

'This has been a terrible worry for you. Sit down, Hanna, and we'll have a much needed cup of tea.' She rang the bell and ordered refreshments for them. 'What did the young man write on the paper he gave you?'

'Oh, I haven't read it yet.' Hanna unfolded the note. 'It's the address of the police station and his name – Alan Rogers. He says I'm to ask for him if I have any more problems.'

'That was kind of him.'

'Very.' The tea arrived and Hanna poured for them, then sat back, feeling quite drained.

'You have told me a little of what happened to you after your parents were killed, but would you mind going into more detail for me? You were so young. How did you manage in those early years, and why did you agree to let Jack go to Talbot, after fighting for so long to keep him with you?'

'That decision will always haunt me.' Hanna took a sip of tea while she gathered her thoughts.

Jane Harcourt waited silently.

'Mrs Harris was in charge when we arrived. She was a kind woman and tried to see the children were as happy as possible. Most people wanted to adopt babies or toddlers, but if anyone showed an interest in Jack he would cling on to me. I told them we wouldn't be separated. Mrs Harris understood and never tried to force me to let Jack go. No one wanted me, so we stayed at the orphanage. Then, five years ago Mrs Harris retired and Mrs Buxton took over. Her aim was to get as many children as possible moved in with families. There wasn't anything wrong with that – an orphanage is not the right place for a child to grow up in. When the Talbots said they wanted a young boy, I was already feeling guilty about keeping Jack with me, wondering if I had deprived him of belonging to a proper family. Was I being selfish? Had I done the right thing? These thoughts were plaguing me.'

Hanna paused, drained her cup and poured another for both of them, then continued. 'Mrs Buxton kept on at us, and made a point of continually telling me that I had no right to deny my brother a proper home. Jack was now old enough to make his own decisions and we talked about it for days. In the end Jack agreed to go to the Talbots. They only lived up the road so we could still see each other every day. But it soon became clear that Talbot was a bully, and had only wanted a strong boy to help with his fruit and veg shop. He obviously thought that taking in Jack would be cheaper than paying an assistant. When I saw how badly Jack was being treated I pleaded with Mrs Buxton to help, but she wouldn't even listen. I wrote to the local councillor, but he ignored my letter. I was at my wits' end when Jack took matters into his own hands and joined the merchant navy. The rest you know.'

There was silence after Hanna finished speaking, then Jane Harcourt looked at her. 'Would you object if I took this to my committee? Your cries for help should not have been ignored.'

Hanna sat back and relaxed her shoulders, trying to ease the tension in her body. 'I don't mind, Mrs Harcourt. It's all over now, but I can't help thinking that Mrs Buxton should not be in charge of the orphanage. I don't believe that she even likes children.'

'I agree. There was something about her I didn't take to, and that's why I didn't feel guilty about trying to employ you, but everything appeared to be in good order when we looked around the orphanage. However, it is not always easy to see exactly what is going on during a short visit. And Mrs Buxton did have advanced warning that we were coming.'

Hanna pulled a face. 'I know. We were kept very busy for days . . .'

The sound of excited chatter and running feet could be heard, and Hanna jumped up. 'My goodness! The boys didn't sleep for long.'

Jane Harcourt smiled and said gently, 'Thank you for being so frank with me. I'll see this is looked into.'

Further conversation was useless as the twins rushed into the room.

Five

Three weeks on and Hanna hadn't seen or heard anything more from Talbot. The police had obviously dealt with him, and she was relieved and grateful. She had settled into the job of looking after the twins, and had quickly fallen under their spell. Not that they were angels – far from it. They had bright, intelligent minds, and a curiosity about everything around them. The questions only ever stopped when they were asleep. They were a constant challenge to keep amused, stretching her to her limits at times, but she loved them dearly. The only worry on her horizon now was wondering how her brother was getting on, and until she received a letter from him she wouldn't be able to relax completely. Mrs Harcourt hadn't mentioned talking to her committee again, so Hanna thought that the subject of the orphanage was closed. She probably couldn't do anything about it anyway, but it had been kind of her to say she would. Perhaps dropping the whole subject was for the best, but she did feel something should be done to save any other children from the kind of abuse her brother had endured. She had done all she could, and would have to put that behind her now. They had both moved on with their lives.

'You look very serious.'

Hanna jumped at the sound of the masculine voice and spun around. 'Oh, you gave me a fright!' she gasped.

'I'm sorry. I didn't mean to, but you were deep in thought.' The policeman frowned. 'Has Mr Talbot been bothering you?'

'No, I haven't seen him again.' She smiled. 'Thanks to you.'

'Good.' He fell into step beside her. 'Where are the children?'

'Having their afternoon nap. We were getting low on baby shampoo so I've been to get some.'

'Do you get an evening off at any time?'

'Yes. Why?'

'I wondered if you'd like to come dancing with me one Saturday?'

She stopped walking and stared at him in amazement. 'Oh, I couldn't do that.'

'Why?'

Now she was flustered. 'Because I've never been on a date before.'

'Then it's time you started.' He gave an engaging smile. 'And I'm quite safe to go out with.'

She shook her head. 'Why do you want to take me out?'

'I'd like to get to know you. You're bright, caring and very attractive. Isn't that reason enough?'

'Er . . .' Hanna shook her head and started walking again. 'It's kind of you to ask, but I couldn't. I haven't got any pretty clothes.'

'You look perfectly all right in the clothes you're wearing.'

'No, it wouldn't be right. I would feel uncomfortable, and I can't spend money on clothes because I'm saving up to make a proper home for me and Jack.'

'And how long is that going to take?' he asked gently.

'Ages, but it's our dream. I expect that's hard for you to understand.'

'No, but you can't deny yourself everything, Hanna. Your brother is making a life for himself in the merchant navy, and it's time for you to think about yourself for once.'

They had reached the house and stopped by the gate. 'I'm sure you are right, but I can't do that yet. I've got to know Jack is really happy first, and then I might be able to consider what to do with my life.'

'All right. I'll take no for an answer this time, but you haven't seen the last of me. I'll keep asking until you agree to come out with me.'

He seemed to be a nice young man and she was tempted, but she couldn't – she just couldn't. There were so many changes going on in her life at the moment, and she didn't feel able to relax enough yet to go out on a date. Hanna smiled kindly at the policeman. 'I'm sorry, but thank you for asking.'

'We'll meet again. You know where I am if you need anything.'

She watched him walk up the road before going into the house. The boys were already up and with their mother in the sitting room. They were spread out on the floor drawing with coloured crayons. They were concentrating very hard so she sat down with them to see what was keeping them so quiet.

David turned his head and smiled at Hanna. 'We're drawing pictures.'

'So I see. They're very good.'

Andrew glanced up, grinned at her compliment and pushed a strand of hair away from his eyes. It was a gesture she had quickly picked up on and marked him out as Andrew. David's hair always stayed in place, as if it wouldn't dare disobey him. David was going to be a force to be reckoned with when he was older, and so would Andrew, but he had a more gentle side to his personality than David.

'David's doing a picture for Daddy and mine is for your brother. Do you think he'll like it?'

Hanna studied it carefully, smiling to herself. They had soon given up trying to fool her once they knew that she could tell them apart. Andrew's picture was of Richmond Park – one of his favourite places, and just like this twin, had a gentle feel about it. 'He'll love it, Andrew. You've drawn the deer beautifully.'

He smiled happily and went back to the drawing.

She was always very careful to treat both boys the same, so she turned her attention to David's drawing. It was the complete opposite to his brother's picture. It was of a ship being tossed around on an angry sea, showing all action and movement. It was really very good. 'Oh, David, your father will love that. I expect he'll put it in his cabin, and my brother will put his by his bunk. It is kind of you both to do this for them. Thank you.'

Seeing that they were happy with her response, and completely absorbed in their artistic efforts, Hanna stood up. 'I got the shampoo, Mrs Harcourt. I'll put it in the bathroom.'

'Take it up when you go. Sit down for a moment and have a cup of tea with me. You are always on the go.'

'I'm used to being busy,' she laughed, taking a cup of tea from Mrs Harcourt, and then sitting down.

'Was that Constable Rogers with you outside?'

Hanna nodded. 'I met him up the road and he wanted to know if Mr Talbot had bothered me any more. Thank goodness I was able to tell him that I haven't seen or heard from him again.'

'That was thoughtful of him,' Jane Harcourt said. 'He appears to be very good at his job, dealing firmly with Mr Talbot. He should go far. And now we are on the subject of that disagreeable man, I want to tell you what I have been doing. I talked with my committee and the chairman paid an unannounced visit to the orphanage. He was not impressed with what he saw this time, and we all agreed that something should be done for the children there. A good friend of mine has just taken over as chairman of Lambeth Council and she would like to talk to you.'

'Oh.' Hanna wasn't sure she liked that idea and it showed on her face.

'You don't need to be afraid, Hanna. Rose Freeman is a formidable woman, but she's understanding, and gets things done. She's already looking into things, and would like to see both of us next week.'

Hanna relaxed a little. 'You will be coming as well, Mrs Harcourt?'

'Yes, we will both be questioned very thoroughly,' she said dryly. 'But we can trust Rose. She knows what she is doing. Are you happy to come with me?'

'Yes.' Hanna nodded. 'Something does need to be done for the children.'

'Good. I'll tell Rose we're coming.'

Six

Bill sat next to Jack. 'We'll soon be going through one of the great wonders of the world – the Suez Canal.'

'Oh, I can't wait to see that.' Jack smiled, excited to be seeing such a marvel. 'When will we be there?'

'The early hours of tomorrow morning, and then it will be on to India where we will be stopping for a couple of days. I'll show you around and see you don't get lost.'

'Count me in as well. I want to buy a silk scarf for my girlfriend.' Frank put a mug of tea in front of Bill. 'You going to get something pretty for your wife, Bill?'

'If I see something I think she'll like.' Bill drank his tea thirstily. 'You could get something for your sister, Jack. It sounds as if she deserves a treat.'

'Oh, I don't know.' Jack looked doubtful. 'I would like to get her something, but I don't want to spend much.'

'Don't worry about that,' Frank told him. 'We let Bill do the bargaining and then we won't have to pay much. He's an expert at getting a good price.'

'In that case I'll see what there is she might like.' Jack smiled at the thought of buying his sister something special. She had told him to spend his money and enjoy himself. Yes, he would enjoy taking home a present for her.

The rest of Jack's day went in a flash, and as usual he fell asleep as soon as he crawled into his bunk, oblivious to the coming and going of other crew members. The ship never slept. The days at sea so far had passed in a blur of activity, and it was so easy to lose track of time, but he loved every moment.

The next thing he knew Frank was shaking him awake. 'Come on, Jack, you've got to see this.'

Jack scrambled into his clothes and ran up the steps, unable to contain his excitement as he rushed to the rail. 'Wow! Look at that! I've never even been out of London before, and here I am in a foreign land. How did they ever build this?' He laughed and stretched out his arm. 'I could almost touch the sides. Is it deep enough?'

Bill had joined them and the two men exchanged amused glances, never bothering to answer the questions pouring from Jack. They all watched in silence as the ship made its way along the canal.

Jack was then called to give a hand with something and he tore off.

The captain came up to Bill. 'Are you taking the boy ashore when we stop in India?'

'Yes, sir. He's anxious to see another country.'

'Keep an eye on him. He's a good kid, eager to please and do well.'

'I will, sir. Cook and me have taken him under our wing and we'll watch over him for the entire voyage. We won't let him go ashore on his own. He's very young and could be taken advantage of in some of these ports.'

'Good. If you have any problems at all you are to come straight to me. I'd swear he's only as old as my son.'

'He certainly doesn't look his age, sir.'

The captain gave a dry laugh. 'You could say that.'

Bill watched him walk away. Captain Stevenson was a good man, one who cared about his crew, knowing them all by name. That wasn't always the way, as Bill well knew from his years at sea.

The sound of running feet caught his attention as Jack erupted back on deck again, eager not to miss anything.

'Quite something, isn't it?' Bill remarked.

Jack nodded, never taking his eyes off the passing scenery. He was fascinated with every sight and sound. 'I never thought I'd ever see anything like this!'

'I know. I felt just the same the first time I came through the canal.' Bill grinned at the excited boy. 'But we still have work to do, so we had better get some breakfast.'

'Yes, of course.' Jack made himself turn away from the fascinating sights. He was reluctant to go below decks, but there was a busy day ahead of them, and they would probably be coming back this way, so he would have a chance to see it again.

Later that day Frank and Bill had managed to grab a quiet cup of tea for themselves, and Bill said, 'That boy was so excited, it was a pleasure to see, but I do wonder what kind of a life him and his sister have had.'

'Pretty grim, I would guess. Poor little devils! But Jack needs looking after, or he could find himself in trouble. He knows nothing about life.'

Bill nodded. 'I saw that straight away, but if the two of us work together we can see he comes to no harm.'

'Good idea, we'll do that. You should have seen them standing on the dock that morning. They looked like a pair of scruffy kids, until you saw the expressions in their eyes – desperation. It fair tore me apart.' Frank sighed deeply and stood up. 'Now, I'd better start cooking, or the crew will be complaining.'

'And that would never do,' Bill laughed.

It was late in the evening before Bill saw Jack again. He was in his usual spot on deck, gazing into the distance, deep in thought.

'Time you turned in, isn't it, lad?'

'Hello, Bill. Just thought I'd take a quiet moment. Some of the men have been talking, and they said there's probably going to be a war. I've heard about the fascists in Germany, of course, but do you think they are that dangerous?'

'It's impossible to say, but I do believe Hitler has ambitions. He's re-arming and building up his forces, and I wouldn't trust him, but at the moment we can only hope it will come to nothing.'

'But you don't think it will?'

Bill shook his head. 'If the worst does happen our country is going to need the merchant navy. You might not have joined at the right time, lad.'

'Oh, no,' Jack said firmly. 'I joined at the right time, and whatever happens in the future we'll face it when it comes.'

'Exactly, so there's no point worrying about it now. Let's

enjoy the voyage and let the world take care of itself for a while. Our next stop will be India and that is an extraordinary country. We'll have a bit of free time there, and there should also be some post waiting for us with the Port Agent.'

The worried expression cleared from Jack's face and he was smiling again. 'I hope there's something from Hanna.'

'I'll take you ashore and show you the sights.'

'Oh, thanks, Bill. It's kind of you to take the trouble.'

'It's no trouble, lad. Now you had better get some sleep.'

'Of course.' Jack straightened up. 'It will be another busy day tomorrow. Thanks for talking to me about things.'

'Any time. Night, lad.'

'See you tomorrow.'

Jack was so tired at the end of each daily shift he was glad to climb into his bunk at night. He knew Bill and the others often had to do night watches, but he hadn't been asked to do anything like that yet. That kind of responsibility would only come with experience, and at the moment he was having enough trouble just finding his way around the ship.

The sound of the engines was soothing and he sighed as he closed his eyes. His last thought before sleep was always with his sister. It was hard not knowing how she was getting on in her new job, and he knew she must be feeling the same about him.

Watching the activity as they docked in Bombay had Jack open-mouthed in amazement. After days at sea the noise and smells assaulted his senses.

Bill dashed up to him. 'The gangway will be going down soon, lad, but don't leave the ship without us.'

'I won't,' he readily agreed.

Grinning at Jack's reaction to his first sight of India, Bill said, 'A bit overwhelming, isn't it? Frank will be here in a few minutes. I'll be back as soon as I can.'

About ten minutes later Frank arrived and joined Jack at the rail. 'Are you looking forward to going ashore?'

'Er . . . I'm not sure.' He gestured to the pandemonium going on below them. 'Is the town anything like this?'

'No.' Frank shook his head.

'That's a relief!'

'It's worse.'

'Frank! You're kidding me. It can't be.'

The man beside him held up his hands, laughing. 'Honest. Would I lie to you?'

'He's telling the truth,' Bill said as he came and stood beside them. 'You stick close to us, lad, and just enjoy the experience.'

With one man either side of him when they reached the main part of the town, Jack was glad they were with him. 'Good grief!' he muttered. 'I thought London was crowded, but this is unbelievable, and all the vivid colours hurt my eyes.'

'That's because you've only seen blue and grey for days.' Bill caught his arm and guided him through the teeming crowds.

'Oh, look at those!' He stopped by an open shop selling silky scarves. 'Hanna would look lovely in one of those. Do they cost much?'

'Not if Bill does the bargaining as I told you,' Frank said.

Jack looked at his friend, eager now to take a special present back for Hanna. 'Would you ask for me, please? My sister deserves something pretty. She's always put me first, and now it's my chance to do something for her.'

'Right, you choose one and I'll get it as cheaply as I can for you.'

There were so many, but he eventually held up one.

Frank studied it and then nodded. 'From what I remember of your sister that orange colour will go well with her dark hair, and the pattern is pretty as well.'

Seeing Jack was decided, Bill took it from him and began to haggle about the price. It went on for quite a while and sounded more like an argument, so Jack stood back and waited to see what would happen.

In the end he only paid a fraction of the original asking price, and they left the trader muttering nasty things about sailors. Jack grinned. 'I don't think he liked us.'

'That's just for show. He's happy with the sale. You never pay full price, lad. As soon as traders see us they double the price of everything.'

'Thanks, Bill, I'll have to remember that.' He watched,

and listened as his friends both bought something on another stall.

They ambled along, allowing Jack to stop and look at anything that caught his attention, and there was a great deal to see. 'Look at that jewellery. Is it real gold?'

'Yes.' Frank pointed to an elaborate ring. 'And that's an Indian ruby.'

'I wish I could buy Hanna something like that.'

'Wait till we get to Ceylon, lad, where we can pick up gems at very reasonable prices. We'll have a look for something you can afford there. I want to get something for my wife as it's our tenth wedding anniversary just before Christmas.' He looked pointedly at Frank. 'What about you buying an engagement ring for your girlfriend?'

'Haven't been going out with her long enough yet,' he grinned.

Jack chuckled at Frank's expression and turned away from the stall. They continued their tour.

When they returned to the ship there was a letter from Hanna waiting for him. It was only short, written after she had been in her job for two days, but it was enough to assure him that she was happy with Mrs Harcourt and the twins. He breathed a sigh of relief to know that things were working out all right for her. Bill had told him that his letter to her was on its way, and he hoped it wouldn't take too long to reach her.

After the excitement of the last stop, and feeling happier now he'd heard from his sister, he settled easily into the routine of the ship again. The next stop would be Colombo in Ceylon, and he was looking forward to seeing something of the island.

Jack wasn't disappointed. They had a couple of days and Bill and Frank took him inland away from the port, and some of the scenery was lovely. On their way back to the ship on their last day they went to a place that sold loose gems and jewellery, and although he had been sure he wouldn't be able to afford anything, Bill had other ideas. He ended up with a small gold pendant set with multicoloured sapphires, and a fine chain to go with it. He couldn't believe how cheap it had been. If it had been on sale in London the price would have been three or four times as much.

Back on the ship he put it carefully with the silk scarf, smiling as he thought how surprised Hanna was going to be when he gave them to her at Christmas.

Seven

Waiting for the postman to arrive had been agonizing, but Hanna was finally holding a bulky envelope in her hands. She gazed at the address written in Jack's neat handwriting, eager to read it, but almost afraid to in case he hated being on the ship. Her biggest fear was that he would be mistreated again. Life on board ship was a strange, and probably a tough world. He would have to deal with things quite out of his experience, and she couldn't protect him there.

Well, there was only one way to find out, so she slit the envelope open and took out the contents. There were pages and pages. Glancing up to make sure the twins were playing happily with their building blocks, she began to read.

Her smile spread as she read his vivid account of what life was like on the ship, and his description of the storm had her laughing quietly. She could picture him trying to keep his balance on a rolling ship. Suddenly she was conscious of quietness in the room and looked up to find both the boys watching her intently.

'It's a letter from my brother,' she told them.

They scrambled to their feet and hurtled towards her. 'Is he all right? Does he like the sea? Where's he been? Where's he going?' Both of them were bombarding her with questions, their faces glowing with eagerness to hear all about it.

'Hold it!' she laughed. 'I've only read the first couple of pages.'

'Read the rest,' David told her, leaning on her knees. 'Then you can tell us what he's been doing.'

'That's if you don't mind telling us,' Andrew said, always polite and mature for his age.

'I'd love to. Just let me read a bit more.'

Andrew smiled and settled on the floor next to her chair, waiting expectantly. David sat the other side of her. They were like a couple of bookends, she thought affectionately.

After reading the letter through quickly and selecting parts she thought the boys would enjoy, she sighed quietly with relief. He was happy, and it sounded as if he had made friends with a couple of the men – one of them they had met on the dock before he sailed. She was pleased about that. Life at sea obviously suited him, and he loved the ship, going into great detail about every new thing he was learning.

Looking down at the twins' upturned faces, she smiled, and began to read. Jack's vivid description about his antics in the storm had the boys rolling on the floor, shrieking with laughter, and then listening intently to his descriptions about the workings of the ship.

By the time she came to the end of the letter the boys were kneeling with their arms resting on her legs.

'Read the bit again about the men going on watch,' David asked. 'Daddy told us about that on his ship.'

Hanna shuffled the pages until she found it, and after reading it she turned to Andrew. 'Would you like to hear something again?'

He nodded. 'That bit where your brother got lost and ended up in the cargo hold and couldn't find his way out again. That was funny.'

As Hanna read Jack's account of the incident again she realized that he had a real way with words. A talent she hadn't known he possessed. She would reply at once and encourage him to keep a detailed record of his voyage.

They were all laughing when Mrs Harcourt came into the room and she listened as her sons explained about Jack's experiences at sea.

'He's going to make a good sailor,' David announced, confident he knew about such things.

'I'm sure he is.' Jane Harcourt looked at Hanna's happy face and nodded. 'I'm so pleased everything is working out well for your brother, and I'm sorry to spoil your day, but we have an appointment with Rose Freeman in two hours.'

'Nothing could spoil this moment, Mrs Harcourt.' Hanna stood up. 'Are the boys staying with Mary?'

'No, they are coming with us. Rose and Bill are their godparents, and Rose hasn't seen the boys for a while.'

'Uncle Bill was a sailor as well,' David told Hanna. 'He was a captain like Daddy, and he fought in the war. When the next one starts he'll have to go back in the navy.'

There was a deathly hush at this announcement, and then Jane Harcourt shook her head. 'There isn't going to be another war, David. Where did you get that idea from?'

'Daddy said there would be. Didn't he, Andrew?'

'We heard him talking before he went back,' Andrew admitted. 'And that's what he said.'

'I've told you boys not to listen to grown-ups' conversations, haven't I?' Jane scolded. 'You only hear part of what is said. Daddy didn't mean that war was inevitable, only that Germany has problems to sort out. Now, we must get ready. We mustn't be late meeting Rose.'

'Ooh, no!' Both boys grinned at each other and then at Hanna, all talk of war forgotten.

Hanna pushed it out of her mind as well. She'd heard talk on the wireless, of course, but she couldn't see what it would have to do with them. Her thoughts turned to the woman they were going to meet. There had been hints that she was not someone you crossed in any way. Could she be as fearsome as they said? Ah well, she would soon find out, but she was so happy after reading Jack's letter that nothing could upset her today.

The council offices in Lambeth were busy when they walked in and a rather harassed looking man came up to them. 'Can I help you?'

'We have an appointment with Mrs Freeman. Harcourt is the name.'

He nodded. 'Wait here and I'll see if she's free.'

Almost immediately a tall, statuesque woman came towards them, and Hanna felt a shock run through her. Mrs Freeman's strong personality was immediately obvious, and she took a slight step back. The dark eyes seemed to be looking straight into Hanna's mind. If she felt intimidated, the twins certainly didn't.

'Auntie Rose,' they cried in unison, delighted to see her.

'Ah, I see you've brought trouble with you, Jane.'

The boys giggled, and each twin grabbed hold of her hands, looking up at her with bright smiles on their faces.

'I couldn't leave them behind, Rose. They would never have forgiven me.'

Rose looked down at the boys. 'If you stay quiet and behave yourselves while I talk to your mum and Hanna, then we can all have tea together.'

'We will – we will! Can we have iced buns, Auntie Rose?'

'Of course. Don't we always?'

They nodded eagerly.

Then Rose turned her attention to Hanna. 'Thank you for agreeing to come and talk with me. Let's go into my office. This way.'

The office was small and sparsely furnished. There was a desk, a filing cabinet and four chairs, and that was all. The carpet was worn in places, but everything was spotlessly clean.

'Sit down,' she ordered before looking out of the door and calling, 'Betty, will you bring an orange drink for the children and some paper and pencils. Thanks.'

Rose settled behind the desk. 'Sorry it's been a while since we've seen you, Jane, but life is hectic at the moment. Is Sam at sea?'

'Yes, and we're not expecting him back for some time. How's the family?'

'They're all fine. Kate's growing fast and is quite a handful.'

'Just like you were, I expect,' Jane laughed.

'True.' Rose grimaced. 'Bill doesn't think I've changed much.'

'I'm not surprised. I thought you'd retired from council work. What are you doing here again?'

'They were having problems and begged me to come back and sort things out for them. I've promised Bill I'll only do a year.'

'And will you?'

'Yes, I should be able to deal with everything by then. Bill is a very patient man and I won't do anything to upset him at this time. He's concerned enough, and will need all my support if there's another war.'

'Do you think there really will be, Rose?' Jane asked, frowning.

Rose didn't hesitate. 'I believe it's inevitable. Hitler wants total domination of Europe, and if that happens then we will be dragged into a conflict whether we want it or not. I don't believe all the talking in the world is going to settle this.'

Jane Harcourt sighed deeply. 'That's what Sam says. If Bill is recalled he will have to fight in another war at sea, and no man should be asked to do that.'

Rose gave a nod and a wry smile. 'But you know me, Jane. I don't trust anyone, especially someone like Adolf Hitler, but this is all speculation. It hasn't happened yet, and we can only hope that it doesn't. Now, we have this business to sort out.'

Hanna had been enthralled listening to the two friends talking, and tensed when the impressive woman turned her full attention in her direction.

'Tell me about the orphanage from the time you were taken there, Hanna.'

'Erm . . .' She was taken back by the request. It was a part of their lives she had tried hard to forget, but she took a deep breath and began. 'I was only eight . . .'

Rose smiled kindly. 'I know this is hard for you, but I must have the whole story before I take any action. You understand?'

Hanna nodded, stumbling over the words at first. This time had been so painful for her and Jack and they never talked about it in detail to anyone.

Nearly an hour later Hanna sat back, exhausted from living once again memories she had tried to block out from her mind.

'Thank you, my dear.' Rose's dark eyes were stormy. 'Is there a member of the staff who would also talk to me?'

'Most of them won't say much in case they lose their jobs. But there was an odd-job man there who has since left, and he might be willing to talk to you.' She gave the man's name and address to Mrs Freeman.

'They'll talk to me!' Rose made a note of the name and looked at Jane. 'This is disgraceful. Someone should have taken notice of Hanna's complaints about the treatment of her brother.'

'I agree, and that's why I brought this to your attention.'

'You did the right thing. I'll sort this out, and heads will roll. Someone hasn't been doing their job properly. But now, I think it's time for tea and buns.'

The twins, who had been so quiet Hanna had forgotten they were there, jumped to their feet, eager for their treat.

Rose smiled at them. 'You've been very good, so I think we'll have our tea in the café across the street. Would you like that?'

'Oh, yes please!'

'That's settled then.' Rose looked out the door and called, 'I'll be out for an hour, Betty.'

With the boys either side of Rose holding her hands, they all trooped across the road.

Later that evening, when the boys were fast asleep, Hanna began to write to her brother. There was so much to tell him, and she knew he would want every detail of her meeting with Rose Freeman. She didn't doubt that something would be done at last, because when a woman like that said the problem would be dealt with, then it would be. Hanna had been in awe of the woman, and it was comforting to know that with her intervention some other children might be spared the brutal treatment Jack had endured.

It was nearly midnight when the letter was finished. She had managed to buy a larger envelope so she could include Andrew's drawing without folding it more than once. After sealing and addressing it, she put it on her bedside table ready to post in the morning.

Eight

It had been July when she had waved goodbye to Jack, and now it was September. Hanna could hardly believe how quickly the time had gone. They had never been parted in their lives before, and she missed him so much that the ache was almost tangible at times. But he was happy – and so was she. They had finally been able to get away from the orphanage and into jobs they both enjoyed. That was all that mattered.

Although autumn was fast approaching it was quite warm, and Hanna smiled as she watched the twins kicking a ball around the lawn.

'Come on!' David dragged her out of the chair. 'You can be the goalie.'

Laughing, she pretended to dive for the balls, allowing most of them past her. As always, she made sure each twin scored an equal amount of goals, though they did their best to confuse her, but by now she was very familiar with the differences in their characters and wasn't easily fooled.

Rolling on the grass in an effort to catch another shot, Hanna heard the boys start to shout with delight. She came to her knees and saw them running to a man and woman who had just come into the garden, accompanied by their mother. She recognized Mrs Freeman immediately and scrambled to her feet, hastily brushing grass from her skirt. Rose Freeman was about six feet in height, but the man with her was even taller. They made a handsome, impressive couple.

The man lifted both twins without any trouble at all, and had them giggling with delight. Everyone was laughing and Hanna joined in.

'Put those kids down, Bill,' Rose said, smiling broadly.

'Where's Kate?' Andrew asked the moment his feet touched the ground.

'In school, where you will be soon.'

'We can read already, Auntie Rose,' Andrew told her proudly. 'Hanna's teaching us how.'

'And we can tell the time,' David said.

'That's very good.' Rose turned to her husband. 'Come and meet Hanna.'

He stepped forward and shook hands with her, and she had a job not to tremble with nerves, but managed to smile. He was very handsome, with a few grey hairs at the temple, and the kindest eyes she had ever looked into. There was an easy-going manner about him, but she sensed that hid a very strong character.

'I'm pleased to meet you, sir.'

He smiled. 'The pleasure is mine, Hanna. My wife has told me all about you. And the name is Bill.'

She couldn't call him Bill!

'Play football with us.' The twins were too excited to stand still.

When Bill and Rose began chasing around the lawn with the twins, Jane Harcourt stood beside Hanna. 'You don't need to be afraid of them, my dear. Rose comes from the slums and had a dreadful childhood. But she was blessed with a brilliant mind and fought for a better life for herself and her family. Against all the odds she became a lawyer, and still fights any injustice she comes across. That's why I went to her with your case. I knew she was the one person who would understand and do something about it.'

Rose came over to them and sat beside Hanna. 'Take them all in for tea, Jane. I want to talk to Hanna.'

Hanna watched them leave the garden, and waited quietly to hear what Mrs Freeman had to tell her.

'The situation at the orphanage has been dealt with. We carried out a thorough investigation, talking to many past and present members of staff and children. As a result of our findings several of the youngsters have been removed from unsuitable places and found other homes. They will be monitored to make sure they are treated well. I'm afraid the matron was taking money and letting the children go to the highest bidder. Her conduct will be taken further, but that need not concern you, Hanna; we have enough evidence to proceed without involving you.'

Hanna nodded. 'Thank you. I'm pleased about that.'

Rose continued. 'Your brother's case should have been dealt with as soon as you reported it. Those responsible have been severely reprimanded and either sacked, or moved to another position. Mrs Buxton has been removed from the orphanage and is also facing further enquiries into her mishandling of the funds.'

'She's been stealing as well?' Hanna gasped.

'Let's just say that she was not using the money wisely. I have personally chosen a replacement and things are already improving.'

'It's a great relief to know that other children will not suffer in the way Jack did.'

Rose gave a wry smile, sadness showing in her dark eyes. 'I can't say that for sure, but we will be keeping a sharp eye on things from now on, and Talbot has been blacklisted. He will never be allowed to take another child into his home.'

'Thank you very much for all you've done, Mrs Freeman.' Hanna sighed. 'I felt so helpless and didn't know what to do next, but my brother settled that for himself.'

'I'd like to meet him sometime. He sounds as if he's got a lot of courage. If you would like to visit the orphanage and see the changes taking place, you would be very welcome to do so.'

'No.' Hanna shook her head emphatically. 'I have put that part of my life behind me and so has Jack. I have no wish to see the place again.'

'I can understand how you feel.' Rose stood up and looked down at Hanna. 'It must have been hard for you to break away from the unsatisfactory life you found yourselves in, and I wish you both a happy and useful life ahead of you. Don't be afraid to reach higher. Impossible is not a word you should accept. I never have.'

Nodding, Rose turned and walked towards the house, leaving that advice ringing in Hanna's mind. She sat where she was for some time, deep in thought. With Jack's announcement that he had joined the merchant navy their lives had changed dramatically overnight. She had been so concerned about her young brother that she hadn't given a thought to her own future, but she ought to, because once the twins were old enough to go to school, Mrs Harcourt probably wouldn't need her any more. What would she do then?

Hanna gazed into space for a while, and then shook her head impatiently. That wouldn't be for a couple of years yet, and she would deal with it when the time came. If she did her job well, Mrs Harcourt would give her a good reference and she could get another job. No point trying to cross that bridge before she got to it. Mrs Freeman was obviously a determined person, and Hanna really didn't think she was anything like her. But to have a goal to reach for was quite a good thing, and her aim was to make a good home for herself and Jack. However, she would take one piece of advice and tell herself that although she had set herself a difficult task, it was not impossible!

Smiling, she stood up and walked towards the house. There was writing paper in her room and she had so much to tell Jack.

An hour later, her letter finished, Hanna was on her way to the post box at the end of the road. Her brother would be so pleased to hear that something had been done about the orphanage and Talbot.

She had just put the letter in the box when she saw the constable striding towards her.

'Hello, Hanna.'

She smiled brightly. 'Lovely day, isn't it?'

'Ah, I guess from your happy face that you've heard from your brother and he's enjoying his life at sea.'

'Yes, he loves being on the ship, and I've just written to him with some good news.' She began walking back to the house and he fell into step beside her. 'Mrs Harcourt contacted a friend of hers and you'll never guess what's happened.'

'I give up,' he smiled. 'You tell me.'

Hanna talked all the way along the road, telling him what Mrs Freeman had done. 'Isn't that wonderful!'

'It certainly is,' he said as they stopped by the gate. 'You must be very relieved.'

She nodded, still smiling.

'I think you should celebrate. There's a dance at the hall next to the cinema tomorrow evening. You told me you couldn't come out with me until you knew your brother was all right. Well, now you know, so will you come out with me?'

It only took her a moment to decide. 'I'd like that. Only I must warn you that I can't dance.'

'Don't worry about that. I'll teach you. See you tomorrow then. I'll come round for you about seven.'

As she watched him walk away, she noted his easy stride, and decided that he was probably a good dancer. Her mind began to whirl at her impulsive decision. She had a little money put aside and would need a new frock for the evening. Nothing expensive, of course, but something pretty. It was time she had some fun, and she wouldn't want to look a mess and let him down.

There was no sign of the twins as she made her way back to the garden, so the Freemans must still be here. The smile was still on her face as she sat down and sighed with relief. Jack was all right, the orphanage and Talbot had been dealt with, and she had a date! Her first ever date, and she was so happy!

'There, you're picking up the steps already,' Alan told her as he guided her around the crowded dance floor. 'You'll be able to manage a foxtrot by the end of the evening. You follow well and have a good sense of timing.'

'That's only because you're an excellent teacher,' Hanna laughed, thoroughly enjoying herself. That morning she had bought a cotton frock in a delicate shade of lemon, which suited her dark colouring, and she didn't feel out of place amongst all the other girls. When Alan had come for her he had immediately told her how pretty she looked, and that had boosted her confidence. He was very good at putting people at ease, she soon realized, seeing the relaxed way he talked to everyone he met.

The evening flew by and she did attempt a foxtrot, but soon decided that she would need more practice before she could glide around the floor like the other dancers.

'Have you enjoyed yourself, Hanna?' Alan asked when they reached the house.

'I've had a lovely time. Thank you for asking me out and for showing me the dance steps.'

He smiled. 'It was fun. Will you come out with me again?'

'I'd like that.'

'Good. I work shifts so it will be a couple of weeks before I get another Saturday off. Perhaps you'd like to go to the cinema then?'

'That would be lovely. I haven't seen a picture for ages. I used to take Jack to the children's matinee when we could afford it, but that wasn't often.'

'There hasn't been much fun in your lives, has there?'

'Not much, but that's all over now.' She smiled up at Alan. 'Thank you again for a fun evening.'

'It was my pleasure, Hanna.' He kissed her gently on the cheek. 'I'll come for you at six o'clock in two weeks' time.'

'I'll look forward to it.'

Once back in the house she ran up the stairs and danced along the landing to her room. Mrs Harcourt and the boys were staying with Captain Harcourt's mother for the weekend, and wouldn't be back until teatime tomorrow. There would be no need to get up early in the morning. What a luxury – what fun!

Nine

How his life had changed. The years at the orphanage and the nightmare of being under Talbot's control seemed like a distant dream. Jack felt as if he had stepped into another world. There was a comradeship among the men, almost like being part of a large family. Although he was new and young he had been accepted. The only concession they made to his youth was to take the time and trouble to explain things to him in detail so he understood exactly what he was being asked to do. It gave him a lovely comforting feeling.

They had made a brief stop to pick up the mail and he had two letters from Hanna on the table in front of him.

'Tea, Jack?' Frank asked as he walked into the mess carrying boxes of supplies.

'Please, I'm gasping.'

'You going to read your letter, lad, or just gaze at it?' Bill took two mugs from Frank and put one of them in front of Jack, and then sat beside him.

Jack gave a nod of thanks. 'I know she's happy where she is, but I left a mess behind for her to sort out, and I'm afraid she might have had trouble with Talbot. He's a nasty brute, and not the sort to let my disappearing go without a fight.' He picked up a letter, weighing it in his hand. 'And I don't like the look of this one. It's rather bulky.'

'There's only one way to find out. Go on, open them.'

'You're right.' He slit open the thick letter first and frowned as he unfolded a child's drawing. When he spread it out on the table all the men in the mess stopped what they were doing to have a look at it.

'Your sister like drawing?' one of the men asked.

'No.' He laughed, suddenly realizing what it was. 'She's looking after two young boys — twins — and one of them must have done this.'

'Read what she says,' Bill urged.

Jack unfolded the letter and began to read quickly, a smile spreading across his face, and he roared with laughter from time to time. He looked up, his face animated. 'The picture is from one of the boys, Andrew, and she said he did it especially for me, so I've got to put it by my bunk.'

'Ah, in that case you must.' Bill picked up the picture and studied it carefully. 'Do you know where this is, or did the boy make it up?'

'That's Richmond Park. Hanna used to take me there now and again as a treat.'

'And I have a feeling you didn't get many of those,' Bill said seriously.

'No, but we really enjoyed them when we did. My sister was very good like that. She tried hard to see I didn't miss out on everything. My favourite time was when we went to the swimming pool.' Jack gulped some of his tea. 'I've always liked the water.'

'We've noticed that by the way you spend your spare moments gazing at the sea.' Bill pointed to the drawing. 'Tell you what, lad, we'll tack it up for you and I'll take a photo so you can send it to the boy.'

'Would you, Bill? That would be wonderful.'

'Easy done, lad. Now, you'd better read your other letter.'

He slit this one open eagerly, and as he read his smile turned to a frown. 'Oh, damn!' he muttered. 'I was afraid of this.'

'What is it, lad?'

'That blasted man has been causing trouble. I knew he would, but he went to the police about me! Can you believe that? A brute like that daring to take the police to question my sister!' Jack was furious that Hanna had had to endure such an ordeal.

The men sitting around him said nothing as Jack continued to read. Slowly his frown eased and he sighed with relief. 'Oh, it's turned out all right – more than all right. Hanna's got friends who are sticking up for her, and they've helped her to deal with him.'

'That's good news.' Frank refilled their mugs. 'Who's been helping her?'

'The woman she works for – Mrs Harcourt, and a friend of

hers who is a lawyer and working at the council offices. Rose Freeman's her name. She's sorted out the orphanage and had Talbot blacklisted so he can never take another kid into his home.'

Bill tipped his head back and laughed. 'If Rose Freeman is involved then you've got nothing to worry about.'

'You know her?'

'I only met her once, but my mother knew her when she worked for the council. That was a few years ago now, but I doubt she's changed much. She's the kind of woman once seen never forgotten. You and your sister won't have any more trouble, lad.'

Intrigued, Jack asked, 'What's she like?'

'Six feet tall, black hair, impressive and absolutely beautiful. She gets things done, and won't tolerate injustice of any kind. Your sister's employer did the right thing by going to her.'

'That's a relief to know.' Jack nodded and put the letters back in their envelopes.

Bill picked up the drawing. 'Let's find a place by your bunk for this.'

Life settled into a busy routine while at sea. Time, and even days of the week merged together, where the only view was the ever-changing sea. Jack loved it, recording every moment of his day as Hanna had suggested for her to read one day.

He sat at the table in the mess, hungry as usual. 'What we got, Frank?'

'Steak and kidney pudding.'

'Lovely, my favourite. I'm ready for it.'

Frank laughed and dished up a generous helping. 'You're always hungry. There will be seconds, if you want it? Though why I ask such a daft question I don't know.'

Bill joined them. 'Your cooking's done the lad a power of good, Frank. He was too scrawny when he joined us, but look at him now. He's filled out nicely.'

Grinning, Jack continued to tuck into his meal. 'I think I've grown taller as well. My trousers are a bit on the short side now. If Hanna was here she could alter them for me.'

'All sailors can sew. We'll teach you how to do things for yourself.'

'You're joking, Frank.'

'No I'm not. How do you think we manage when we're at sea for weeks?'

Everyone round the table was nodding, so Jack pulled a face. 'In that case I'd better learn, I suppose. Can I have some more steak pudding, Frank?'

Jack was just wiping his plate clean for the second time when silence fell on the mess, everyone listening intently. 'Why have we slowed down, Bill?'

'Don't know.' He stood up and strode out.

Fifteen minutes later he was back. 'Engine trouble, but the engineers think they can fix it. We'll have to stop for a while so they can make repairs.'

'What happens if they can't fix it?' Jack wanted to know.

'Then we radio for help, lad.' Bill smiled. 'But don't worry, no captain likes to do that, and the owners like it even less. It can cost money, but we've got some clever engineers on board. If it can be repaired they'll do it.'

'Can you swim, Jack?' one of the men asked.

He nodded, looking puzzled.

'In that case you can get out and give us a push if we need it.'

Everyone in the mess roared with laughter, including Jack. 'I might need a bit of help to do that. It would be a job for more than one person.'

Chuckling, Frank poured more tea for those who wanted it, and winked at Jack as the engines fell silent.

It was an eerie feeling being on a silent ship, but it was a new experience for Jack, so when he had finished his allotted work for the day he went up on deck. He leaned on the rail and gazed at the sea – something he never got tired of doing. They were miles and miles away from England now, and he couldn't remember ever feeling so fit and content. Never in his life had he ever had the peace of mind he now felt as he gazed at the ever-changing sea.

A mug of tea was put in front of his face and he took it, looking up. 'Thanks, Bill, I need that. It's been a busy day even if we aren't going anywhere. How are the repairs going?'

'Nearly done, but we'll see how successful they are when they try to start the engines up again.' Bill laughed softly. 'A few of the men are praying we can get going soon. The old ship wallows a bit when she isn't moving and that doesn't do their stomachs a lot of good. We're lucky we don't suffer like that.'

They stood there for some time enjoying the quiet, then the peace was shattered when there was a roar and the ship shuddered, and then fell silent again. It took three attempts before the engineers were able to start up again, and Jack could hear cheers coming from various places on the ship.

The two men grinned at each other, and Bill said, 'That's another experience you'll be able to tell your sister about.'

'I know, and I've got plenty to tell her. When I get home I'll be talking for days.'

Ten

It seemed to Hanna as if Jack had been away for years, but of course it was only a few months. She had looked after him from the moment their parents had been killed, and this was the first time they had ever been apart. Things were different now though. They were older and Jack had to make his own way in life, she knew that, but she missed him so much and really hoped he would be home in time for Christmas. If he wasn't she knew he would have a good time on board ship, or at whichever port they were in, but she would be lonely without him. Mrs Harcourt had already heard that her husband would be home and they were going to spend the holiday with his mother, so she wouldn't be needed. The rest of the staff all had their own plans and she would be the only one left here.

She read Jack's last letter through again and then carefully put it back in the tin box. It was unlikely that would happen, but if it did then she would go to the library and get out some books. It was a long time since she'd had a good read, and would enjoy that.

She would also enjoy going dancing with Alan this evening, and she had better start getting ready. They had been out together a few times now and she liked him very much, they got on well together, but she didn't dare think beyond that. They had learnt while in the orphanage that it wasn't wise to hope for too much as it could easily lead to disappointment. Things were going so well for her and Jack at the moment, and she couldn't ask for more. Their lives had changed dramatically − and for the better.

They were steaming at full speed, proper repairs having been made to the engines while they were in New Zealand, and that had delayed them. But everyone wanted to be home for Christmas. Jack pulled his collar up and blew on his hands. The sea was churning, angry looking and grey as he braced himself against the pitching of the ship. Such a change from the blue waters they had been in. Due to the delay they had spent more time in New Zealand than originally planned, and they had been able to explore quite a bit. It was a beautiful place, and he looked forward to going there again so he could see more. There was no doubt in his mind now that the merchant navy was where he belonged and he would make this his career. One day he might even be able to study for a master's certificate, and that thought made him grin to himself. Such lofty ambitions! But what was it Mrs Freeman had told Hanna – nothing is impossible? He straightened up. Quite a thought, but now his stomach was telling him it was time to eat.

The mess was nearly empty when he arrived. 'Where is everyone?' he asked Frank.

'Been and gone.' Frank eyed him. 'I can see from your red nose that you've been gazing at the sea again.'

He nodded and sat down. 'I like to watch it, whatever its mood.'

'Phew! Cold out there.' Bill came in blowing on his hands. 'Shame we've got to make a detour instead of going straight home, but we managed to pick up a cargo for Germany on our way back.'

'Will we have a chance to go ashore?' Jack was always eager to see another country.

'Probably.' Bill's expression sobered. 'But you're not to go ashore there unless the two of us are with you. Promise?'

'All right, I promise.' Jack was puzzled by their serious expressions, but didn't ask why. They had looked out for him ever since he'd joined the ship, and he trusted them. In fact, Bill had become like a father to him, and Frank an uncle. He followed their advice without question. They were experienced travellers, and he wasn't, so he was happy to do as they said.

They reached Hamburg the next day and Jack watched the activity on the dock, and it wasn't long before Frank, Bill and three more men joined him.

'We've only got three hours, and then we'll be under way again, so it will have to be a quick look round.'

'That will be enough,' Frank muttered.

'At least I'll be able to say I've set foot in Germany.' Jack smiled at the group of men. 'Are we all going?'

'Yes, and we'll stay together. Come on, let's go.'

They caught a bus into the centre of the town and began to walk along a street. Jack frowned. 'Are all those men in brown police?'

'No lad, they are members of the Nazi Party.'

'There are quite a few of them.' There was a sound of breaking glass and Jack spun round, pointing in amazement. 'They've just broken that shop window!'

'None of our business.' Frank urged Jack to keep walking when it seemed as if he would go over to the commotion.

'Why isn't someone calling the police?' he asked, looking back over his shoulder.

They stopped round a corner and Bill turned Jack to face him. 'This is what's going on here, lad. The fascists are gaining the upper hand and no one is trying to stop them. If we interfere we'll end up in prison – or worse.'

'That isn't right, Bill. They shouldn't be allowed to get away with it.'

'We know that, Jack,' Frank said. 'But this isn't our country, or our problem – yet.'

The truth suddenly dawned on Jack. 'So this is the reason for all the talk about war?'

'It is. There's a lot going on in this country, and it could spill over to involve other countries. It's worrying.'

Jack grimaced. 'You know, I haven't taken much notice of all the talk, but I understand more now.'

'That's why we brought you ashore, lad, and why I was insistent that you shouldn't come alone. You could easily have got yourself into real trouble.'

'I could, and thank you all for looking after me, but I hated walking away from there. Why did they pick on that shop?'

'Because it was a Jewish tailor's shop, I expect.'

'That's terrible!' Jack shook his head. 'I don't like it here. Can we go back to the ship?'

They all readily agreed and caught the next bus back to the docks.

The memory of what he'd seen lingered, and Jack knew he

would never dismiss the speculation about what might happen with Hitler and his party again. That brief visit had been an eye-opener, and he was glad the men had taken him ashore.

They arrived back three days before Christmas, and after receiving the pay due him, Jack signed on for the next voyage, and made his way to Kensington, eager to see his sister. They would have so much to talk about.

The house was just as his sister had described, and excited to be seeing her again, he went round to the back door and knocked.

A young girl opened the door and stared at him. 'Yes?'

'Could I see Hanna Foster, please?'

'Oh, you must be her brother!' Smiling broadly she opened the door wide. 'Come in. She'll be so pleased to see you. Cook, look who's here!'

An elderly woman looked up from the pastry she was rolling, dusted the flour from her hands, and said, 'Sit down, Jack, you look perished. I've got a pot of stew on the stove and a bowl of that will soon warm you up. Mary, go and tell Hanna she's wanted down here, but don't say why.' She beamed at Jack. 'Don't stand there, my boy. Sit down.'

He felt quite bemused by the welcome. 'Thank you, madam.'

She was busy filling a bowl with stew and looked over her shoulder. 'My name's Gladys Potter, and you can call me Mrs Potter or Cook like everyone else does.'

The food looked and smelt delicious, and as always, he was starving. 'This is wonderful, Mrs Potter,' he said between mouthfuls.

'I expect it is after the food on the ship.'

'We have a very good cook.' Jack looked up and smiled. 'Not as good as you though.'

'So polite,' she laughed. 'Just like your sister.'

At that moment the kitchen door opened and Jack scrambled to his feet and gazed at Hanna. She had two children with her, one either side holding her hands, and they made such a picture that he burst out laughing. 'Oh, it's so good to see you. And you're right. They are like bookends.'

Letting go of the twins Hanna rushed to throw her arms

around her brother, then she stepped back, looking him up and down. 'You're taller, you've filled out and are tanned. You look so different I hardly recognized you.'

He wrapped her in his arms again and rocked her gently, choked with emotion. 'We took a terrible risk, didn't we, Hanna? But everything has turned out all right for us.'

She nodded, her eyes misty. 'I think we were due a bit of good fortune, Jack. Now, say hello to the boys, but I warn you, they are going to want to hear all about your voyage.'

He stooped down and found himself looking at identical faces. 'Which one is Andrew?' he asked.

'I am,' they said in unison.

'Ah, that poses a problem then. One of you sent me a lovely drawing, and I can't thank you properly if I don't know which one of you it is.'

Andrew pushed a strand of hair away from his eyes. 'It was me. Did you like it?'

'I certainly did.' Jack sat on the floor and took something out of his pocket. 'One of the sailors had a camera and he took these photos for you. This one shows my bunk with the picture stuck up so I can see it, and the others are of the ship. They are for both of you to keep.'

'Wow! Thank you. Look at these!' They began running around the kitchen showing them to Mary and Cook.

'There's a lot of noise going on in here.'

The twins stopped immediately, spun round to face the man who had just come into the kitchen, and rushed over to him.

'Daddy!' They threw themselves at their laughing father, nearly knocking him off his feet, and holding out the photographs. 'Look what we've got!'

He disentangled himself from them and stood up. 'Give me a chance to greet Hanna's brother and then I'll have a look at those.'

Jack watched in bemusement and not a little heartache. How wonderful it must be to belong to a family like this.

'I'm pleased to meet you, Jack.' Captain Harcourt shook Jack's hand. 'Glad you made it home for Christmas.'

'It was a close thing, sir.' Jack smiled at the impressive man who had only just arrived and was still wearing his uniform.

'We had engine trouble, and that delayed us while repairs were made in New Zealand.'

Mrs Harcourt also came up to Jack, smiling warmly. 'Welcome home. There's a room ready for you in the annex. It's yours any time you want it.'

'That's very generous of you, and we're both grateful.' He slipped his arm around Hanna's shoulders and grinned. 'We've got so much to tell each other.'

'I'm sure you have. We are going to my husband's mother for the holidays so Hanna will be free to spend the next few days with you undisturbed.' She cast her sons an affectionate smile as they talked excitedly to their father. 'And thank you for giving the boys the photographs. They will treasure those. Hanna, show your brother to his room and get him settled in. The boys will stay with us until it's time for them to bath and go to bed.'

'Thank you, Mrs Harcourt.'

Jack watched the family leave and let out a deep sigh.

Understanding how her brother was feeling, she took hold of his arm, and said quietly, 'They are good people, Jack, and we've been very lucky to find them. Come on, let's get you settled.'

Lifting his bag on to his shoulder, he turned to Cook. 'Thank you for the food, Mrs Potter.'

'My pleasure, young man. I'll expect you both back here at eight o'clock for dinner.'

While the family and all the staff were away, Hanna moved into the annex. It contained a small kitchen and they had great fun cooking a Christmas dinner for themselves. Neither of them had ever had to prepare their own food before, but Cook had left copious instructions, along with a chicken, Christmas pudding and a cake.

They never stopped talking and laughing. It was a wonderful time for them and Hanna knew she would remember this as the best Christmas they had ever had. They were finally free of the orphanage and all the unhappiness it represented.

After washing up they sat by a log fire in the sitting room, relaxing with a nice cup of tea.

'Well, that wasn't bad, considering we didn't know what we

were doing.' Jack sighed with contentment, stretching out his long legs in front of him.

Hanna watched him relax, smiling gently. Her little brother was so grown-up now, and she couldn't believe just how tall he had grown in such a short time. He was also strong and muscular looking. Life at sea clearly suited him.

Draining his cup, Jack put it on the floor beside his chair and began to search through his pockets, until he found two small packages. He handed them to her. 'I bought these for you on my travels.'

She took them from him and asked, 'What are they?'

'Open them,' he grinned. 'Then you'll find out.'

She opened the soft one first and gasped when she saw the beautiful silk scarf, immediately draping it around her shoulders. 'This is so lovely. I've never had anything as fine as this. It feels like real silk, Jack?'

'It is, and I was right, the colours do suit you. I bought it in India. Open the other one. I got that in Ceylon.'

'All these exotic places,' she teased as she eagerly unwrapped the other package and carefully opened the small box. 'Oh, Jack, this must have cost a fortune!'

'Not as much as you'd think, especially when you have Bill doing the negotiating,' he laughed. 'Put it on and see if you like it.'

Lifting the delicate pendant on its fine gold chain out of the box, Hanna went over to the mirror on the wall and let Jack fasten it for her. 'I've never seen anything so beautiful. I'm lost for words.'

'That makes a change,' he joked. 'But seriously, it looks really nice on you. Hey!' He turned her to face him. 'You're not going to cry, are you? I didn't want to upset you. I just thought it was time you had something pretty to wear.'

She blinked away the moisture from her eyes and hugged him. 'Of course I'm not crying. Thank you for buying me the most beautiful presents. I love them both.'

'Good. And you can stop frowning, Hanna. I know what's going through your mind, but I didn't spend all that much because Bill bargained a very good price for me on both of them – and yes, I could afford them.'

'You know me too well, little brother, but I've always had to be careful with what little money we had, and it's hard to break the habit of a lifetime.' She reached behind the settee and gave Jack a bulky parcel. 'Happy Christmas, Jack.'

'Oh, thanks.' He ripped it open eagerly and pulled out knitted socks, gloves, a jumper and a woollen hat, all in navy blue. 'Wow! Just what I need. Did you make these yourself?'

She nodded. 'I only hope they fit. You've grown a lot more than I anticipated. Try them on.'

On went the socks, jumper, gloves and even the knitted hat, each a perfect fit. They both roared with laughter as Jack paraded in front of the mirror, and then spun round in front of her so she could inspect every item.

Then they found some dance music on the wireless and Hanna began to teach Jack how to waltz, being careful not to step on his stocking feet.

Eleven

September 3rd, 1939

Hanna felt as if her world had been torn apart, as did everyone else as they listened to Prime Minister Chamberlain tell them that they were now at war with Germany. Jack had returned to his ship after a lovely Christmas, and they had both been full of hope that a bright future was ahead of them. During this year he had come home a couple of times for brief visits, and had made friends with Alan, which had pleased her. Alan was now very much a part of her life, and they had even talked about marriage some time in the future.

'Damned man!' Cook exploded as she switched off the wireless. 'Hitler should never have been allowed to gain so much power. Now look what's happened. We've got another war to fight!'

Hanna was numb and fingered the pendant around her neck. What would happen to Jack? Would he leave the merchant navy? He was still so young, but knowing her brother she guessed that was unlikely. He loved his ship, the life it offered him and the friends he had made. He wouldn't leave them. And what about Alan? Could he avoid call-up by being in the police force? Her thoughts went out to everyone she knew. Rose Freeman's husband, being an experienced navy officer, would certainly be called upon again, and Captain Harcourt would be in it right from the start. Poor Mrs Harcourt, she must be feeling sick with worry, as would just about every family in the country.

'What are you going to do?' Mary sat beside Hanna at the large kitchen table.

'I haven't had time to think about it yet, but I'll stay with Mrs Harcourt and the twins, if I can.'

'They might make you do something else. They're already saying that women will have to take the place of the men as they join the forces.'

Hanna shrugged. 'I'll wait and see what happens. What about you?'

'I'm not going to wait.' Mary took a deep breath. 'I don't want to work in a factory so I'm going to join up straight away. I'll try for the Wrens first, and if I can't get in there I'll take any of the other services. I'm happy here, and Mrs Harcourt is a kind employer, but I don't want to spend my life in service. This is my chance to do something else, and I'm going to take it.'

'I hope you get what you want.' Hanna smiled sadly. 'We're going to miss you, but I want to stay with Mrs Harcourt and the boys. They are going to need me. If the Government tries to make me leave then I'll enlist the help of Rose Freeman,' she joked.

Mary and Hanna laughed softly and it was a good sound on such a sombre day.

'We're all going to have to adjust to new changes,' Mrs Potter said, 'but for now, Mary, you can help me. Mrs Harcourt and those little rascals will be home soon, and they'll be hungry.'

Needing to do something, Hanna stood up. 'Shall I go and lay the table in the dining room, Mrs Potter?'

'Thank you, my dear, and you'd better set a place for yourself. Mrs Harcourt will be needing a bit of company when she gets home.'

It was two hours later when Jane Harcourt arrived, and Hanna went immediately to help with the boys.

'A terrible day,' Jane said as she removed her jacket.

'It is,' Hanna agreed, looking down as Andrew slipped his hand in hers. Even the boys looked subdued, but could they really understand the enormity of what had happened this day? She doubted it, but they were bright enough to sense that everyone around them was worried.

Stooping down, she smiled. 'Did you have a nice time with Grandmother?'

They nodded, and David was the first one to speak, as usual. 'Mummy told us that we are at war now and Grandma was upset, so is Mummy, but she pretends she isn't.'

Mrs Harcourt had gone into the sitting room so Hanna

crouched down to the boys' level. Andrew said nothing but snuggled closer to her. 'We were all hoping and praying that this wouldn't happen, but in the end it couldn't be avoided. Your mummy's being brave, and that's what we've all got to do. Your daddy, and everyone involved in defeating Hitler, are going to need our love and support. Do you understand?'

They nodded again, and Andrew's little face was serious. 'What's going to happen, Hanna?'

'No one knows yet, sweetheart.' She smiled, trying to ease their concern, knowing how hard it must be for them to understand. Seeing their grandmother upset had obviously troubled them. 'We carry on as usual and pray that it will not last too long. If you are worried about anything at all then you can come to me and we'll talk about it together. All right?'

Their expressions relaxed at last.

'Now let's go and see your mother, and be just like you always are, two noisy boys,' she teased.

'We're not noisy! We're ever so good.' The broad smiles were back.

'Really? I've never noticed.' When she saw the devilish gleams in their eyes as they silently communicated with each other, she turned and ran for the sitting room with them right behind her.

'Help! Save me,' she shouted in mock terror, allowing them to catch her just inside the sitting room. She pretended to collapse on the carpet and they pounced on her, shrieking with delight.

'We're not noisy! We're good!'

'All right, I give in,' she gasped. 'You're very good boys.'

They sat on the floor for a moment, laughing at the fun, and then she scrambled to her feet.

'Mummy, Hanna said we were noisy. We're not, are we?' David's face was wreathed in smiles.

'I can't think where she got that idea from,' Jane said dryly. 'Now, why don't you boys go and ask Cook for a drink of orange?'

They took off at high speed, chatting away to each other as they ran.

'Thank you, Hanna.' Mrs Harcourt indicated she should join

her. 'I'm afraid we couldn't hide the shock and grief at the announcement, and ever sensitive to the moods of people around them, the boys were troubled.'

'That was obvious as soon as you came in.' Hanna sat down. 'There are worrying times ahead of us, but we must keep the boys' lives as normal as possible.'

'I agree. When are you expecting Jack home?'

'Should be within the next week, but after today's news I really don't know when we'll see him again.'

The news that they were now at war with Germany came as no shock to the men aboard the *North Star*. They had seen and heard enough on their travels to be sure this was coming.

Bill found Jack in his usual spot on deck, gazing at the sea, deep in thought. 'We're making full speed for home, and our lives are going to change from now on. Britain is an island and all our supplies have to come in by sea, so we are going to be needed. There won't be any more relaxed and pleasant trips like this one. What are you going to do, lad?'

'Do?' Jack frowned at Bill.

'You know what I mean. You're too young to get caught up in this. It's going to get dangerous.'

'I know that, but I'm not going to leave the ship, or the friends I've made. Whatever happens, we're in this together.'

'That's what I thought you'd say.' Bill's smile was wry. 'But I'm not sure it's a wise decision. However, you're a sailor at heart and we're going to need every man we've got. I'm just glad you had the experience of voyages in peacetime because things will be very different from now on.'

'I've enjoyed every minute of it and learnt so much, thanks to everyone on board, especially you and Frank.'

'We've enjoyed being a part of your enthusiasm.' Bill slapped Jack on the back. 'You're going to make a fine sailor. Now, I'm on watch in ten minutes.'

Jack watched him walk away and smiled to himself. Bill and Frank made light of what they had done for him, but he'd never forget their kindness. He had come aboard as a frightened young boy, running away in desperation, and they'd helped him put the past behind him. Bill had included him when he'd said they were going to need every man. That made him proud – and feel needed. He had found somewhere that he belonged, and nothing was going to make him walk away from it.

Two days later Jack walked up the path of the Harcourts' house, and before he reached the side door it burst open and the twins rushed out to meet him.

'Jack's home!' they shouted together. 'Hanna!'

'I'm right behind you,' she laughed, trying to get past the boys to welcome her brother. Because he was a sailor like their father, they had immediately adopted him as belonging to them.

It was a tussle, but Jack eventually managed to get into the kitchen. One twin was still holding on to his jacket and he grinned at Hanna. 'Which one is this? I still can't tell them apart.'

'That's Andrew. The one running and shouting to tell his mother you're here is David.'

'Ah.' He removed his bag from his shoulder and swung Andrew up. 'You're the one who drew that lovely picture for me.'

'I did,' he giggled, legs swinging in the air and looking over his shoulder. 'Mummy! Jack's here.'

'So I hear, and the whole street must know from the noise you two are making. Welcome home, Jack.'

'Thank you, Mrs Harcourt.' He put Andrew down, pursing his lips. 'Now, where did I put my bag?'

'Here it is.' David tried to drag it along.

'Ah, yes.' He stooped down and began to search inside with two little faces pressing to see what was in there. 'Gosh! What's this?' he said in mock surprise, bringing out two small packets and looking at the boys. 'What do you think these are?'

They shook their heads in unison, beaming with pleasure as Jack handed one parcel to each of them.

The paper was eagerly ripped away to reveal two carved wooden warships, and with whoops of delight they thanked Jack. After that everyone in the room had to admire the boats.

'You really shouldn't, Jack.' Mrs Harcourt was shaking her head. 'But that is so very kind of you.'

'It's nothing.' Jack stood up, smiling to see how delighted the twins were with the simple gifts. 'On a long voyage the men have various hobbies, and one man loves to make things from wood. He's very good.'

'He is indeed. Now, let's all have a nice cup of tea, shall we, Mrs Potter?'

'Kettle's already boiling, and I've got a fruit cake just out of the oven.'

'Perfect. We'll enjoy that.' Mrs Harcourt sat at the large kitchen table. 'Let's have it here together.'

Jack always marvelled at the way he had been accepted into the household. Mrs Harcourt had said 'welcome home', and it did feel like home to him. He had a room of his own and everyone always seemed pleased to see him. And more importantly, Hanna was happy here. She had changed from a worried, harassed girl, to a pretty young woman who smiled a lot, and he was so relieved about that. He had run away and left her to pick up the pieces, but as always, she had coped beautifully.

'Here you are, Jack.' Cook put a large slice of warm cake on his plate.

'Thanks, Mrs Potter. That looks and smells delicious.'

'Did you hear the news about the war while you were at sea?' Mrs Harcourt asked.

'Yes, the captain anticipated it and we were already at full speed for London.'

'What are you going to do now, Jack?' Hanna asked.

'Stay with the ship. This country has got to be fed and kept supplied with necessities if it's going to survive, and that will be our job.' He looked intently at her. 'I've got to do this, Hanna.'

'I know.' She squeezed his arm. 'I wouldn't have expected you to do anything else.'

He nodded, knowing she would support him as she had done all through the years. His sister was a very special person. Then he turned his attention to Mrs Harcourt. 'Do you know where your husband is at the moment?'

'No, but I received a message from him saying that all leave had been cancelled, and that was only to be expected. I'm afraid we will have to get used to not knowing where any of you are. Secrecy will be rigorously enforced.'

'No doubt. We've been told that we won't find out where we're going next until we are at sea.'

'When do you have to go back?' Hanna asked.

'I've only got two days.' He smiled gently at her. 'Sorry.'

'That's better than nothing. I'm going dancing with Alan tonight, so why don't you come with us?'

'He might not care to have me tagging along,' he joked.

'Of course he won't mind. We all need to relax and have a bit of fun.'

'Well, it would be nice, and you have taught me how to do the waltz.'

'Good, that's settled then.'

'I've never known two days go so fast.' Hanna tried to hide her fear for her brother's safety, and wasn't very successful.

'Don't look so worried, Hanna. I'll be fine. I'm on a good ship with a crew who know what they are doing.'

'Sorry,' she sighed. 'But it's hard. Why did this have to happen, Jack? For the first time in our lives everything was going well for us, and there seemed to be a hopeful future ahead of us. Now that's all gone and there's a war to fight.'

'Come on, Hanna, this isn't like you.' Jack placed an arm around her shoulder. 'The future's still there, we just don't know what shape it will take, or where it will lead us. We've got to take each day as it comes and do the best we can. It isn't going to be easy, but we've overcome tough times before, and we will this time.'

She looked up and smiled. 'When did you become so wise?'

He shrugged and grinned. 'The sea makes me think. Anyway, look, the sun is just rising on another new day.'

They were standing in the garden and Hanna lifted her head. 'I remember another time when we watched the sunrise together before you boarded the ship for the first time. It seems a lifetime ago. We had no idea what that day held in store for us, and just when we felt everything was going well for us, we find ourselves in that position again.'

Jack looked down at her. 'And remember we welcomed that new day with hope in our hearts, and it turned out all right, didn't it?'

'Better than we could have expected,' she agreed.

'Well, so will this one, you'll see.' He hugged her, slung his bag over his shoulder and walked out of the garden and up the road.

Twelve

Christmas had come and gone, and disappointingly neither Jack nor Captain Harcourt had made it home, but they all knew that was how it was going to be from now on. It was May now and Winston Churchill had taken over as Prime Minister, but apart from that it had been a quiet few months at home. Hanna couldn't help feeling that this was the lull before the storm. Things were not going well in France and Captain Harcourt had sent a message to his wife saying that she should leave London for the country, so he obviously knew something was about to happen.

All they could do was to take each day as it came, and today she had a date with Alan. She had bought a new skirt and blouse in the hope that it would lift her spirits a bit. She mustn't be gloomy today, but it wasn't easy to push aside the worry. Jack had only managed to get home once for a short visit since war broke out. He hadn't said anything about where he'd been, and she didn't ask, knowing that everything was secret now. The movement of ships or troops was never mentioned, and she understood that that was for their safety and the security of the country. Just about everyone she knew or met was concerned about someone, and they managed to stay cheerful. Alan said it was no good fretting because no news was good news, and he was right of course.

After brushing her hair one last time she checked that she looked all right, and went downstairs, a smile on her face. She always enjoyed her time with Alan, and they had nearly a whole day in front of them.

Alan came to the side door on time as usual, and after greeting her with a quick kiss, they walked up the road arm in arm.

'You look lovely, Hanna.'

Her smile broadened as she looked up at him. 'Thank you, but you always say that.'

'Well, it's always true. I think you're the prettiest girl I've ever met.'

'And you are the most handsome man I've ever been out with,' she teased.

He tipped his head back and laughed. 'Considering I'm the only one you've ever been out with I don't think that's much of a compliment.'

'Ah, but I also mean it.' They were both smiling happily when they reached the bus stop. 'Where are we going today?'

'The weather's good so why don't we go for a walk by the river, have tea somewhere and then go dancing?'

'That sounds lovely.'

'Ah, here comes a bus for the Embankment. We can go there and then dance the evening away at Hammersmith.' They got on the bus and went upstairs so Alan could smoke, then he turned to her, his expression serious. 'I don't want to spoil our day, Hanna, but I must tell you that I've joined the army, and will be leaving as soon as they call for me. Probably in about two weeks.'

The news wasn't unexpected, but she clasped his hand and managed to smile. 'I thought you would; you're not the kind of man who can stand on the sidelines, are you?'

He shook his head and squeezed her hand. 'Will you wait for me, darling, however long this damned war takes?'

'Of course I will, and we'll see each other when you come home on leave.'

He sighed with relief, and kissed her gently. 'It was my lucky day when I met you.'

'And mine. You dealt with that awful man so firmly.'

'That's all behind you now.' He smiled at her. 'Let's try and forget all the unpleasant and worrying things and just enjoy ourselves.'

'Good idea.' Hanna knew they weren't going to get many more carefree days like this once he was away in the army, so they would make the most of any time they had together. 'Are you joining the Military Police?'

'No, I didn't want to do that. I'm just going to be an ordinary foot soldier.'

That surprised her because he was a policeman through and

through, but he must have his reasons, and she didn't ask. If he'd wanted to explain, he would have told her.

When they reached their destination they walked hand in hand along the Embankment, neither speaking. She gazed at the river and smiled to herself. It was a pleasant day and they weren't the only ones out to enjoy themselves. The river was very busy.

After a while Alan stopped walking, a deep frown on his face, and Hanna nodded towards the river. 'Lots of boats out today.'

'Hmm, too many.' He pulled her down some steps towards the river until their feet were almost in the water, then he cupped his hands to his mouth and shouted, 'Where are you all going?'

'The coast. We've all been requisitioned by the navy,' a man called back.

'Why?'

'We haven't been told why they need our boats.'

Alan was immediately moving with purpose. 'Come on, Hanna, I've got to find a police station.'

She had to trot to keep up with his long strides, but said nothing. Alan wasn't the sort to worry over nothing – and he was worried.

He showed his card and asked directions from a passing policeman, and they were soon inside the station. 'Wait here, darling. I won't be long.'

She watched him show his police identity card again, talking earnestly to the sergeant on the front desk. Then he was taken into another room.

'Would you like a cup of tea while you wait?' the sergeant on the front desk asked.

'Thank you, that would be welcome. Do you know what's going on?'

'That I couldn't say, Miss. Sugar in your tea?'

'No, thank you.' Of course he wouldn't answer even if he knew, but she hadn't been able to stop herself from asking.

The tea arrived, she drank it, and still Alan hadn't appeared. She sat quietly, and waited, and waited. Patience was a quality she had in abundance, so the waiting didn't worry her, but her curiosity was running riot. What on earth could this be about?

An hour later Alan came out of the room, and she had never seen such a grim expression on his face. 'I'm sorry, darling, but I'll have to take you home. I've got to report for duty at once.'

She stood up. 'Can you tell me what's happening?'

He just shook his head. 'You'll find out soon enough, but I can't say anything at the moment.'

'I understand, but how do you know you've got to report back at once?'

'I phoned my station from here. Everyone is being recalled in case we're needed.'

The journey back was mostly silent, neither of them wanting to talk much. When they reached her house he held her tightly for a moment, and then said, 'I'm sorry our day out has ended like this. I'll be in touch when I can.'

'You take care,' she told him.

'I'm not in any danger.' He grimaced. 'Not like thousands and thousands of other poor devils. Tell Mrs Harcourt to do what her husband asked, and get the children out of London.'

With those last worrying words he turned and strode up the road, his stride long and urgent.

'You're back early, Hanna,' Mrs Harcourt said as soon as she walked in. 'I thought you were spending the day with Alan?'

'He's had to report back for duty at once.' Hanna then told her what had happened, and the advice Alan had given. Jane Harcourt rushed to switch on the wireless.

'Jack! Where the devil are you?'

A head covered in a navy-blue knitted hat appeared through a hatch. 'I'm here, Frank.'

'Quick, come on. The captain wants to talk to us.'

'Do you know why?' Jack scrambled back on deck.

'Not a clue, but it must be something important. Careful now!' Frank caught hold of Jack as the ship plunged and then rolled. 'Damned Atlantic can be nasty at times.'

'Where's the meeting taking place?' Jack shouted above the howling wind.

'In the mess.'

When they got there it was crowded with all those not on duty, and they managed to squeeze in at the back.

Captain Stevenson nodded when they arrived, his expression grim. 'There's bad news. Belgium and France have capitulated, and our army is trapped on the beaches at Dunkirk.'

There were murmurs of dismay, and after a pause, the captain continued. 'We don't have any more details at the moment, but there's bound to be attempts to rescue as many as possible. Unfortunately we're only a day out of New York and unable to give any help. I'll let you know as soon as we have any further news, but I'm sure you are all aware that with France as a base the Germans will have easy access to the Atlantic.'

'Things are going to get very rough,' one man muttered.

'I'm afraid so.' The captain looked at the men crowded round him. 'But we've got to get the supplies through if our country is going to survive.'

There were grim faces all round when the captain left, and Jack was stunned as he struggled through the men to reach Bill. 'How could this have happened? There will only be the Channel between the Germans and us. If we don't find a way to get our troops off those beaches, then we could end up without much of an army as well. What's going to happen now, Bill? Will Hitler now invade Britain?'

'I really don't know, lad, but that stretch of water won't be easy for the enemy to cross. We've got the air force and the best navy in the world.' Bill gave a grim smile. 'We aren't beaten yet.'

'No, of course not.' Jack nodded. 'The Germans will face huge losses if they try to invade that way.'

'Tea up!' Frank called, and there was a stampede for the counter, everyone talking at once.

'As long as we don't run short of tea we'll be all right,' Bill joked, handing a mug to Jack. 'You're filthy, lad, what have you been doing?'

After wiping his hands on an equally dirty rag from his pocket, Jack took the mug. 'Chief Harris has been showing me how they look after the engines.'

'I thought you were off duty now?'

'I am, but there's so much to learn, and the crew are happy to show me how the ship works. They're very good to spare the time to show me things.'

Bill shook his head in amazement. 'You thinking of studying for your master's certificate some time?'

'Why not?' Jack took a gulp of the hot tea, and then grinned at Bill. 'This is what I want to do for the rest of my life, so I might as well aim high.'

'You might as well.' Bill slapped him on the back, drained his mug and put it back on the counter. 'Duty calls. All watches have been doubled.'

They were diverted to Liverpool instead of London, and Jack watched the cargo being unloaded with Bill and Frank beside him.

'Our convoy got through without losses this time,' mused Frank, leaning on the rail. 'But those bloody subs won't have so far to come now and they'll be after us.'

'They'll do whatever they can to cut off supplies to Britain.' Bill turned to Jack. 'You can still get off this ship, lad. We'll all understand.'

'Don't start that again, Bill. I'm staying, and the threat of more danger isn't going to make me change my mind. I know what the fall of France means to us.' He straightened up and faced his two friends, determination written across his young face. 'I'm not leaving!'

'I didn't think you would, but I had to make sure you understood how rough it could get now.'

'I've seen ships go down, so I understand.'

'All right.' Bill nodded, respect showing clearly in his eyes. 'The subject is closed. We're in this together and that's how it's going to stay. Now, we're only here for two days and that isn't enough time to get to London and back, so let's go ashore and see if we can catch a newsreel at the pictures. I want to find out what they're doing to get our troops home.'

The gangway was in place and quite a few of the crew were making their way off the ship, all anxious for more detailed information.

Thirteen

Three weeks later Hanna was standing on the station platform with Alan's parents, waving as the train pulled out. Thousands of troops had been rescued from Dunkirk, but Britain was now in a perilous position, and all the forces needed to be strengthened. The question on everyone's mind was – would Hitler give us the chance to do so, or invade immediately? But no one knew.

Hanna dropped her arm as the train disappeared from sight. She was going to miss Alan so much, and now she had someone else to worry about. Jack hadn't been home for some time, but the worst part was not knowing where he was.

'Thank you for coming, Hanna.'

She had been so lost in thought that she jumped slightly, but turned and smiled at Alan's parents. 'I wanted to see Alan off, Mrs Rogers.'

'And he wanted you here.' Alan's father took his wife's arm. 'Would you join us for a cup of tea at the café across the road, Hanna?'

'I'd like that, thank you.' She couldn't rush away while Mr and Mrs Rogers looked so sad. She had only met them a couple of times, but knew they had been hoping their son would be able to stay in the police, and not have to go into the forces. That wasn't Alan though, and she doubted he would have stayed out of the forces even if he'd been able to. He was a doer and not a watcher, so his going into the army had been inevitable.

'We've never had a chance to talk to you,' Mrs Rogers said, once they were settled at a table by the window. 'Alan always whisked you away before we could say more than a couple of words. We know a little about you, of course, but Alan hasn't said much. Would you tell us a little about yourself and your brother?'

Hanna talked mostly about her brother and her job of looking after the twins, avoiding going into detail about their years at the orphanage. Although those years were behind her now, she still didn't talk about them easily.

'It sounds as if your brother is happy being a sailor now,' Mr Rogers said.

'He is,' she nodded. 'It's a shame the war had to come along and spoil everything, but he's determined to stay in the merchant navy and make it his career.'

'And what are you going to do now?' Mrs Rogers asked. 'Are you thinking of going into the forces as well?'

'I've considered it, of course, but I would like to stay with Mrs Harcourt. I feel as if the Harcourt house is my home now and I don't want to lose that, so I'll just wait and see what happens.' She sighed and shook her head. 'Everything is changing so fast and I don't even know what Mrs Harcourt's plans are. She might not want to keep me now. I'm afraid everyone is facing tough decisions.'

They talked for another ten minutes, and after promising to visit Alan's parents whenever she could, Hanna made her way back to the house.

The boys were having their afternoon nap, so Hanna opened the sitting-room door and looked in. Mrs Harcourt was there alone. 'Anything I can do for you, Mrs Harcourt?'

'You can keep me company for a while.' She smiled. 'Alan's on his way then?'

'Yes, and his parents were a bit upset so I stayed and had a cup of tea with them. They wanted to talk, and I was happy to get to know them better.'

'And I'm sure they appreciated your company.' Jane Harcourt sighed. 'I know my husband won't be happy until he knows the boys are away from London. We have a small farm in Suffolk, and the main house is quite large so there's plenty of room for all of us. Would you mind coming with us, Hanna? The boys would be very upset to lose you now, and so would I.'

'Oh, I'd love to.' Hanna sighed quietly with relief.

'Thank you, Hanna, I'm glad that's settled and you want to stay with us. We are leaving tomorrow, so there's quite a bit of packing to do. I'll inform everyone of our new address.' She handed Hanna a paper with the Suffolk address on it. 'You will need to let Jack and Alan know where you are. They will both be welcome at the farm whenever they come home on leave.'

'Thank you, Mrs Harcourt. What are you going to do with this house? Close it up?'

'No.' She shook her head. 'Mrs Potter will be staying here. She says that no one is going to move her out of London, so tell Jack he can still use his room here if he can't get to Suffolk any time.'

'He'll be pleased about that, and it's very kind of you.'

'Not at all, my dear.' Mrs Harcourt smiled sadly. 'This is going to be a big upheaval for all of us, but the boys' safety must come first. I fear that there are rough times ahead. All that separates us from the German army now is a small strip of water, but it won't be easy to cross without huge losses, and we can only hope it will be our saviour.'

Hanna agreed. 'Our army took a terrible beating in France, but we still have the air force and navy.'

The door burst open and in tumbled the twins, bright and full of energy after their sleep, and all talk of the war stopped.

'Hanna! We're going to the country.' Andrew was bubbling with excitement. 'Mummy said there's sheep, pigs, cows, chickens and all sorts of animals. Won't that be exciting!'

'My goodness, I've never been on a farm before.' She laughed at their excitement.

'You'll like it,' David told her. 'There are lots of fields and gardens as well.'

'Really? It sounds a lovely place.'

David nodded. 'Daddy told us we've been there but we were too young to remember. And we're going on the train!'

Jane Harcourt stopped the boys chatting. 'Come and sit down and have your drink of milk, and then we must all do our packing.'

Unable to sit still for more than a minute or two the twins finished their milk as fast as they could, then they were towing their mother and Hanna upstairs to decide what to take with them.

They weren't interested in the clothes; their only concern

was which toys to choose, and that was a serious business. They began to gather up all of their toys.

'Remember we're going on the train,' their mother reminded them when she saw how much they wanted to take with them. 'Only your favourites, please, boys. I shall be coming back here from time to time and I'll collect a few of the others each time. You can only take a few tomorrow.'

This needed a great deal of thought and discussion, but eventually a small heap was put on one side. Hanna noticed that every toy their father and Jack had given them were the ones they didn't want to be parted from. Hanna's packing didn't take any time at all because she still had little in the way of personal possessions. After years of being frugal she found it hard to spend money on herself, even though she was now in a position to do so. In a modest way, of course.

Later that evening Hanna wrote to Jack and Alan giving them the new address. She would post the letters in the morning when she popped round to see Alan's parents to let them know she was leaving London. They weren't catching a train until eleven o'clock in the morning, so she would have time to visit Mr and Mrs Rogers.

'All ready?' Jane Harcourt asked, when she came in to see if the twins were sleeping peacefully.

'Yes, I've written my letter, and all I've got to do is see Alan's parents in the morning.'

'I wish we didn't have to do this.' Jane sat down, a worried expression on her face. 'If our men get the chance of a short break they might not have time to come and see us. I don't want to leave London, but Sam is insistent.'

'He's only concerned for your safety,' Hanna said kindly. 'No one knows what is going to happen now.'

'You're right, of course, and it's hard to see family and friends leave, knowing they are in danger. I don't think I told you that Bill Freeman is back in the navy, did I?'

'Oh, I'm sorry to hear that. His wife will be upset.'

'Upset is hardly the word I'd use.' Jane Harcourt chuckled softly. 'If the Germans dare to invade, Rose will take them on – and win.'

Remembering the strong, determined woman Hanna had

met, she could well believe that. She also laughed at the picture that conjured up in her mind.

'Hanna, I've lost Mary and don't want you to leave as well, and I know you want to stay with us, but I'm sure that eventually everyone will be called upon to do war work of some kind. The farm is short-handed because all the young men have been called up. If you did some work around the farm that might be considered essential work.' Jane Harcourt was hesitant. 'Of course, I can't tell you what to do, and please feel free to refuse if you don't like the idea.'

'I've never been out of London, but I'll be happy to do anything I can. I desperately want to stay with you and the boys as well.'

'Thank you, Hanna, that is a relief. I know it isn't compulsory yet, but it could become so, and I wondered how you felt about it. Now, we'd better get some sleep.'

The twins were excited about going on the train, and Hanna had no trouble getting them ready. Carrying the luggage was harder, but two soldiers at the station took pity on them and stacked it all in a carriage for them.

After settling the boys so they each had a window seat, Hanna sat back. 'Phew! Those men were very kind. I hope we find someone that helpful at the other end.'

'We'll be all right then. Someone from the farm is meeting us.' Mrs Harcourt gave her sons a suspicious look. 'I think a few more toys were slipped in the cases when we weren't looking.'

Both boys glanced at their mother with expressions of pure innocence, then turned back to watch the passing scenery. Hanna chuckled quietly to herself. How many times had she seen that expression? It was a sure sign they had been up to something.

They had brought sandwiches and orange drinks with them, and these were welcome during the journey. No one was talking much, not even the boys, and Hanna was grateful for the silence. She was very apprehensive about leaving London, and wondered what it would be like living in the country.

'We're here.' Jane Harcourt was on her feet as soon as the train stopped, throwing open the door and stepping out.

Hanna caught hold of the boys to make sure they didn't try to get off the train by themselves. Their mother was already on the platform and talking to an elderly man and a young boy of around fourteen.

'Hanna, this is George and his grandson, Pete,' Mrs Harcourt said, bringing them over to her.

'I'm pleased to meet you.'

'And you, Hanna.' George smiled down at the twins who were studying him very carefully. 'My goodness, how you've grown. The last time I saw you was when you were babes in arms.'

David spoke first, as usual. 'We've come because Daddy said the Germans might come to London.'

'Ah, and that was very sensible. They'll never get this far. Now, come on, Pete, let's get this luggage into the cart. While we're doing that, Mrs Harcourt, you make your way outside.'

The boys stopped in amazement when they saw what was waiting for them, and so did Hanna. 'A horse and cart!'

She only just managed to hold on to Andrew, who was pulling to get away from her so he could get closer to the horse.

'It's a bit more than that,' George told them as he stacked the cases under the seats in the back. 'We brought this instead of the farm truck because it's more comfortable and we knew you'd have a lot of luggage with you. In you get.'

Hanna couldn't help smiling. There were steps which folded down to make it easy to climb into the back, two seats in the front for George and Pete, and two long padded leather seats in the back for passengers. It was like a coach of olden times, but without a roof, and everything was dark polished wood. 'This is beautiful, Mrs Harcourt.'

'Yes, my husband found it in a barn when we bought the farm and he restored it himself. It took him a long time because he could only work on it when he was on leave, but it was worth all the effort.'

'Have we got far to go?' David asked as the horse moved off at a gentle trot.

'About five miles, and it's a good job it isn't raining.'

'I'm glad. This is perfect.' Hanna was enthralled as they made their way along country lanes. She had never been out of London before, and she could now understand how Jack felt when he travelled to all those different places.

The boys were talking to each other and pointing out things of interest to them. It wasn't always easy to understand them when they were like this, for they seemed to have a language of their own.

Hanna was almost sorry when the journey was over, but when they pulled into the farm she studied the house with interest. It wasn't as large as the house in Kensington, but certainly large enough for all of them.

Unloading and settling into bedrooms already prepared took some time, and by the time they were finished, the boys were very tired. They stayed awake long enough to drink milk, and then Hanna tucked them up for a nap. They were asleep as soon as their little heads touched the pillows.

Jane Harcourt smiled down at her children, and sighed. 'This is all a huge adventure to them. At least they are too young to really understand the dangers of war.'

'And we'll try to keep it that way,' Hanna said, as they tiptoed out of the room. 'From what I've seen they will have plenty here to occupy their young minds.'

'Yes, I didn't want to leave London, but Sam was right. Their safety must come first. Now, Hanna, dinner won't be for another hour, so why don't you go and have a look round. I'll listen for the boys.'

'Thank you, I'd like to do that.'

Once outside Hanna took a deep breath of fresh air, tinged with all sorts of strange smells, none of them offensive. Looking round the first thing she saw was a high brick wall with an ornate iron gate and, curious, she opened the gate and went in. 'Oh, my,' she gasped, 'I never expected anything like this on a farm.'

'Lovely, isn't it?' Pete scrambled to his feet, brushing soil from his hands. 'We grow everything here. Those are fruit trees and fruit bushes all along the wall, and the beds are full of every kind of vegetable you can think of. The small patch at the other side is for flowers. My gran says we must have flowers even if there is a war on. There's a seat in the corner there if you ever want to have a quiet place to sit. Nice and warm in that spot it is because it catches the sun most of the day. The high wall protects the garden and everything grows well.'

'It's beautiful.' She smiled at the boy. He was obviously so proud of the garden.

'I love growing things. Do you?'

She shook her head. 'I've never even tried. Mrs Harcourt said I could do some work around the farm, so would you show me how while I'm here?'

'I'd love to. There's a spare plot right down the end you can start on, and the kids might like to get their hands dirty as well.'

'I'm sure they would,' she laughed, 'but you might not want them running around your lovely garden.'

He grinned. 'I was out here as soon as I could toddle. I'll see they don't do any damage. You come along any time and I'll get you started. I'm here most of the day.'

'Thank you, Pete. We'll be here some time tomorrow morning.'

She had only just begun to walk towards the gate when it swung open and the boys were running full pelt towards her, leaving their mother far behind. She always marvelled at how little sleep they needed before they recovered from their tiredness.

'Keep to the path,' Jane Harcourt called.

'We will!' they shouted, never slackening their pace as they shot past her to reach Pete. Their never-ending questions began to pour out.

'Oh, dear, I'd better go and rescue Pete,' she said dryly.

'He seems to be coping well,' Jane laughed. 'This is my favourite spot on the farm. You soon found it.'

'It's lovely. I've been talking to Pete and he said we could have that spare plot at the end and he'll teach us how to grow things. I thought the boys might enjoy having a little piece of garden each. What do you think?'

'That's a splendid idea. Let's go and have a word with him.'

Pete grinned as they approached. 'I think we could have a couple of budding gardeners here.'

'Hanna's been telling me you would be willing to teach them how to grow things, Pete.'

He nodded. 'That's if it's all right with you, Mrs Harcourt?'

'It certainly is.' She gazed around the garden. 'This place is a credit to you. We won't be short of fresh vegetables.'

'Ah, well, growing things has always been my passion.'

'It shows.' Hanna could see the pride in the young boy's eyes after hearing Mrs Harcourt's praise, and just managed to catch David before he stepped on to new plants just showing above the ground. 'What are these?'

'They're cauliflowers. Be ready for the winter. Come with me and I'll show you the plot you can have.'

As they walked to the end of the garden, Hanna smiled with pleasure as she noted the neat rows and rows of plants.

'Here we are. You can take half, Miss, and I'll divide the rest into two for the boys. It will need to be dug over first, and I'll do that for you.'

'Oh, no, you must let me do that,' Hanna protested. 'If this is going to be our plot then we must do everything ourselves, following your instructions, of course.'

He picked up a fork and began turning over the soil. Hanna watched for a while and then stopped him. 'Let me try.'

The twins thought it was hilarious to see her digging the garden, and although it was hard work, she loved doing it. There was a kind of satisfaction in seeing the newly dug ground.

When she had a patch that looked almost as good as the piece done by the experienced gardener, she looked up. 'What do you think, Pete?'

'Very good, but you do a little at a time until you're used to it. You will find it makes you ache at first.'

'I will, and thank you.' She stooped down to the boys who were obviously finding the whole thing fascinating. 'We are all going to have our own piece of garden and grow food for the war effort. That will help all the sailors who have to bring in their precious cargo to keep everyone fed.'

They nodded, serious for a moment. 'Can we choose what we grow?'

'Of course you can, Andrew. When I've got the ground ready we'll talk it over with Pete, and then he'll show us what to do.'

'Ah, there you all are!' Mrs Green came into the garden. 'Dinner's ready, Mrs Harcourt. Pete, you find your grandfather and tell him.'

Every spare moment Hanna had she was in the garden digging. It took her three days to finish, and her muscles certainly knew about the unusual activity.

'You've made a grand job of that,' Pete said as he inspected the plot. 'I'll divide it up for you now. I've got some spare planks of wood. How do you feel?'

'I ache in every joint,' she laughed, 'but I've really enjoyed doing it, and can't wait to start planting things. The hard work has helped to ease my worries about my brother. He's in the merchant navy, and I don't know where he is, or what he's doing.'

Fourteen

An enormous flash lit up the sky, and Jack remained rooted to the spot, knuckles showing white as they grasped the rail. 'There goes another one, Bill. Looks like a tanker this time. Poor devils. I hope a ship near them will stop and pick them up?'

'Everyone's been told that they must not drop behind the escorts.'

'I know that, but if we were closer do you think the captain would disobey that order?'

'I wouldn't be surprised. They are our men and I don't believe he could just sail past and leave them in the water.' Bill put the binoculars to his eyes. 'One of the escort ships is there. He'll pick up as many as he can, but he's taking a hell of a risk.'

Jack took the glasses from Bill and focused on the burning ship. 'You're right. Good for him.'

'Why don't you try and get some sleep, lad? You've been on the go for hours.'

Jack snorted. 'So have you and everyone else in this convoy, Bill. Do you really think anyone can sleep when at any moment a torpedo might hit you?'

'You're right.' Frank joined them carrying mugs. 'Thought you might like a cuppa. There must be more than one U-boat stalking this convoy. Since the fall of France it's easy for them to gather in packs. Wish we could see the buggers!'

'How many ships have we lost?' Jack thirstily drained his mug and handed it back to Frank. 'Is anyone keeping count?'

'No, this is a sizeable convoy and is spread over a large area of ocean, but we've lost far too many,' Bill replied. 'We've got another two days before we reach Liverpool and we'll be lucky if there's half the convoy left.'

'Hope the RAF comes out to meet us.'

'They will, lad. Now, you really must get some rest. You're exhausted.'

Giving a deep sigh, Jack nodded. 'You're right. Wake me if a torpedo hits us.'

'You can be sure of that.' Bill gave a grim smile at Jack's feeble joke, and watched as Jack walked away.

'That kid's made of solid stuff, Bill. It's bloody dangerous out here, and yet he can still joke. It makes you wonder if the kind of life he's led so far has made him tougher.'

Bill nodded. 'I've no doubt he's learnt to bend with the blows. He's scared, like all of us, but he's kept his head and shown no sign of panic. He's gaining a lot of respect from the crew, but this is a hell of a way for him to grow up.'

'True, but he isn't going to quit, however much we wish he wasn't putting his young life at risk.'

Both men lapsed into silence, looking out at what remained of the convoy. The sky was getting lighter and another day dawning.

'Hey!' Jack waved frantically as the Hurricane roared overhead, followed by two more. 'We've got our escort home, Bill!'

'That's a welcome sight.' Bill glanced at the men crowding the deck, smiling now. Only about a third of the original convoy was steaming towards the coast. 'A few hours and we'll be home, lad. Battered and bruised, but some of us have got through, and I've got some good news. We've got five days before we join the next convoy.'

'Well, I know what I'm going to do,' Frank said. 'Sleep!'

'Pity we aren't docking in London, but I'll be able to see Hanna for a couple of days.'

'And we could all do with the rest. This trip has been hell, and things aren't going to get much better any time soon.'

'I'm afraid you're right, Bill.' Frank gazed up at the planes circling overhead. 'But if our country is going to survive, we've got to keep bringing in vital supplies. The trouble is the Germans know that as well, and they're going to be after us all the time.'

Jack and Bill nodded, their faces drawn and tired.

★　　★　　★

When what was left of the convoy reached Liverpool, the dock workers were waving and ready to unload as soon as they could.

'They're pleased to see us,' Jack said, waving back. 'But not as glad as we are to see them.'

As soon as they had docked, a line of ambulances turned up next to them. Everyone watched in silence as the injured survivors were carried off the ship.

'They picked up a lot of men. From the state those poor blokes are in they must be from the tanker, but I thought the escort ship was doing that?'

'It was hard to see,' Bill said, 'but she might have been providing protection while the cargo ship hauled the men on board.'

Jack nodded and turned away from the distressing scene. 'Where are we going to get a bath? I can't get on a train like this.'

'There might be a public baths here, if not we'll find somewhere. We all need a good brush-up before we're presentable again.'

It was an hour before they could leave the ship, and Bill asked the first dock worker they met where they could get a bath.

'There's a place just outside the gates, mate. It's been opened to help sailors when they come ashore. You'll be able to clean up there and get a meal. They also have beds if you're stuck for the night.'

'Thanks, that sounds perfect.'

The dock worker studied the three men, his eyes resting on Jack. 'You've had a rough trip by the looks of it.'

'Hah.' Jack grinned and turned to his companions. 'It was a pleasure cruise, wasn't it?'

'Never had one like it,' Frank replied with a perfectly straight face.

'Some pleasure cruise when you need a fleet of ambulances to meet you.' The man shook his head, frowning. 'I don't know how you do it, but we're grateful you do.'

Bill hoisted his bag on to his shoulders, thanking the man again, and the three of them headed for the gates.

The Women's Voluntary Service running the centre was very helpful, and they were soon clean and sitting down with a tasty meal of vegetable pie in front of them. Feeling refreshed and more presentable they made for the station to catch the first train to London.

Jack was looking forward to seeing Hanna again, and although he was feeling exhausted, there was a smile on his face as he rapped on the kitchen door and stepped inside.

Mrs Potter was busy at the sink and she turned. 'Jack! How lovely to see you.'

'It's good to be here. Is Hanna around?'

'No, she's in Suffolk with the family. The captain insisted that they take the children out of London to a safer place. Didn't you receive her letter?'

He shook his head. 'I'm afraid not. Do you have the address?'

'Of course.' She looked him over carefully. 'But you can't go today, Jack. You look as if you can hardly stand. Stay here for the night, and then you can catch an early train in the morning. Mrs Harcourt left instructions for your room to always be kept ready, in case you wanted to stay here when you came home.'

'That's good of her.' Eager as he was to see his sister, he knew Mrs Potter was right. He was in no condition to make another journey today.

'Sit down, son, and I'll get you something to eat.' Mrs Potter ushered him into a chair. 'And then you can go and have a nice sleep.'

Jack didn't even remember getting into bed, and he slept so soundly that he woke up feeling more refreshed. He hadn't caught a train as early as he'd intended because Mrs Potter had let him sleep until he woke at nine o'clock.

Stopping at the gate of the farm he gazed around, drinking in the beauty and tranquillity of the place, pleased his sister was staying in such a safe place. His stay would be short, but he was glad he'd made the journey.

There wasn't a sign of anyone around as he walked towards the house, so he made his way round to the back. It was then he heard children laughing and he followed the sound to a walled garden. He opened the gate and stepped in. Hanna was on her hands and knees planting something with the twins chatting and laughing as they watched. A young boy was with them, obviously giving advice. It was such a happy, normal scene after the mayhem at sea that he watched for quite a while before one of the twins turned and saw him.

'Jack!' he yelled, already running with his brother right behind.

He dropped his bag and braced himself for the onslaught. The next thing he knew he was on the ground with the boys climbing all over him. 'Let me up!' he laughed.

Giggling and laughing, they allowed him to scramble to his feet so he could greet Hanna. He engulfed her in a bear hug, holding her longer than he would normally have done, because it was now he realized how close he had come to never seeing her again. That last convoy was the most dangerous they had been on so far, and the next one could be just as bad. But he wouldn't think about that now. His ship had come through without a scratch, and he would enjoy this short time with his sister.

'Let me look at you.' Hanna stepped back so she could look him up and down. 'My goodness, Jack, you've grown even taller. I would hardly have recognized you if I had seen you in the street. Oh, it's good to see you. How long can you stay?'

'Only a couple of days because I've got to get back to Liverpool.'

Hanna's disappointment showed for an instant, but was quickly wiped from her face. 'Never mind, at least we'll have a little time together.'

He nodded and turned his attention to the twins who were waiting patiently by his side. 'And what have you two been up to while I've been away?'

'We're learning to grow things,' Andrew told him. 'It's fun.'

'I expect it is.' Jack turned to the young lad hovering near them. 'Are you the one who has taken on the task of teaching them?'

Pete stepped forward. 'Yes, sir.'

Being called sir took Jack by surprise. He wasn't much older than this youngster, but he did feel ancient in comparison. 'Please call me Jack. I'm Hanna's brother.'

'My name's Pete, and I'm pleased to meet you.'

At that moment the garden gate opened and Mrs Harcourt walked in. 'Welcome, Jack. It's lovely to have you home.'

'I'm afraid it's only a short visit, but it's good to be here.' He had a lump in his throat at her greeting. They'd never had a home before, but everyone here did make him feel welcome, as if he belonged. It was a good feeling.

Jane looked at the would-be gardeners. 'Why don't you all rinse your hands under the tap and then we can take Jack inside for a drink?'

'I think that's an excellent idea.'

All eyes turned towards the gate, and the twins squealed in delight.

'Daddy!'

After the greetings had been made and some kind of order restored, Captain Harcourt said, 'Now we all deserve a drink. You as well, Pete.'

They piled into the large kitchen and Mildred Cooper set about getting the drinks, helped by Hanna. As they all settled down Jack couldn't help noticing the dark shadows under the captain's eyes, just like his own. The strain was showing on both of them, and Jack wondered if he had been one of the escort ships on that dreadful voyage. He'd ask him later if he got the chance to speak to him alone, but this happy family scene was no place to discuss such a horror.

That chance came when Mrs Harcourt and Hanna were bathing the boys and getting them ready for bed. They were in the sitting room on their own.

Captain Harcourt held up the whisky decanter. 'Drink, Jack?'

'No thanks, sir, but I'll have a soft drink if you've got one.'

'Orange?'

'That will be fine.'

He handed Jack the glass with a wry smile on his face. 'I forgot you are only very young. Are you still on the *North Star*?'

Jack nodded.

'Glad you made it then.'

'So am I.' Jack gave the captain a studied look. 'Were you part of our escort? The one who stopped when those survivors were picked up from the tanker?'

'Yes.'

'That was a brave thing to do, sir. That sub was probably still lurking nearby.'

'More than one. They are beginning to operate in packs now, and that convoy took a beating.' The captain emptied his glass and put it on the small table beside him. 'But we're not the only ones facing a struggle. The RAF is also fighting a tremendous battle. Hitler can't invade unless he knocks out our air force first.'

'He can't win. Whatever it takes we can't let him.'

'No, it's unthinkable.' The captain poured himself another small whisky. 'Are you staying on the Atlantic convoys?'

'As far as I know. We haven't been told anything different.' Jack grinned. 'I'm hoping to get ashore in New York next time. We couldn't this trip because the return convoy was already gathering, so we were loaded and on our way back before we had a chance to see anything.'

'The Germans are going to sink as many cargo ships as they can, Jack,' the captain told him, studying him carefully.

'I know that. Thank goodness I'm a strong swimmer, eh?'

'Well I'm not.' The captain gave a dry laugh. 'So if you see me in the water give me a hand up, will you?'

'That's a promise, sir.'

They both laughed, relaxing for the first time in a long while.

All the excitement had tired the boys out and they were fast asleep in no time at all. Hanna and their mother crept out of the room.

'They couldn't even stay awake to say goodnight to their father,' Hanna said.

'Yes, that's a pity, but I didn't want to disturb Sam. I had the feeling he wanted to have a quiet chat with Jack.'

A worried frown crossed Hanna's face. 'They both look so tired, and although Jack appears the same, making quiet jokes as usual, he's changed. Now and again there's a look in his eyes I've never seen before – like sadness. I don't know how to describe it. Neither of them have said where they've been or what happened on their last trip.'

'And they won't, Hanna. We mustn't press them. They'll talk if and when they want to. They are only home for a short time and we must make it as happy and enjoyable for them as we can.'

Fifteen

It had been wonderful to see Jack and the captain, and Hanna sang to herself as she dug over another piece of vegetable garden. She was getting so good at this now that Pete was allowing her to use another small plot. Much to her surprise she loved gardening, and the farm was a constant delight to her and the twins. After living all of her life in London, this place was paradise, but she couldn't help feeling guilty about being so happy here when others were suffering. The men at sea were facing terrible dangers, and the airmen were engaged in a desperate fight in the skies. And when Alan had finished his basic training he would also be facing all kind of unthinkable dangers.

Slamming the fork into the ground she leant on it. Was she doing enough? Should she have joined the forces, or something else? She shook her head. No, producing food was absolutely essential, and she was working very hard to do just that.

'Had enough of digging?'

She looked up and smiled. 'No, Pete, I was just thinking. I love the farm, and growing food is vital to the war effort, but I was wondering if I should be doing more?'

'That's how I feel. I tried to join the Home Guard, but they won't take me because I've only just turned fifteen. They told me that we all have a different role to play in this war, and being a farmer is very important. Still, your brother isn't much older than me and he's in the merchant navy bringing in needed supplies on the Atlantic convoys.'

'Did he tell you that?' She had guessed that was what he was doing, but he hadn't said anything to her.

Pete nodded. 'I was telling him how frustrated I was not being allowed to fight, and he said I was already doing a great job, but it didn't make me feel any better about it. I just wish I was a few years older.'

'You mustn't feel like that, Pete. This could be a long war

and we are all going to be needed. There's a place and a right job for all of us. We just have to find out where we fit in.' Hanna looked around the garden that was flourishing with every kind of vegetable. 'And I believe this is where we belong.'

'You're right, of course.' He smiled then. 'And the country has got to be fed. If we starve we can't fight, can we?'

'Exactly!' The conversation with Pete had settled her own mind, and she went back to her digging with renewed energy.

The sound of children's voices and running feet made Hanna grin. 'The twins are awake and need me.'

'We're going to have a party!' They hurtled towards Hanna and Pete, shouting with one voice.

'How exciting,' Hanna laughed, catching them before they trampled all over her freshly dug ground. 'When?'

'Saturday!'

Hanna kept the smile on her face although she felt a pang of sadness when she remembered that her brother hadn't been much older than them when she and Jack had been put in the orphanage. But when she looked at the two identical, happy faces, it was a joy to know that these precious little boys wouldn't have to face such an ordeal.

'Mummy said we could ask the children from the village school to come.' Andrew couldn't stand still he was so excited.

'Ah, I see they've told you.' Jane joined them. 'I was trying to keep it a secret, but I was discussing it with your grandmother, Pete, and they came into the kitchen. The little imps can move very quietly when they want to.'

David and Andrew gave each other knowing glances, looking smug.

'I've made an appointment to see the head teacher at the nursery school in the morning, Hanna. We'll take the boys with us and they can meet some of the children. It's time they had others of their own age to play with. They can start attending the school next term.'

'Won't that be lovely! You'll make lots of new friends.'

The twins gave each other one of those strange looks, and David said something that only Andrew understood. Then with a look of mischief on their faces they dragged Pete off to tell them why the plants were taking such a long time to grow. They expected to plant them one day and have them fully grown the next.

Jane sighed and shook her head. 'I wish they wouldn't do that. I swear they can read each other's mind, and that's why I want them to mix with other children. I thought a party might be a good way to start.'

'I'm sure they'll grow out of it, but I know what you mean. They seem quite content in each other's company, but this is a complicated world and they've got to learn to live in it.'

'Yes, and it isn't a nice one at the moment. They've got to be able to cope with the good and the bad life will throw at them, and the sooner we start that the better. Have you heard from Alan lately?' Jane asked, changing the subject.

'I had a letter yesterday. He's nearly finished his basic training and looking forward to coming home on leave.'

'When he does, Hanna, you must go to London and spend a few days with him. You can stay at the house in Kensington while you're there. When you came to work for me we agreed that you should have at least a day and a half off a week, but you never take it. You work so hard it's time you had a break.'

'I wouldn't know what to do with spare time, but thank you. Alan has been asking if I could get a couple of days free, and it would be so lovely to see him again and not have to rush away.'

'Then you shall go. Just let me know when he's home,' Jane told her. 'And you mustn't worry about the boys. I'll be here and Mildred is always happy to look after them if necessary, so you go and enjoy yourself.'

There were only ten children in the kindergarten class, and they all stared at the identical twins as if they couldn't believe their eyes.

'Children.' Their teacher, Miss Preston, called them to order. 'Andrew and David will be joining us next term, and they have something to ask you.'

Hanna and their mother had briefed them on what to do, but they still looked uncertain. Jane bent down to them. 'Ask them to come to your party on Saturday.'

They nodded, stood shoulder to shoulder and spoke together quite clearly and in perfect unison.

When they had issued the invitation one little girl left her desk and stood right in front of them. 'I'll come. What time?'

'Two o'clock,' Jane told her. 'What is your name?'

'May,' she told them. 'That's when I was born. Is it a birthday party, and should we bring presents?'

Hanna was impressed. May was certainly very mature and sensible for her age.

'There is no need to bring presents or anything else,' Jane told the class. 'This is just a chance for you all to get to know David and Andrew.'

May nodded her approval of this, and then turned her attention to the boys, who were watching everything very carefully. 'You both look the same. I can't tell who is who.'

'I'm Andrew.'

'And I'm David.'

Hanna smothered a laugh and she heard Jane almost groan. That was the wrong way round, and they looked so innocent, but they were up to their old tricks again.

'They're going to have the children in a real tangle,' Jane murmured to Hanna.

All the children had gathered around the boys now, asking questions, but May sidled over to Hanna. 'Do you know which one is which?'

Hanna stooped down to the little girl. 'Yes, it's quite easy when you get to know them.'

'How? Will you tell me?'

'Well, look at them carefully. See how one of them has a small lock of hair coming down on his forehead? That's Andrew. David's hair always stays in place.'

May nodded, pursing her lips in concentration. 'That's not what they said.'

Oh, this was one bright little girl, Hanna thought as she shook her head. 'They try that on everyone they meet, but they won't be able to fool you now, will they?'

She grinned and shook her head, then went back to join the rest of the children.

When the teacher motioned that they should leave the room,

they left together. Miss Preston said, 'We'll leave them alone together for a couple of minutes, Mrs Harcourt, but it looks as if they are going to get along just fine. I know you are both able to tell them apart, so would you mind telling me what to look for.' The teacher shook her head. 'They're going to have me in a real mess if I don't know which boy I'm dealing with.'

'Oh, they will indeed!' Jane laughed, and then explained the slight differences the teacher needed to look for.

Every one of the children turned up on the Saturday, along with their mothers, and it was a blessing that the weather was good so they could be in the garden. The noise was unbelievable and for two hours Hanna never stopped running around. Jane Harcourt couldn't have any more fears about her children fitting in, Hanna thought wryly. They were in the thick of things, though never far from each other. Still, it was good to see them laughing and playing with the other children. They had grown quite a lot in the short time she had been with them, and once they were at school she would help more in the garden, and also help George with some of the other farm work. She felt strongly that she must make more of a contribution to the war effort. She hadn't expected the boys to be going to school for a while yet, so this would be a good opportunity to do something useful with the extra time she would have on her hands.

Finally they waved off the last child, May, who seemed reluctant to leave the twins, and when her mother had at last persuaded her daughter the party was over, Jane and Hanna collapsed on to kitchen chairs with a sigh of relief.

'I'll give you a hand with the clearing up, Mildred,' Hanna said as she surveyed the mountain of dishes, all empty.

'You'll do no such thing. I can soon put this place to rights again. The best thing you can do is see if the boys will sleep for an hour or so after all the excitement. That will help all of us.'

'Good idea.' Hanna dragged herself out of the chair. 'They must be tired, but I think the party was a great success.'

'I agree,' Jane said. 'It's a shame Sam wasn't here. He would have loved it.'

'So would Jack.' Hanna stretched. 'I'll see if I can persuade the boys to take a short nap.'

They were still in the garden, sitting quietly on the grass, and surprisingly there wasn't one protest from them.

A week later, Hanna received a letter from Alan, saying he would be home on leave in two days' time, and she went straight to see Jane Harcourt while the boys were busy in the garden with Pete. They did love getting their hands dirty and spent quite a lot of time out there.

'Alan will be home on leave tomorrow and has asked if I can spend a couple of days with him, Mrs Harcourt. Will it be all right if I go to London tomorrow?'

'Of course it will, Hanna. You can stay at the house, and Mrs Potter will be pleased to see you.'

'Thank you so much. It will be lovely to see him again.'

After the beauty and tranquillity of the country it was strange to be back in London again. Nearly everyone seemed to be in some kind of uniform, and the train coming up had been packed with service men and women. There had been British, French, Canadians, Australians, and others she couldn't make out.

The house looked just the same though, as imposing as ever, but so quiet now there was only Mrs Potter living here. She tapped on the back door, opened it, and walked in.

'Hanna!' Mrs Potter hugged her. 'How lovely to see you. Are you staying for a while?'

'Only for two days. Alan's home on leave.'

'Ah, that's splendid.' She took Hanna's bag. 'Let's get you settled, then we'll have something to eat before you go and see your young man. How's that fine brother of yours?' The elderly lady chatted away, smiling all the time, and obviously pleased to have a bit of company for a while.

'His letters aren't very regular, but the last time I heard from him he was fine.'

'Good, good. Worrying times, my dear, but let's hope it won't last too long.' She gave Hanna's hand a reassuring pat. 'We got through the last one and we'll survive this one as well. You'll see.'

Hanna nodded, but after the fall of France she didn't hold
out much hope of a speedy end to the war. These thoughts
she kept to herself though.

Mrs Potter insisted she eat before she went out, so she did,
letting the housekeeper talk away. It turned out that Mrs Potter
was far from lonely, as Hanna had first thought. She had many
friends, and quite a social life going on. No wonder she had
refused to leave London.

As soon as the meal was finished, Hanna went straight round
to Alan's. She had just opened the front gate when the front
door crashed open, and the next instant she was swung off her
feet.

'You made it!' He buried his head in her shoulder, and then
rained kisses all over her face. 'Oh, how I've missed you.'

'I'm happy to see you as well,' she laughed when he put her
down. Stepping back, she studied him. 'You've lost a bit of
weight, but you look very fit.'

'So I should after that training, but let's not talk about that.
It's Saturday night, so let's go dancing.'

'Sounds like a good idea.' Hanna couldn't stop smiling.
'Hadn't I better go and say hello to your parents first?'

'Be quick then. We've got to make the most of our time
together.'

Mr and Mrs Rogers were standing by the door, smiling.
'Glad you could get here, Hanna.'

'Mrs Harcourt insisted that I come. How are you?'

'Very well,' Mr Rogers said. 'But you don't want to waste
your time talking to us. Off you go and enjoy yourselves. It's
only four o'clock, so you can have a nice long evening together.'

They didn't need any more persuading, but they had only
taken a few steps up the road when the air-raid sirens sounded.
Alan stopped, gazing up at the sky, and Hanna said, 'I expect
it's just a practice.'

'I don't think so, not this time. Listen, can't you hear the
drone of planes?'

'Yes . . . What was that?' she exclaimed.

'London's being bombed.' Alan turned her round and they
went straight back to the house. 'Where's your nearest shelter?'
he asked his parents.

'At the end of the next road, but we're not going there, Alan,' his father said firmly. 'Not unless they start dropping bombs right here, but it looks as if they are after the docks.'

Alan's father was right, and by around five o'clock the docks were blazing. They stood in the back garden looking at the glow in the sky. It was six o'clock before the all-clear sounded and the raid was over.

'Oh, those poor devils,' Mrs Rogers said, shaking her head. 'I think we all need a cup of tea after that.'

'I need a brandy!' Alan's father stated. 'What about you, Alan?'

'Just the thing,' he agreed.

They sat in the front room with their chosen drinks, and Mrs Rogers said, 'Well that seems to be all over now. Hanna has come all this way to be with you, Alan, and I think you should still go out and enjoy yourselves.'

Alan drained his glass and nodded. 'We'll go if you and Dad promise to go to the shelter if they come back again tonight.'

'That's unlikely, but we'll do as you say.' His father raised his glass. 'Go and enjoy yourselves.'

The dance hall in Hammersmith was packed, and as they danced they talked non-stop. Alan wanted to know everything she had been doing and any news she had of Jack. He let her talk all the time and said very little about the camp he was in, or what he was likely to do now his basic training was finished. However, she wasn't surprised, knowing that security was of the utmost importance. It was accepted that people involved in the war effort didn't talk about what they were doing.

The raid certainly hadn't stopped people from coming out for the evening, and they were so lost in enjoying themselves and being together again that they were surprised when the music suddenly stopped in the middle of a dance.

A man in ARP uniform stepped up to the microphone and announced that the air-raid warning had sounded. 'It looks as if they are dropping their bombs anywhere this time, and we advise you to make your way to the shelters,' he told them.

Some people began to leave, but many just stayed where they were even though the sound of explosions could now be heard in the silence.

'Come on, Hanna.' Alan caught her hand and began to move towards the door. 'Let's see what's happening.'

The sight that greeted them was unbelievable. The sky was alight not only with fires, but also searchlights, and the anti-aircraft guns were blasting away.

'Looks like they're hitting civilian targets this time.'

Hanna's heart went out to the people living in the East End, where it looked as if most of the bombs were falling at the moment. It was an area she knew well and she prayed that the children in the orphanage had been taken to safety.

'Will Jack be in London?' Alan asked.

'Unlikely. They've been docking at Liverpool, and anyway I think he's still at sea.'

Alan nodded. 'I'd better get you to a shelter.'

'Down there, mate,' an air-raid warden told them. 'And I'd hurry if I was you. Those damned planes are coming over in waves, and there's no telling where they're going to drop their bombs.'

The shelter they found was crowded, but they managed to squeeze in on one of the long wooden seats. Alan couldn't settle and kept going to the door to see what was happening, standing outside for quite a while.

'Your young man wants to get out there and help,' a woman sitting next to Hanna said. 'I guess the only thing keeping him here is you.'

'I think so too.' Hanna grimaced. 'He was a policeman before the war and he isn't used to waiting on the sidelines. If he had the room he would be pacing up and down. I'll go and have a word with him.'

When she stood beside him he placed an arm around her shoulder. 'Just look at that, darling. It looks as if the whole of the East End is ablaze, and it sounds as if even more bombers are coming over. You must go back to the country tomorrow. I don't want you in London now this has started.'

'I'm not going to let them stop us spending some time together, Alan. Even if we do have to keep dodging into shelters.'

He smiled down at her. 'We'll try to keep away from the bombs then.'

She squeezed his arm, pleased he hadn't argued with her about staying.

They didn't appear to be in much danger where they were, so they stayed just outside the shelter, ready to dive in if anything got too close. It was almost dawn before the sound of the bombers eventually ceased, and after a while the all-clear sounded.

'I'll take you home, Hanna.'

'And then I suppose you are going over there.' She pointed towards the glow in the sky.

'I might be able to help. I've had first-aid training in the police. I can't just ignore this, darling.'

'I know, but you're not leaving me behind. I'm good with children and I think they are going to need all the help they can get. I grew up in the East End, Alan, and if I can do anything then I will.' She glanced up at his face and put her finger on his lips to stop him protesting. 'How are we going to get there?'

He shrugged, accepting her decision even if he obviously didn't like her being in the danger area. 'That won't be easy, but we'll find a way.' He clasped her hand tightly and they headed for the main road.

The first thing they saw was a taxi, so Alan waved him down.

'Where do you want to go, mate?'

'Get us as near to the East End as you can, please.'

The driver pursed his lips. 'Hop in. I'll see what I can do, but the roads are probably closed around there.'

'Do the best you can.' They got in and gave each other a grim smile.

'Looks like that swine has changed his tactics and is going to try and bomb us into submission,' the driver said, when they were on their way. 'Wasting his time, of course. All he's going to do is make us bloody mad!'

The driver continued to chat and Hanna and Alan were content to sit back and listen. Their progress was good at first, and then they began to come up against blocked-off roads. After many twists and turns the driver pulled up. The road in front of them was strewn with rubble and the smoke from burning buildings was overpowering.

'What a bloody mess,' the driver muttered, and then turned back to look at them. 'This is as far as I can take you. Will it do?'

'Yes, thanks very much.' They climbed out and Alan took out his wallet. 'How much do we owe you?'

'Nothing, mate. Can't charge you on a night like this. We've all got to do our bit.'

Hanna shook her head as the taxi turned and roared away. 'That's the first time I've ever known a cabbie refuse to take his fare.'

'Hmm.' Alan was preoccupied, scanning the street in front of them. 'We can't go down there. That building is blazing and there are firemen everywhere, so we mustn't get in their way. Let's see if we can get through down a side street.'

'Oh, look!' Hanna gasped, breaking into a trot to keep up with Alan. 'These houses have been flattened, and people are trapped, by the look of it.'

'Need some help?' Alan asked as soon as they reached a group of men trying to move heavy rubble.

Another soldier looked up and nodded. 'Help me shift this, but be careful. We think there's someone under there.'

Hanna stood back for a moment wondering what she could do, and then she saw a woman stepping over rubble with a toddler and a baby in her arms. She hurried over. 'Do you need a hand? Where are you going?'

A policeman came up to her with another woman and two small children, both boys. 'Miss, take these to the church hall, down the road and turn left.'

'Right.' She held her hand out to the girl who was about the same age as the twins. 'Let's find this place, shall we?'

'Where's our house, Mum?' One of the boys was staring up and down the road, refusing to move.

'It ain't there no more, Jimmy,' his mother told him with a break in her voice. 'A bomb fell on it when we was in the shelter.'

Hanna stooped down to the bemused child and took his hand. 'I'm going to take you somewhere where your mum can get help. They'll give you food and find you somewhere to stay.'

He stared at her, his bottom lip trembling. 'My dad ain't 'alf gonna be mad when he finds out.'

Keeping hold of him with one hand and the little girl in the other, Hanna urged them along, and easily found the hall. It was crowded.

'Ah, come in, my darlings.' A WVS woman hastily pulled the blackout curtain back in place, making sure not a chink of light showed.

That struck Hanna as slightly unnecessary considering the whole area was lit up with burning fires, but she realized there was no point in getting careless. Seeing that her charges were now being taken good care of, she went out to see if she could find any more women who needed a helping hand.

Hanna was kept busy, and it was well into the morning when she returned to the hall where the volunteers were serving tea for the rescue services. After gulping down a welcome cup of tea, she was just about to look for Alan when he walked in the door. His uniform was torn, and he was covered in dust.

He downed two mugs of tea without stopping, and then he held his hand out to her. 'We'd better be getting back.'

They were both given heartfelt thanks for their help, and they walked up the road, too weary to talk.

It wasn't until they reached the main road that Hanna gave a short laugh of disbelief. 'Look at that! The buses are running!'

Sixteen

The bombers came again the next night, but Hanna was determined that she and Alan would spend the two days together. She was well aware that as the war went on she would see less and less of him, so she was not going to allow anything to stop them spending a couple of precious days together.

When it was time for her to return to the farm, Alan took her to the station and kissed her goodbye. She got on the train feeling troubled and sad, not only about the destruction she had seen, but also because they had no idea when they would see each other again.

As soon as she walked into the yard, Jane hurried out to meet her. 'Hanna, we are so relieved to see you. We've heard the news about the bombing, and it must have been frightening. Are you all right?'

'I'm fine, but it wasn't pleasant.'

'Come in and sit down, my dear. We want to hear all about it.'

Mildred already had the kettle on, and George and Pete were also waiting in the kitchen anxious for news. They listened intently to Hanna's account of the bombing, and what they did after the raids.

'Oh, those poor people.' Jane's expression was one of sadness and anger. She began to pace the room. 'I feel so helpless being here, but Sam has told me very firmly that my job is to keep the boys and myself safe. He said that if he didn't survive the war and I put myself in danger, then our little ones could lose both parents.'

'He's right.' Hanna was on her feet in alarm. 'It's devastating for young children to find themselves suddenly orphans, as Jack and I know only too well. You must stay here. London is a very dangerous place now, and Hitler has threatened to destroy it, along with other cities. No, no, you mustn't take any risks.' The thought of those two lovely boys ending up orphaned like her and Jack was horrifying.

Jane nodded, sitting down again, sighing deeply. 'You're quite right, of course, but I've got to do something, Hanna.'

'I've been thinking about that while I was on the train. I spoke to women with young children whose homes were just rubble, and every one of them had a husband in the forces.' Hanna hesitated, wondering if she had the right to suggest this.

'Go on,' Jane urged.

Taking a deep breath, she continued. 'There are two cottages on the farm. Pete said they used to be for farmhands, but haven't been occupied for a long time and are in a state, but if we could make them habitable then they would do for two families.' When Jane just stared at her, Hanna thought she might have overstepped the mark, and said hastily, 'You don't have to agree if you think it's a daft idea.'

'I think it's a splendid idea!' Jane pulled Hanna out of her seat. 'Let's go and have a look at them now. Mildred, the boys are having a nap, but would you keep an ear out for them? We won't be long. And George, your advice will be welcome, and you can take us there in one of the trucks.'

In no time at all they were trundling along in the ancient truck and George said, 'This is a grand idea, but it will take a deal of work to make the cottages fit to live in, even if it's at all possible.'

'We'll make it possible.' Jane smiled at Hanna, a determined glint in her eyes. 'What does Rose Freeman always say, Hanna?'

'Nothing is impossible.'

'Exactly!'

The first inspection of the cottages had Hanna doubting that statement. She had only ever seen them from the outside. 'Perhaps this wasn't such a good idea after all.'

'It can and must be done,' Jane said, undaunted by the mess. 'What do you think, George?'

'Well . . .' He rubbed his chin, and then walked around knocking on walls. 'Seem sound enough, but we need to get the rubbish out first and then have a proper look. First job after that will be to repair the roofs. Looks like rain has been getting in.'

'Can you get some men from the village to do the work?'

'No trouble there, Mrs Harcourt. I know a couple of builders who would be glad of the work.'

'Good. Go and see them now. I want these ready as quickly as possible.'

The next two weeks flew by in a flurry of activity. The two cottages were almost ready, and much needed because the intensive bombing of London was still going on. Andrew and David had started at the nursery school and appeared to be settling in well, although it wasn't without problems. Some mornings it took a lot of persuading to make them go to school. They often wanted to work in the gardens and couldn't understand why they had to go every day.

After one such morning, Jane and Hanna collapsed into chairs, exhausted. When the twins decided on something it was a hard task talking them out of it.

Mildred put a tray of tea in front of them. 'I thought you could do with this.'

'Oh, bless you.' Jane sat up straight. 'Just what we need.'

Hanna poured for both of them. 'I don't think I've ever seen the boys be that stubborn before.'

'I have, but not for some time.' Jane sipped her tea. 'We've tried never to force them to do something without explaining why it should be done, but they were determined this morning. You were very good, Hanna, and finally got through to them. It was a relief to see them go into the school quite happily in the end. Sam and I realized early on that they weren't going to be easy children to bring up, and we decided that we wouldn't fight with them, or give them orders they didn't understand. I swear that as soon as they were born they looked at us in their knowing way, and silently said, "All right, we're here, and from now on we're the boss."'

Hanna laughed along with Jane and marvelled at her good luck in finding this job. She had been included in the family as soon as she had arrived, and now there was a lovely feeling of companionship. The usual formality of mistress and servant didn't exist in this household, and that was unusual. The war was breaking down a lot of the old ways, as everyone was in this conflict together, but she doubted that the Harcourt household had ever been any different.

There was a rap on the front door and Mildred went to answer. She was soon back. 'There's someone to see you, Mrs Harcourt.'

The door opened wide and Jane jumped to her feet, a wide smile of pleasure on her face. 'Rose! I thought you were in Wales.'

'I'm on my way to London and you mentioned in your last letter that you had two cottages for victims of the bombing. Can I see them?'

'Of course. Mildred, can we have a fresh pot of tea, and then would you ask George if he would bring the truck round?'

'Right away.'

'Hello Hanna.' Rose Freeman turned her dark eyes on Hanna. 'I hear this was your idea.'

She nodded. 'I was in London the first night of the bombing and saw the plight of those made homeless. Two homes are a mere drop in the ocean, but it would help a couple of families.'

'Quite right.' Rose sat down. 'Are the cottages ready?'

'Just about,' Jane told her.

'Good. Would you like me to find you suitable tenants?'

'That would be a big help, Rose,' Jane agreed, handing her a cup of tea. 'We weren't sure how to go about getting someone.'

'You can leave all that to me.' Not wasting any time Rose drank the tea and was on her feet, heading for the yard where George was waiting to drive them to the cottages.

Hanna jumped into the back of the truck, leaving the two women to squeeze in the front. Work was still going on when they reached the cottages, but the workmen had said that all would be finished in another couple of days.

After a thorough examination of the homes, Rose pronounced them excellent. 'I'll be in London for three days so I'll find you two families and bring them back with me. Have you got enough petrol to drive me to the station, George?'

'I've got enough for that, Mrs Freeman.'

'You're not going at once, surely?' Jane protested. 'Can't you stay for lunch?'

'Thanks, but I can't spare the time.'

Jane and Hanna got out at the house and waved to Rose as she left.

'Phew!' Hanna shook her head. 'Does Mrs Freeman ever stop long enough to draw breath? She didn't say what she was going to do in London.'

'Whatever it is she'll be in the thick of things. She's always been like that. Like us, her family have moved to the country, but I didn't think she would stay there all the time. She'll be back and forth, helping in any way she can, and we're lucky because she will choose carefully for us from the most needy.'

'She's never forgotten her roots, has she?' Hanna said thoughtfully.

'No.' Jane looked at her, a sad smile on her face. 'Just as you never will. That's why you went to the East End after that first raid.'

'I suppose you're right.'

'Now, I don't know about you, but I'm hungry. Let's go and see what Mildred has managed to find for our lunch. I don't know how she manages to produce such delicious meals with the meagre rations we have today.'

'She's an excellent cook,' Hanna agreed. 'But we are better off than a lot of people because of the fresh vegetables from the farm.'

Jane nodded. 'Sam was right to make us come here. Not only is it keeping the boys safe and happy, but we are all still having wholesome meals.'

Three days later Rose returned with the families for the cottages. They looked battered and uncertain, but Rose ushered them forward. 'This is Jean Walters and her kids, Joy and Doug. And this is Pat Aldridge and her girl, Hazel. Their husbands are both in the army.'

'Welcome.' Jane smiled encouragingly at the obviously nervous Londoners. 'The cottages are ready for you now and we hope you'll be very happy here.'

'We gonna live here, Mum?' Hazel asked in a loud whisper.

Hanna stooped down to the bewildered child. 'We have a nice house for you and your mum, and your dad can live here as well when he comes home. You'll be right next door to Mrs Walters and her children, so you won't be alone.'

'Oh.' The girl gave Hanna a hesitant smile. 'It's pretty here. Do the bombers come over every night?'

'No, you'll be quite safe here.' Hanna smiled at the other two children who had also gathered around her. 'And when you're all settled in I'll show you round the farm. We've got lots of animals for you to see.'

All three children brightened up at that thought.

'Right,' Rose nodded to Jane. 'Let's get everyone settled, shall we? I have to get back to Wales today if I can.'

The new families only had a few bundles of possessions with them, but they had to use two trucks to get them all to the cottages. The children were tired and Jane didn't want them to have to walk any more today. George drove one of the trucks and Rose handled the other one with expertise.

There was silence when the women saw the cottages, and even the children were gazing around in disbelief. 'Where's all the other 'ouses?' one of them whispered. 'These are in the middle of a field!'

Hanna knew how incredible this must seem to youngsters from the East End of London. There they lived surrounded by concrete; here it was all open fields. 'You'll have lots of space to run around in,' she told them, and they nodded, not being able to take their eyes off the fields.

Mrs Aldridge dropped the bundle she was holding and turned to Jane. 'Oh, this is very kind of you, but we can't afford nothing like this. We ain't got nothing left. You made a mistake bringing us here, Mrs Freeman. We'd better go back.'

'That isn't necessary,' Jane said quickly, ushering them inside the first cottage. 'I'm not going to charge you rent while the war is on, and there is everything here you will need.'

Hanna opened the larder. 'And there is enough food here to last you for a while.'

'Cor, Mum,' Hazel tugged at her mother's hand. 'It's smashing here. Can we stay, please? I don't want to go back to the bombs.'

'Well, I'm not going back!' Mrs Walters declared with determination. 'And you shouldn't be thinking such a thing, Pat.

This is very good of the lady, and we was lucky Mrs Freeman picked us.'

'I know that, Jean,' Pat said hastily, casting Jane an apologetic look. 'But it's all a bit overwhelming.'

'I understand you've been through a terrible ordeal and need time to adjust. Why don't you settle in and see how you like it here. The village is just a short walk away, and there is a school for the children.'

'You're right, Mrs Harcourt.' Jean Walters gave a wry smile. 'But we can't take all this without giving something back. We're both strong, so could we earn our keep by helping with the farming? Don't know much about it, but we'd learn quick and we ain't afraid of hard work.'

George spoke for the first time. 'With your permission, Mrs Harcourt, that would be a good idea. After the other farmhands were called up Pete and me have been doing all the work. Hanna has been helping a lot, but we'd welcome two more workers.'

'Well, if you're sure, give it a try, but if you don't like it, or it gets too much for you, then you must stop. And only work when your children don't need you, and you will take a small wage for the hours you do. I insist on that.'

'Fair enough,' Jean agreed. 'You want this house, Pat?'

'They're both exactly the same,' Hanna told them.

'Right, I'll go next door then. That all right with you, Pat?' Pat nodded and smiled for the first time.

Young Doug was gazing out of the window. 'What's them?' he asked George.

'Cows.'

'Cor, ain't they big! Are they dangerous?'

'No, they're very gentle, but you must keep out of their field in case they don't like you being there.'

Doug nodded vigorously. 'I think I'm gonna like it here.'

'Good, that's all settled then. Now I must see if I can catch a train. I'll drive one of the vans back, George, and leave it by the barn. Jane, you contact me if you need anything.' Rose began to move towards the door, and then stopped. 'George, you might consider teaching Hanna to drive. Could be useful for all of you.'

'I'll do that, Mrs Freeman.'

'Me, drive!' Hanna gasped as soon as Rose drove away.

'It's a good idea, and one I was already considering.' George gave Hanna a steady look, laughter in his eyes. 'And it's no good you arguing about it because Mrs Freeman said you should learn.'

'Oh well, if that's the case then I wouldn't dare protest.'

They all laughed at the ridiculous idea of anyone opposing Rose Freeman. You would have to be a very brave person indeed to do that!

Jane and Hanna were busy showing the women how the stove worked and where everything was when the truck returned. Hanna frowned, wondering who was driving it, when she saw Pete get out and help the twins down.

'I didn't know Pete could drive,' Hanna remarked.

'He can manage the farm vehicles,' George told her, 'but he's too young to do more. It's only a short hop from the house and he's quite safe doing that. I expect the boys pestered him to bring them down here.'

When the twins came into the kitchen, Hazel, who was about the same age, stared at them as if she couldn't believe her eyes. 'Er . . . Mum, look . . . they're the same!'

Andrew and David were quite used to this kind of reaction and stood there grinning, holding small boxes in their hands.

Joy was the quietest of the children, but she was the first to speak to the boys. 'Why do you look the same?'

'Because we're twins,' they said in unison, holding out the boxes to the mothers. 'Mrs Cooper said we were to give you these.'

'Thank you.' Pat was smiling broadly now. 'What are they?'

'Blackcurrants,' Andrew explained. 'Mrs Cooper said if you put them with some apples they make a nice fruit pie. The apples are in your larder.'

'That's very kind of her.' Jean took the gift. 'You must thank her for us.'

They nodded. 'Do you like your houses? We helped get them ready.'

'They are lovely,' Pat told them.

'These are my sons, Andrew and David, and Pete is George's grandson,' Jane told them.

'Pleased to meet you all.' Jean gestured to the open larder door. 'And we've never seen so much fresh food, and eggs! What luxuries. You've all been more than generous to us, and we are truly grateful. We had nothing left in London and really didn't know how we were going to manage.'

'You're living on a farm now,' Pete told them. 'We produce all our own food. I grow all the fruit and veg, so you just let me know if you need anything.'

'Oh, my,' Pat shook her head. 'I'm having a job taking this all in. One minute we're in London going through the rubble to see if we could find anything of ours, and the next we're here. You'd better pinch me, Jean, in case I'm dreaming.'

'It's real enough, and I can't wait to start working on the farm. I always did hanker after green fields instead of concrete.'

'We'll give you a few days to settle the children in school and find your way around. Then you can see George and he'll decide what you can do.'

'Thanks, Mrs Harcourt.' Jean shook Jane's hand. 'Now don't you worry about us. You've done enough, and we'll soon settle in.'

Seventeen

The next few weeks flew by. George had declared that Hanna was now competent enough to drive around the farm, but forbade her to go out on the roads without him. Being able to get around easily she could do more on the farm, especially now the boys were at school. Coming from the East End herself, Hanna was quite at ease with Jean and Pat, who had thrown themselves into country life with great enthusiasm. The two women now had colour in their cheeks and laughed a lot. It was heartening to see the change in them and their children in such a short time.

Christmas was fast approaching and it was cold, but that didn't dampen their enjoyment. Even their children were doing their bit. They had been so impressed when they had seen the twins' gardens that with Pete's help they had already planted winter vegetables in their own small gardens at the back of the cottages. They loved doing this no matter how cold the weather because in London all they'd had was a concrete yard.

Hanna lifted the feed from the back of the truck, smiling when she saw the sheep running towards her.

'Just look at that!' Pat laughed when the animals surrounded her. 'Tell you something, Hanna, I ain't never going back to London. This place has been a real eye-opener to Jean and me, and we're hoping that when our husbands come back they'll see we could have a good life here. They'll turn their hands to any job; they've had to so we could survive through the times it was hard to get work. My Bob's good with anything mechanical, and Pat's Jim is a builder, but he'll do any job going.' Pat sighed and gazed around. 'We've written and told them all about it, and they'll like it here I'm sure. Can't wait for them to come home on leave and see all this.'

'Are you expecting them home any time soon?'

'Can't say. They could turn up out of the blue. Be nice if

they could make it for Christmas though. Do you think your brother will get home?'

Hanna shrugged. 'I'm in the same position as you. I never know where he is or when I might see him.'

'Bloody war! November's been a bad month what with bombs raining down on London and other cities. And on top of that the bugger is trying to starve us by sinking our ships. It must be terrible for you to hear about shipping losses on the news all the time.' Pat's mouth set in a firm line. 'But we'll beat him in the end, no matter how long it takes.'

Nodding agreement, Hanna took a deep breath. 'We have to, Pat. Hop in the truck and I'll take you back. The kids will be coming out of school soon.'

Christmas was only two days away, and they all waited anxiously to see if any of the men would be able to get home.

The first to arrive was Captain Harcourt, much to the delight of his family, and then Pat and Jean's husbands made it just in time for Christmas day. Hanna was pleased for everyone, but there was no sign of Jack or Alan, and although her disappointment was crushing she remained cheerful, not wanting to spoil the festive season for the others. She would be having Christmas dinner with George and his family, and enjoying Mildred's excellent cooking, so that would be a treat, she thought, as she gathered sprouts from the garden.

'Hanna!'

Looking up she saw the boys hurtling towards her, waving their arms frantically. 'What's up?' she asked when they skidded to a halt in front of her.

'Jack's here!' They began pulling her back towards the house.

The kitchen was crowded when she tumbled through the door and hugged her brother. 'You made it! Oh, it's so good to have you home. Let me look at you.' Stepping back she held him at arms' length, and apart from tiredness showing around his eyes, he looked well. But he had grown and matured so much that it was hard to believe that this was the little boy she had loved and protected all those years in the orphanage.

He laughed at her careful scrutiny and pointed to the sprouts rolling around the kitchen floor. 'I'm pleased to see you as well, but there's no need to throw the vegetables away.'

'Oh dear!' Hanna began to pick them up. 'I'm sorry, Mildred, but I was so pleased to see my brother I forgot I was carrying these.'

With everyone helping they were soon rescued and placed in the sink.

'No harm done,' Mildred said. 'Now, why doesn't everyone sit down while I make us all something to eat?'

'Glad to see you made it home as well, Captain Harcourt,' Jack said when they were all settled.

He nodded, sighing softly. 'It's good to have a few days to relax.'

'How long can you stay?' Hanna asked Jack.

'I've got a whole seven days. They have to do some work on the ship.'

'What kind of work?' she asked, frowning, wondering if they had damage from an attack.

'Just general maintenance,' he said dismissively, turning to the twins and changing the subject. 'And what mischief have you two been up to while I've been away?'

Their faces wore identical innocent expressions. 'We don't get into mischief.'

When everyone around them roared in protest, they just grinned.

'Ah well, in that case, as it's Christmas day I'd better see what I've got in my kitbag for you.'

'Can we look?' They were already clambering off their chairs. This was a little game Jack always played with them, and they thought it was huge fun to rummage through his bag.

Jack nodded. 'My bag is over by the door. See what you can find.'

Giggling with excitement they fell on the bag. The first thing they found was a brightly wrapped package, and held it up for Jack to see.

'Not that one.' He took it from them and gave it to his sister. 'Happy Christmas, Hanna.'

'It will be now you're here.' She leant over and kissed his cheek, and then opened her present. It was the most beautiful pair of leather gloves she had ever seen. They were light brown with flowers stitched around the cuffs in a darker shade. 'Oh, they're so lovely, and the softest leather I've ever felt. Thank you, Jack. I'll keep these for best. I've got something for you in my room.'

'You can give it to me later.' He smiled, clearly pleased she liked the gloves.

Their attention was brought back to the boys when they let out squeals of delight, each clutching a parcel. 'Are these for us, Jack?'

'They are. See if you like them.'

Before the paper was ripped off Hanna noticed the words 'New York' all over the wrapping, and realized that must be where her present had come from. She watched with interest as the boxes inside were opened.

'Gosh! Look at this, David.' Andrew showed his brother a model of a New York cab. 'The doors open and there's even people inside. What's yours like?'

'The same.' David dived into the box again and brought out a small key. 'What's this for?'

'Boys!' their father said sharply. 'Don't you think you ought to thank Jack for the lovely presents?'

They scrambled to their feet, looking apologetic. 'They're smashing, Jack. Thank you. Would you show us how they work, please?'

After winding up both the cars, Jack got down on the floor with the twins, quickly joined by the rest of the men in the room, all wanting to see the toys run around the room.

'Your brother is so kind,' Jane said quietly, 'but he shouldn't be spending his money on the children.'

'He likes to do it, and it gives him a lot of pleasure so I wouldn't like to tell him not to buy the little gifts.'

'No, of course, you're quite right.' Jane smiled at the men all crawling around the floor. 'It's hard to tell the difference between the men and the boys.'

Hanna grinned, and then was immediately serious again. 'But those men have been facing dangers we can only guess at, and they need to relax for a while. Playing with the boys is a good way for them to forget the war for a few days.'

Jane picked up a piece of the wrapping and smoothed it out. 'This tells us Jack has been on the Atlantic run, and I wouldn't be surprised if that's where Sam has been as well.'

'And that's a very dangerous place to be, but they're both home safe and sound, and I'm going to enjoy the holiday season. It doesn't look as if Alan is going to make it, but I've got my brother home for a few days, and I'm grateful for that.'

'We will all enjoy ourselves, and the war will not be mentioned even once while they're here.'

It was the happiest Christmas Hanna could remember. She showed Jack what they were doing on the farm, and one day proudly drove him over to meet Pat, Jean and their families. They had only intended to stay for a few minutes, but everyone decided that the visit called for a party and it was midnight before they got back to the house. After a few days Hanna was pleased when the lines of strain disappeared from Jack's face, and he was relaxed and laughing.

They didn't see a lot of the Harcourts, but Hanna knew they were enjoying being together for a short time. Moments like this were precious now, and they all made the most of them.

'Ah, there you all are.' Jane came into the kitchen. 'If you haven't got any plans, we would like you all to join us to see the New Year in together.'

'That would be lovely,' they all agreed. 'Thank you.'

'Good. Hanna, would you ask Pat and Jean if they and their families would also join us. They can bring the children, of course.' She gave an amused smile. 'We are allowing the boys to stay up as a special treat, but if they would prefer the children to be in bed early they can have one of the spare rooms while they are here.'

'I'll tell them.' Hanna stood up. 'What time tonight?'

'Ten o'clock. George, would you pick them up and drive them home again after? You might have to make two journeys, but I don't think Hanna should drive that late at night.'

'I'll do that all right, Mrs Harcourt.'

The London families were delighted to accept the invitation

when Hanna told them, and decided that the children could also stay up.

On the dot of ten they all gathered in the sitting room where Mildred had laid out enough snacks and drinks to feed twice as many people. Living on a farm did have its advantages, Hanna thought wryly, as did having a cook as inventive as George's wife.

At first the three children from London seemed overawed by their surroundings, but David and Andrew soon drew them into play with them.

There was a huge grandfather clock in the corner of the room, and as midnight approached they held full glasses ready to make a toast. They watched the seconds tick away.

As it struck twelve they all raised their glasses, and Captain Harcourt said, 'We don't know what this year will bring, but I wish you all a safe and happy New Year.'

'Hear, hear,' everyone agreed, clinking glasses.

Looking round at the smiling faces, Hanna's insides tightened. What would 1941 hold for each person here?

Eighteen

'This is the biggest convoy we've been a part of,' Jack remarked, scanning the sea with binoculars. 'The ships are spread out over a large area and the escorts have their work cut out keeping this lot in order.'

Bill nodded. 'And God help us all if the U-boats find us.'

'Let's pray they don't.' Jack lowered the glasses. 'We've been lucky so far and survived the winter. There's even a bit of warmth in the sun.'

'Hmm, but the sea's still mighty cold.'

Jack gazed down and then looked up, grinning. 'Still pretty though.'

Laughing with amusement Bill gave Jack a playful shove. 'Even with evil predators lurking beneath its depths you're still in love with the sea.'

'Of course. It isn't the sea's fault.' Jack hung the binoculars around Bill's neck. 'Come on, it must be time for dinner. Did you hear we could have as much as seven days' leave when we reach Liverpool? It will be good to see Hanna again. I'm glad she isn't in London. They've been taking a real pasting, according to the reports.'

'Yes, there was an all-night raid in April apparently. My wife and mother won't leave London, though I've tried to make them.' He gave a grim laugh. 'They said I was a fine one to tell them what to do when I kept going back to sea, and anyway they were quite safe in the Underground stations. Much safer than I was. I do wonder though if my house will still be there when I get home this time.'

They reached the mess, sat down, and Jack looked at the men around the table, knowing that many of them were worried about their families, and probably cursing the delay they'd had in New York, waiting for this convoy to form up. Finally they had sailed two days ago, but the going was slow. Their ship had a respectable turn of speed if need be, but others were slow and they had to match their speed. If any dropped behind they were likely to be picked off by the subs.

'Hey, Frank!' one of the men, Tim, called, pointing to his plate. 'What's this?'

'Spam fritters. What did you expect, steak?'

'Would have been nice,' he muttered. 'Those steaks in America were huge and delicious.'

'I'll say,' another one of the crew agreed. 'They don't seem to know there's a war on.'

'That's because they are not at war, Harry. They're doing what they can to help us out though. Our cargo hold is full of desperately needed food.'

'Let's hope we can get it home safely.'

'Amen to that!' Tim muttered, taking a bite of his fritters. 'Hey, Frank, these aren't bad. Quite tasty in fact.'

'Praise indeed.' Frank raised his eyebrows, and then winked at Bill and Jack. 'I've got a blueberry crumble for afters. Now we don't get those at home.'

That announcement brought murmurs of approval.

'Bill, did I tell you my sister's got a regular boyfriend?' Jack said, as he tucked into his dinner. He was always so hungry he never questioned what was put in front of him.

'No, you didn't. What's he like?'

'Seems a nice bloke. He was a copper before he got called up. Now he's in the army, but they seem really keen on each other. Hope it works out for them. Hanna deserves to be happy and have children of her own. She'd make an excellent mother. She loves kids.'

'You think the world of her, don't you?'

'Of course. I was only five when our parents were killed, and I don't know what would have happened to me without her. I want her to be happy now.'

'I'm sure she will be.' Frank put a large dish of crumble in front of Jack. 'You eat that. Can't have you going to bed hungry.'

Everyone laughed. Jack's appetite was a standing joke with the crew.

Jack did sleep quite well that night, and after another quiet day he was preparing for bed again. Removing his shoes he began to unfasten his trousers – and stopped. He had a niggling feeling that he should keep his clothes on. Many of the men already did, but until now Jack had undressed at night. He stretched out on the bunk. Not tonight though. Silly, but he would follow his instinct and laugh about it in the morning.

At the first explosion his feet were on the floor and he was running before the sound had finished reverberating through the ship.

They were already listing badly by the time he reached the upper deck. A fire was raging at the stern and Jack ran to help crew members trying to launch lifeboats and rafts. Once they had managed to get two over the side he began to look around frantically for Bill and Frank. It was impossible to single out anyone in the chaos going on around him. The two friends had told Jack that if this happened he was to save himself and not worry about them, but he had hoped he would be able to find them. He wasn't at all happy about the thought of leaving them behind.

The ship was now at a perilous angle and going down fast when the 'Abandon Ship' call came. There was nothing for it so Jack stood on the rail and jumped, then began to swim away from the sinking ship as fast as he could. The next thing he knew hands were plucking him out of the sea and dragging him on to a raft. Gasping, he muttered his thanks and sat up just in time to see the bow of the ship rise out of the water, shudder, and then sink out of sight.

'That was bloody quick!' one man cursed. 'Wonder how many managed to get off in time?'

'Let's see who we can find.'

Jack spun round at the sound of the familiar voice. 'Frank! Do you know where Bill is?'

'Afraid not. We can only hope he got off before she went down.'

Turning his attention back to the sea Jack could see men everywhere, so he began to yell. 'Bill . . . Bill!'

For an hour they dragged as many men on to the raft as it would take, but there was no sign of Bill. Jack was getting frantic. Dawn was just beginning to lighten the sky when he spotted two lifeboats, and they paddled towards them.

'Bill . . . Bill!' Jack was calling when they got close. 'Are you there?'

When a figure waved back, he grabbed Frank's arm. 'He's there. He's all—'

'Catch him! Hell, the boy's bleeding. Why didn't he say he was hurt? We need a bandage here. Have you got any in the lifeboat?'

'Tie the raft to us and pass Jack over. We've got a medic with us.'

Jack felt himself being lifted up and wondered who was hurt. Bill and Frank were safe, and that was a relief. Wouldn't like to lose his two friends. Lost his drawing though. Still, Andrew would do another one for him . . . Why did his leg hurt?

'I've stopped the bleeding, but goodness knows how much blood he's lost. Try and make him drink some water, Bill. And keep him awake.'

Someone's in a poor way . . . so tired . . . must sleep . . .

'Jack! Wake up!'

'What?' He opened his eyes and smiled at Bill. 'Been looking for you.'

'Well, you've found me. How did you hurt your leg? Talk to me.'

He frowned and peered at his legs. One trouser leg was ripped up to the thigh and a bandage wrapped around the lower part of his leg.

Bill shook him. 'How did you do that?'

'Don't know. Only a scratch . . .'

'Drink this and listen to me, Jack. You've lost a lot of blood and we must get some fluid into you. Come on, lad, do it for me and Frank.'

A couple of sips was all he could manage before he began to drift off again, conscious only of the murmur of voices around him, and the rocking of the lifeboat as someone else came and sat beside him.

'Sit him up straight and prop that leg up.'

Who was that? Ah, it sounded like Harry. He'll be busy looking after the men who have been injured.

'Thank God it's morning at last. Only hope it's not too long before we're picked up. I'm worried about the boy, Bill. He might not last long if we're adrift for days. All you can do is try to keep him awake and give him as much water as we can spare.'

He was being told to wake up again. Why did they keep doing that? He only wanted a little doze . . .

'Are you listening to me, lad? Open your eyes.'

With a mighty effort he dragged his eyes open and looked around him. He was in a lifeboat with Bill and Frank holding him up. He took a deep breath. 'How did I get here? I was on a raft.'

'You passed out, lad, and we lifted you over so Harry could see to you.' Bill held a tin mug to his mouth. 'Drink this.'

Jack peered at the scene around him, his mind clearing as he recalled the disaster and horror of seeing their ship sink below the waves. There were two lifeboats and three rafts lashed together with rope, and packed with men. This was by no means the entire crew and his heart ached with sadness for the loss they were all feeling, but not showing. He turned his head away from the mug. 'No! We must be careful with water. The convoy's long gone and it might be days before someone finds us.'

'And if you don't drink you could die,' Bill said bluntly. 'That gash on your leg is deep and should have been seen to immediately.'

'I didn't know I'd been hurt nor when it happened. You needn't worry about me, I'm already feeling better.' His eyes began to close and he forced them open again.

'That's a good thing,' Frank said. 'But you must try to stay awake, Jack.'

'Why? I'm tired and there's nothing to do but wait. Unless you'd like me to swim away and try and find help?' he joked.

Bill shook his head, the corners of his mouth turning up slightly. 'Be serious, Jack. Harry said that if you go to sleep you might not wake up again, and we're not going to let you drift away like that, lad. All three of us are going to come out of this alive. So drink the water. It's been allocated to you.'

He was too tired to argue so he obediently took a few sips, and it did help a little . . . Just a little . . .

'All right, let him sleep now, Bill. He's over the worst, I hope.'

That was Harry's voice. 'Thanks, Harry . . .'

'Jack!' He was being shaken awake. 'It's breakfast.'

'Ah.' Pulling himself upright he shook his head to clear it, then asked, 'What we got, Frank? Eggs and bacon, don't forget the fried bread, will you?'

'Sorry, but you'll have to do with a hard biscuit this morning, but it will fill a corner.' Frank began handing out the rations.

'Not much of a one,' he joked, munching on the hard tack. He flatly refused to take more than two small sips of water to help the biscuit down, and then made sure that the other men also had a little to drink. He knew very well that water was the most important thing. If that ran out then they really would be in danger of losing some of the weaker men. He sat up straight and took a deep breath, gritting his teeth in determination. He was young and strong . . .

'How you feeling, lad?' Bill asked, studying him carefully.

'I'm fine, Bill. Can't even feel any pain from the gash in my leg now.'

Bill looked worried at that remark. 'Well, you hang in there, Jack. Think about your sister. You don't want to die out here and leave her alone, do you?'

'Mustn't do that. Not going to do that.'

'Hope it stops raining soon.' Hanna stepped into the kitchen and shook the umbrella through the open door before putting it in the rack. 'Our poor plants will get washed away if it doesn't ease up soon. Oh, hello, Jane, I think the boys were glad to go to school today.'

When no one answered, she looked up. As well as Jane, Mildred, George and Pete were also there, all looking upset.

'Sit down, Hanna.' Jane guided her to a chair, and a hot cup of tea was placed in front of her. 'This has just arrived for you.'

When she saw the telegram she went icy cold and just stared at it, hardly able to breathe. She was well aware what these things meant, but not her brother . . . Please God, not her darling little brother . . .

'Would you like me to read it for you?'

She shook her head, took the telegram in her hands, and without hesitation she slit it open. A moan of agony escaped her lips as she read. 'Jack's missing – presumed dead.'

'I'm so sorry, my dear.' Jane held her as the silent tears ran down Hanna's cheeks.

Hanna's mind was a whirl as she read the dreaded words again. 'Missing – presumed dead.' She gulped down the tea and shook her head. 'No! They don't know if he's dead. Until they tell me for sure then there's still hope. I'd have known if he had died. I'd have known!'

The next week passed in a mist of pain for Hanna as she waited for definite news, refusing to let the glimmer of hope fade.

Nineteen

'Your garden is a picture.'

Hanna looked up, her face ravaged with despair and sleepless nights after ten days with no news. 'Thank you, Mrs Freeman. Pete is a very good teacher.' She scrambled to her feet, brushing dirt from her hands. 'I enjoy the work and it's very satisfying to eat the things you've grown yourself, isn't it, Jane?'

'It certainly is.' Jane smiled. 'Rose has some news for you.'

'Oh, about the orphanage?'

'No. Let's sit on the seat in the sun.' When they were settled, Rose said, 'I've received a message from my husband. He sent it from his ship and insisted that I be informed immediately. It was brief. "Survivors picked up. Jack Foster among them."'

Hanna was laughing and crying at the same time. 'Thank you! Is he all right? Where is he?'

'I'm afraid you'll have to wait for all the answers. Bill couldn't send a detailed message, and as far as I know they are still at sea, but you can be sure they are being well looked after. My husband will see to that.'

Nodding, Hanna grasped Rose Freeman's hand. 'Thank you for coming to bring me this wonderful news. I'm very grateful. Thank your husband for me. I'm well aware how careful they have to be about sending messages while at sea.'

Rose gave a wry smile. 'Bill knew you would be worried sick about your brother and the message was very brief. I'll certainly thank him for you. Now, I think we can all do with a nice cup of tea.'

'How is he?'

'Doing fine, Captain. There's no sign of infection to his injured leg, but they are all weak after days in the boats.'

Jack opened his eyes and sat up suddenly, gazing at the captain, a tall impressive man with a kind face.

'Ah, good, you're awake. How are you feeling?'

'Much better, thank you, sir. It was a wonderful sight when we saw your Royal Navy ship steaming towards us. We shouted until we were hoarse, frightened you would miss us. After so long we had begun to think we were invisible,' he joked.

The captain smiled. 'I've managed to get a message to my wife and she will tell your sister that you are all right.'

'Thank you, sir.' Jack was puzzled. 'Er . . . does she know Hanna then, sir?'

'I should have introduced myself, Jack. My name is Freeman.'

'Rose Freeman's husband!' Jack couldn't believe it. 'I'm so pleased to meet you, sir. Your wife has done so much for Hanna and me. Thank you, thank you both.'

'It's been our pleasure. Now, you just relax and get your strength back. We'll be in Portsmouth in a couple of days.'

Jack watched Captain Freeman stride away, marvelling at the strange turn of fate.

'You've got friends in high places, lad.'

He grinned as his friends came and sat by his bunk. 'He's sent a message to let Hanna know I'm all right. And I am, so I think it's time to get up and have a look at this ship.'

'What do you think you're doing, young man?' a stern voice asked as Jack swung his legs over the edge of the bunk.

'Need some exercise, Doc. I've been sitting around for days.'

The medic gave a dry laugh. 'I suppose you have. All right, but I want you back here in one hour.'

'Two.'

He bent down and checked Jack's leg. 'All right two, but no running up and down the deck. We don't want that wound to open up again.'

'We'll see he doesn't do anything daft,' Frank said. 'We haven't kept him alive just so he can do himself an injury now.'

With the help of Bill and Frank they reached the upper deck, and Jack hobbled towards the rail, taking a deep breath as he gazed at the sea.

'Still think she's beautiful, lad?'

He nodded. 'Nothing will make me change my mind about that, but I remember what you told me in the beginning, Bill. Love her, respect her, but never take her for granted.'

'And we never will take her for granted after this experience, will we?'

All three nodded in agreement, happy to have survived the
ordeal. But there was sadness for all those who didn't, including
their greatly respected captain. The ship went down so quickly
that many just didn't have time to get off. Seeing her disappear below the waves was not a sight they would ever forget,
nor the horror of knowing some of their friends were still on
board. They had loved the *North Star*, and now she was no
more.

For the next two days they relaxed, tucked into good food,
and used this short time to try to come to terms with what
had happened. Though deep down they all knew this was
something that would stay with them for the rest of their lives.

As the warship made its stately way into Portsmouth, the
survivors of the *North Star* watched in silence. They were a
ragged-looking lot, but every one of them had a smile on their
faces as they disembarked. There were helping hands every
step of the way, and they accepted gratefully, as they were still
weak, and some unable to walk at all.

'This way, mate,' a young navy doctor said, steadying Jack
as he swayed slightly. 'We've got to check you over before you
can go home.'

Jack held on to him as they made their way towards a
building. 'Bit unsteady on my feet. The dry land seems to be
moving,' he joked, noticing that some of the others were having
the same problem. Must be because they had spent so much
time in a small boat without proper food, he thought.

Only three were considered in need of hospital treatment,
and the rest were told that after a night's rest in the accom-
modation block, they could go home.

No one protested because when the examinations were over
they were all feeling exhausted, and fell on to the bunks with
sighs of relief.

The sailors brought in piles of clothes. 'When you're feeling
up to it, men, you can see if anything here fits you. Leave
your old clothes on the spare bunk and we'll dump them for
you.'

Jack dragged himself off the bunk. He needed a pair of

trousers. His were torn up to the thigh, and he certainly couldn't get on a train wearing them. Then something dawned on him. 'Hey, Bill, how are we going to pay the train fare? Everything we owned went down with the ship.'

'Don't worry about that,' a sailor told them. 'You'll be issued with travel warrants.'

'Is there any chance of a drink?' Bill asked. 'I could murder a pint.'

The young sailor laughed. 'Dinner will be in an hour and I'll have a word with the officer in charge.'

'This is a navy base so there must be plenty of pubs around here.'

'There are, but we have strict instructions not to allow you off the base until tomorrow. But don't worry; we've got our own supply of beer.'

'Ah, well, that's good news. We'll leave it to you then.'

The sailor nodded and then left them to sort out something more respectable to wear. Jack found himself a pair of trousers and a shirt that just about fitted, and he settled on those.

'Blimey! We look as if we're in the Royal Navy now,' Harry remarked, as he shrugged into a navy blue jacket. 'Except there aren't any badges on the clothes. That should confuse anyone who sees us.'

'I don't think anyone will take us for Royal Navy,' Jack laughed, looking at his ill-fitting clothes. 'If we were in the navy we'd be put on a charge for untidy dressing.'

'Wonder how long it will take them to find us another ship?' Frank mused, stretching out on the bunk.

'Don't know, but I hope it's quick. I've never spent much time ashore, and I don't want to now – U-boats or not. How do you feel about going back to sea, lad?' Bill asked.

'I feel the same as you; the quicker the better. They do say you should get straight back on a horse after it's thrown you, don't they?' Jack pulled a face. 'I don't want too much time to think about what happened.'

'Grub's up!' came the call. 'Follow me.'

The mess was large, and many of the tables were already occupied, but they arranged three in a line so they could all sit together.

'I'm starving,' Jack said, sitting back and gazing around the room. 'The smell of the food is making my mouth water.'

'Oh, he's getting back to normal,' Harry chided. 'This lad is a bottomless pit where food is concerned.

'We went days without food and I've got a lot of making up to do.' He grinned at his friends. 'And whatever they're cooking here smells heavenly.'

A sailor came up to their tables. 'We've got sausages and mash, or fish and chips. Tell me what you want and it will be brought to you.'

Everyone opted for the sausages, and then a cheer went up when a sailor approached carrying a large tray holding pints of beer. One was put in front of Jack and he was thirsty enough to tackle it even if he wasn't used to strong drink.

'Thanks, mate,' Harry said as he held up his glass to the sailor.

'Enjoy,' he told them, 'you men have certainly earned it. There's more where that came from.'

Bill stood, glancing at the men around the long table. 'We should make a toast with our first pint. Men, the *North Star* was a fine ship with a first-class crew. Lift your glasses to the best captain I've ever served with, and all our other friends who did not make it. God bless them.'

The chairs scraped back as every man stood, glasses raised. 'To the *North Star* and all those who went down with her.'

Out of respect, Jack saw that every man in the mess also stood, and didn't sit again until the survivors did. This was the first time any one had mentioned the losses, though each had been grieving silently. 'That was well done, Bill,' Jack said quietly. 'It's been too painful to talk about.'

He nodded. 'And some of us will not for a very long time – if ever – but we needed to acknowledge their sacrifice.'

Their meals began to arrive and the general talk around the table resumed. The men seemed a little more relaxed now, and Jack could see the wisdom of what Bill had done. Something had to be said, and no one else had been able to take that step. Now it was done, Jack felt better, and so did everyone else.

Frank nudged Jack. 'Here comes Captain Freeman.'

He looked up and saw the tall man approaching.

'May I join you?'

'Of course, sir.' Bill grabbed a chair from another table, and everyone shuffled round so that the captain could sit beside Jack and Bill.

'Thank you.' Captain Freeman sat down and called an orderly over, who almost ran to his side. 'I'll have the sausages and a pint of beer as well.'

'Do you want it served in the officers' mess, Captain Freeman?'

'No, here will do fine.'

'Yes, sir.'

As the sailor hurried away, the captain turned to Jack. 'How are you feeling now?'

'Stronger, sir, but still a bit unsteady on my injured leg, though it's healing well. One of the doctors gave me a stick and told me to use it on my way home tomorrow.'

'That's good advice. I wish I could come with you, but that isn't possible, I'm afraid. Remember me to your charming sister, won't you?'

'I'll do that, sir.'

Bill rapped the table for silence. 'Men, if you have any beer left in your glasses please raise them in thanks to Captain Freeman and his crew for finding us in that wide expanse of ocean. Without him I doubt that any of us would be here now.'

'To Captain Freeman and his crew!' The toast was heartfelt.

'I'm only too pleased we found you in time,' he said, lifting his own glass of beer. 'But I am the one who should be toasting your courage in bringing needed supplies to this country, and your determination to stay alive. Gentlemen, to you.'

Captain Freemen stayed with them long enough to finish his meal, and have a few words with every one of the survivors. He was just draining his pint when a Petty Officer hurried over.

'Sorry to disturb you, sir, but I've been ordered to find you. You are needed.'

The captain nodded and rose to his feet immediately. 'It's been a pleasure spending time with you.'

'And you, sir. And thanks again for all you've done for us,' Bill said. 'But I hope we don't meet you again under similar circumstances.'

'Amen to that. The U-boats seem to have the upper hand at the moment, but that won't always be so. We'll find a way to stop them.' With a nod to everyone he strode towards the door of the mess and disappeared from sight.

'I must say I've always wondered what kind of a husband Rose Freeman had, and now I know. That is one strong, impressive man, but he has a quiet air about him. They must suit each other admirably.'

'He seems a good man, Bill, and we were damned lucky he found us.' Frank drained the last of his beer and stood up. 'We'd all better get some rest if we're going to be up to travelling tomorrow.'

'Where's your stick, lad?' Bill frowned when he saw Jack was ready to leave the next day.

'I don't need it,' he protested. 'The leg is healed now.'

'But not very strong.' Bill glared at Jack. 'Do you want to fall down and break it? If you do a daft thing like that we'll have to sail without you next time, because I don't think we'll have to wait long for another ship.'

'Ah, I can't have that.' Frank was holding out the stick and Jack took it, rested on it and grinned. 'All right, am I out of trouble now?'

'For now. Come on, Frank, let's get this lad home so his sister can take care of him. He looks like a scarecrow in those ill-fitting clothes.'

Jack roared with laughter. 'Have you taken a look at yourselves?'

The survivors all gathered outside intending to make the journey together. They were all still feeling exhausted after their ordeal and agreed it would be best if they stayed together so they could help each other where and when needed.

'Which way is the station?' Harry asked as a truck roared up to them.

'Hop in. I've got orders to take you to the station.' Two

sailors jumped down and helped the men into the back of the truck.

One of them frowned as he looked them up and down. 'Are you sure you blokes should be travelling yet?'

'We'll be all right, and we need to get home. You understand?' Bill asked.

The sailor nodded. 'Yes, of course you do.'

When they reached the station the two Royal Navy sailors came on to the platform with them, striding around until they found seats for those of the group still unable to stand for long.

'Thanks,' Frank said. 'We'll be all right now.'

'Our orders are to stay with you until you're safely on the train to London. Captain Freeman tried to get you transport all the way to your homes, but it just wasn't possible today. He said we were not to leave you until you were on your way.'

'That was good of him,' Jack said, leaning on the stick, and glad his friends had made him use it.

'Fine man, and respected by his crew. Ah, this is the London train.'

As soon as it came to a halt one of the sailors jumped on, moving up and down the corridor until he found two nearly empty carriages together. Then he beckoned to them. 'It's crowded, but there are nearly enough seats here for you.'

When they had seated as many as they could, the sailor jumped out, stood on the platform as the train began to move and saluted smartly.

'I must say the Royal Navy has treated us very well,' Frank said, sighing as he sat back. 'It will be good to get home. I began to have my doubts that I was ever going to see my parents and girlfriend again.'

Jack propped himself against the door of the carriage and smiled. 'How long have you been going out with her?'

'Nearly three years.'

'I told him he should marry the girl,' Bill remarked.

'I was going to, but war was looming, and I didn't like the thought that I might make her a widow so young.'

'That's a chance thousands of couples are taking,' Harry told him. 'Marry her, Frank. We survived this time and you know what they say – lightning doesn't strike twice. The next time those buggers shoot at us they are going to miss.'

'Wish I had your confidence,' Bill snorted. 'But he's right, Frank; marry the girl now.'

'Perhaps you're right.' Frank looked up. 'You all right, Jack? Do you want to sit here for a while?'

'I'm fine,' he lied. Frank was looking very drained and Jack didn't want to make him stand.

'You can have my seat, young man.' A woman who had been sitting quietly by the window stood up.

'Oh, no, madam,' Jack protested. 'I wouldn't dream of taking your seat.'

'You need it more than I do.' She smiled. 'Come on, son, you look as if you can hardly stand.'

'Take it, lad.' Bill took his arm and guided him to the seat. 'Thank you, madam.'

'My pleasure.' She stood by the door next to Bill and said quietly, 'He's just a boy.'

Bill glanced at Jack already dozing in the corner, and shook his head. 'He looks that way, but he's a man now, if you know what I mean.'

'Yes, I think I do.'

They stopped at a station and Jack woke up suddenly, thinking he was still in the lifeboat for a moment. He straightened up and glanced around the carriage. Some were staring into space, others still asleep, and Bill was now sitting on the floor.

Two young soldiers, obviously new recruits, peered into the carriage hoping to find seats, and stared at the ragged assortment of men in disbelief.

'Hey, will you look at this!' one said in a loud voice. 'Did you ever see such a scruffy bunch of layabouts? Been on the booze all night from the look of you. Too tired to let a lady sit down?'

'Some people,' the other one remarked in disgust, 'don't know there's war on.'

Bill slowly stood up. 'We are very aware of that, probably more than you, and I would suggest you move along the train.'

'You going to make us?' they taunted.

Seeing that the two were spoiling for a fight, Jack stood up, so did Frank and a couple of the others. Jack gripped the stick and hobbled over to Bill.

'Oh, did you fall down the pub steps and hurt your leg?' The two young soldiers were obviously not going to give up.

'Do you know I really can't remember where I did it.' Jack gave Bill a broad smile. 'Can you remember, Bill?'

'Well, I'm not sure.' He rubbed his chin thoughtfully. 'I think it must have been when the second torpedo hit the ship and you had to jump overboard.'

'You're probably right.' Jack nodded to the men and shrugged. 'Does that answer your question?'

The lady who had been watching silently now turned on the young soldiers. 'You two louts ought to watch your tongues. These men are merchant navy, risking their lives every day to bring in desperately needed supplies to this country. It's clear to any fool that they are wearing clothes given to them because everything they had went down with their ship. They are still recovering from their ordeal, and you should be ashamed of yourselves.'

'Er . . .' They backed away. 'Sorry, didn't mean any harm. Just having a bit of fun after being stuck in camp for ages.'

'Then I suggest you go and have your fun elsewhere.' The lady waved them away. 'You are a disgrace to your uniform.'

The survivors from the *North Star* were all grinning as the men scuttled away, and Bill was openly laughing. 'I thank you, madam, but even though we're not at our best we could still have defended ourselves.'

'I don't doubt that,' she smiled, 'but I did enjoy putting those idiots in their place. And I think I can remove this now.' She unbuttoned the plain navy-blue coat she was wearing, slipped it off and removed a hat from the bag she had with her, placing it at the correct angle on her head.

There was silence when the men saw the Royal Navy nurse standing there, and seeing their stunned expressions, said briskly, 'The medical officer was not happy about some of you travelling today, but he understood how much you all wanted to get to your homes, so we are here to see that you do just that. There is another nurse in the next carriage.'

'But why the masquerade?' Bill wanted to know.

'The MO thought you might not like being openly escorted by nurses until you were safely on the train. He said you appeared to be a tough bunch and would probably object to have attention drawn to you by having nurses with you. Transport will be waiting for us in London to take each of you to your homes.'

'But I'm going on to Suffolk,' Jack told her.

'We are aware of that,' she smiled again. 'Jack Foster, isn't it?'

He nodded.

'Captain Freeman was insistent that you were all taken safely to your destinations, no matter where. Now, why don't you all rest, and sleep if you want to. I'll wake you when we reach London.'

'How can we refuse with such a gorgeous guardian angel looking over us?' Bill muttered, sliding down to sit on the floor once again. He was instantly asleep.

Twenty

There had been no further news about Jack, and Hanna couldn't settle to anything, so she was wandering around the farm being of little use to anyone. She knew he was safe, but had no idea where he was, or if he'd been injured. Until she actually saw him for herself she wouldn't be able to concentrate on anything.

'Give us a hand to get this food to the pigs!' Pat called.

'Coming.' Hanna hurried across the yard. With the boys at school now she was doing more work with the animals, as well as tending the vegetable gardens, and she really enjoyed it.

'Try to stop fretting, Hanna,' Pat told her. 'You know he's been found, and all you can do now is wait.'

'I know,' she sighed, helping to fill the troughs, 'but I don't know if he's injured, and the waiting is hard. I wouldn't even know he had been rescued if it hadn't been for Mrs Freeman. I would have expected a letter or telegram by now to say he was all right.'

'The authorities seem slow to deal with these things, but you think about the amount of notifications they have to send out. You're not the only one in this situation,' Pat told her gently.

'Pat, I'm so sorry to be making such a fuss.' Hanna lifted her hands in exasperation. 'Don't take any notice of me. In my mind he's still the little brother I've been looking out for since we went to the orphanage, but he's all grown up now and out in a dangerous world. I feel so helpless, but I know he's safe, and should be jumping for joy, instead of carrying on so.'

'It's understandable that you still feel responsible for him, but he's decided what he wants to do with his life, and he's a sensible and mature lad for his age. This is a difficult time for all of us, Hanna, but we'll get through it.'

'Of course we will.' Hanna smiled at Pat, appreciating her kind words, and the reminder that she had much to be grateful for. 'Would you and Jean like some vegetables for the weekend?'

'Please.'

'Right, let's go and get them now.'

They headed for the walled garden, and were just about to open the gate when a lorry rumbled into the yard.

'That's Royal Navy,' Pat said, shading her eyes against the sun. 'Wonder what they want? Let's go and find out.'

Hanna had only gone a few yards when she saw a familiar figure get out of the cab, and with a cry of delight ran as fast as she could to reach her brother. 'Jack!' She threw her arms around him and hugged him tight, and then stepped back in alarm as he swayed and she saw the stick he was holding. 'Oh, you're so thin, and you're hurt!'

'He's going to be fine, Miss Foster. It's been a tiring journey, but all he needs is rest and regular meals.'

Hanna stared at the nurse who had just climbed out of the cab.

'Let's get Jack to his room so he can have a nice long sleep.' The nurse took Jack's arm. 'Come along, young man, you can talk to your sister when you've had a rest. And don't try to argue with me,' she scolded when he looked about to protest. 'You've had quite enough excitement for a while.'

Jack winked at Hanna, and although the ordeal he'd been through was clear to see, the amused glint in his eyes was still the same.

Taking his other arm they went into the house and straight to his room, not giving anyone a chance to say much to him. His bed was ready for him and he sat on the edge with a sigh.

Mildred came in carrying a tray laden with tea, sandwiches and cakes. 'Welcome home, Jack. I thought you might like something to eat and drink before you have a rest.'

'Thank you.' He reached for a sandwich immediately and smiled at Mildred when she put a cup of tea beside him on the small table.

'Would you like something as well, Nurse? Your driver is in the kitchen having a snack.'

'That is kind of you.' The nurse took one of the sandwiches, and then bent down to remove Jack's shoes. Seeing he could hardly keep his eyes open she took the cup from his hands. 'Sleep now, young man,' she ordered.

'I am tired,' he admitted, giving an apologetic smile, lifting his legs on to the bed and stretching out. 'Thank you for all you have done for us, Nurse.'

'It has been a pleasure, Jack, and Captain Freeman would have our hide if he thought his orders hadn't been carried out to the letter. You rest now.'

'He's already asleep,' Hanna whispered, and they all left the room quietly.

Nurse collected her driver from the kitchen and Hanna went with them to the truck. Before getting in the nurse took hold of Hanna's hand for a moment. 'Don't be alarmed by your brother's appearance. A few days' rest and he'll be back to his usual self. He's had an injury to his left leg, but it's healing well and shouldn't give any trouble. Don't try to make him talk about it – he won't – and don't fuss too much over him. Treat him as you normally would, and let him heal in his own way and time. I have dealt with men who have suffered in this way. Only a few of the crew of his ship survived, so the loss is greatly felt. Give him the time he needs to come to terms with the tragedy.'

'I'll do that, Nurse, and make sure everyone else understands as well. Thank you for your advice.'

She hesitated before climbing into the lorry. 'Your brother won't tell you this, but I think you ought to know. He has spent many days in an open boat with no food and precious little water. They were in a poor way by the time they were picked up. They have all made light of their ordeal, but don't be fooled by Jack's jokes. He'll be hurting inside, so give him space.'

'I'll see he has all he needs.'

The nurse nodded and climbed in the truck, then leant out of the window. 'From what I've seen of Jack and his friends this will not deter them from going back to sea as soon as they can. Once fully recovered I believe they will all be anxious to get back on a ship again. I have seen it before, Miss Foster, and know the signs. You can be proud of your brother.'

'Oh, I am, and always have been.'

The nurse smiled, lifting her hand in a wave as the truck drove out of the farm.

'Grandpa told me Jack's back. How is he?' Pete asked, coming to stand beside her.

'He's going to be fine, and is resting after his journey. We mustn't bombard him with questions though, because he won't want to talk about it.'

'I don't suppose he will. I knew a couple of blokes who had been at Dunkirk, and they never said a word about it, not even to their wives.' He shrugged, and then smiled. 'How about asking Gran for a cup of tea before you go and pick the boys up from school?'

'Good idea. I'll just peek in at Jack as well, but I think he's going to sleep for a while. He's very tired.'

'Sleep is very healing, they say, and the farm is just the place for him to relax.' Pete nodded thoughtfully, then grinned. 'But knowing Jack, I expect it won't be long before he's looking for something to do.'

'Well, there's plenty here to keep him occupied.'

Hanna only had time for a quick cup of tea before dashing off to collect the boys. It was a lovely day and she sang softly to herself as she walked to the village. For the moment the worry and tension had disappeared.

The boys were the first through the door as soon as the school bell sounded, tearing towards her. 'Careful!' She caught hold of them before they ran into the road. They were both talking at the same time, and it was almost impossible to understand them when they did that, but they seemed to know what each other was saying without any trouble.

Taking each one by the hand she began to walk the short distance to the farm. 'Have you had a good day?' she asked, and listened while they told her about the lessons they'd had. Jane had been wise to put them in the nursery school so early because they had inquisitive minds and needed the stimulation the classes gave them.

They talked non-stop until they had almost reached the house, so Hanna stopped and bent down to them. 'I've had a good day, as well. Jack's home.'

'Oh, goody!' Their faces lit up.

Hanna caught them before they could tear into the house to see him. 'He's asleep at the moment, but you will be able to see him when he wakes up.'

'Is he tired then?' Andrew asked.

'Yes, sweetheart, he's very tired, and I want you both to do something for me.'

They waited expectantly, and she took a deep breath. The boys hadn't been told that Jack's ship had been sunk, but in an effort to make them understand how things were, they needed to know now. 'Jack's ship was sunk by the German U-boats and it was days before he and his friends were rescued. They didn't have any food so he's very weak, and he needs to rest. There won't be any little presents this time because everything went down with the ship, and I'm going to ask you not to talk about this with him, no matter how much you want to. He probably doesn't want to talk about it yet. We must give him time and treat him just like we always do.'

Their little faces were solemn now and Andrew's eyes glistened with unshed tears. 'Is he all right?'

'Yes, he will be – with our help.'

'What do they want to sink our ships for?' David pulled a face. 'It isn't right.'

'No, it isn't, but they will be stopped.' Then she smiled. 'And do you know who found Jack and his friends?'

They shook their heads in perfect unison.

'Your Uncle Bill.'

'Wow!' That pleased both of them and they were smiling again when they rushed into the kitchen.

'Mummy!' David went straight to his mother who had just arrived after visiting friends. 'Jack's home, and Uncle Bill found him! Isn't that terrific?'

'That's wonderful news!' Jane smiled at Hanna. 'How is he?'

'Sleeping at the moment. All he needs is rest and plenty of good food.'

'He'll get both from us,' Mildred said, busy chopping vegetables.

'Jack's ship was sunk, and Hanna said he won't tell us about it.' David looked puzzled. 'I'd really like to know.'

'I'm sure you would, darling.' Jane sat beside the boys at the table. 'But try to be patient. Do you remember how upset you both were when our cat, Scampy, died? It was a long time before you could talk about him, wasn't it?'

'Is that how Jack feels?' Andrew asked, and when his mother nodded he said: 'But we can talk about Scampy now.'

'Yes, and I'm sure Jack will tell you all about his ship when he's feeling better, but you mustn't bother him at the moment.'

Both boys nodded, happy with that explanation, and Hanna said a quiet thank-you to Jane. That had been the perfect example, and something they could understand because it had happened to them.

'Would you boys like to go and pick me some more peas?' Mildred asked. 'I don't seem to have enough for dinner tonight. Jack will need extra because I expect he's very hungry.'

'He always is,' they laughed, already scrambling off their chairs and heading for the door. Hanna was right behind them. She certainly got plenty of exercise when the twins were around. They never seemed to do anything at normal pace.

When dinner was almost ready, Hanna peeked into Jack's room, but he was still fast asleep, and reluctant to wake him she went back to the kitchen. 'Sorry, Mildred, he's still spark out and I don't like to disturb him.'

'Best not to. Don't worry, Hanna, the pie will keep until he's ready.'

When everyone was seated, Hanna helped to serve the meal, and was just about to sit down herself when the door opened and Jack came in.

'Hello everyone. Sorry I'm late but I've only just woken up.' He grinned at the boys who were gazing at him with huge smiles on their faces. 'My goodness, you two are growing so fast.'

They jumped down and gave him a hug, and then rearranged the seating so he could sit between them. 'We've got steak and kidney pie. Special for you because you're home at last.'

'That's very kind of you, Mildred, and it smells delicious.'

She placed a generous helping in front of Jack. 'Help yourself to vegetables, and we've got plenty more if you need another helping.'

The boys began to chatter about their gardens, school and the things they had been up to, and Hanna watched and listened as the conversation flowed. George and Pete related some amusing stories about the farm, making Jack laugh. Everyone contributed to the talk, never mentioning the war once, and Hanna began to relax as she studied her brother carefully. He had lost a lot of weight, but that could soon be put right, and although he had a rather haggard look about him, he was talking and laughing. He was still the same person, and whatever horrors he had locked inside, he would deal with them. He'd always had a strong, determined character, and that would see him through this now. Of that she was very sure.

Twenty-One

It was only a week before Jack was playing football with the boys, digging the garden and helping generally with the farm work. Pat and Jean made a great fuss of him, pretending they needed his help, when in fact they were more than capable of tackling most of the jobs around the farm. George took him to the pub some evenings, and Hanna was grateful to everyone because all this was helping him to relax. She could sense the tension draining from him, and see the lines of strain on his face fading. He was looking better, but what horrors he was dealing with on the inside was something he kept hidden.

It was June and the weather was good, and what more could she ask, Hanna thought, as she watched Jack working in the garden with the boys. In such a short time he had put on weight and had lost the slight limp completely. The village doctor had examined him yesterday and declared him fully recovered from his injury.

Jane ran into the garden, calling, 'Jack, Hanna, I've just heard some astounding news!'

'The war's over?' Jack joked, striding over to them with the boys either side of him.

'Not yet, but Hitler has invaded Russia.'

There was a stunned silence before Hanna managed to say, 'But they are allies. Didn't they sign a non-aggression pact?'

'Yes,' Jane nodded and looked up at Jack. 'Will this take the pressure off us, do you think?'

'It could, because the German forces will now be fighting on another front.' Jack took a deep breath. 'I can't believe he would do such a thing. The fool!'

Over the next week Hanna watched her brother become increasingly restless, and knew that it wouldn't be long before he was on his way again, so she increased her efforts to provide him with clothes. He had turned up with only the things he was wearing, and they didn't fit properly. Fortunately he had a few clothes at the farm, but they weren't nearly enough. Pat, Jean and Jane had given him quite a few things and Hanna was knitting every spare moment she got. At the village shop they had been able to buy him a pair of trousers and two shirts, but everything was in short supply and they had to buy what was available.

'Ah, there you are.' Jack came into the shed where they stored fruit and vegetables, carrying a bag George had given him. 'I'm going to London for a couple of days to see Bill and find out if there is a ship for us yet.'

'Oh, right.' Hanna stopped what she was doing and stood up. She knew he had received a letter from Bill the other day, but he hadn't said what was in it, only that Bill was all right. 'Have you got enough money?'

He nodded and smiled. 'You've made sure of that already. There is a house by the docks for seamen so I'll stay there overnight. It won't cost much.'

She had hoped he would stay at the farm for longer, but the signs were clear and she knew he wanted to be on his way again. 'If there is a ship for you will you come back here before you sail?'

'I won't leave without coming back to see everyone.' He smiled at his sister. 'You've all been marvellous. I've been given money from you, clothes from the others, but most of all I've been given understanding. Not one of you has questioned me about the ship sinking, not even the boys, bless them, though I know they are bursting for the details. I've been so grateful for that, but now I need to see Bill and Frank, and get back to sea.'

'Of course you do.' She gave him a hug, smiling. 'I want to meet your shipmates sometime.'

'We'll have to arrange it one day.' He slung the bag over his shoulder, then bent to kiss her cheek. 'I have to do this, Hanna.'

'I know, and you have my support and blessing, Jack. You know that, don't you?'

'I do, and I love you for being so unselfish. You've always been there for me, and when this is over I'm going to take care of you for a change.' He winked. 'Unless Alan beats me to it, of course.'

She laughed, slipping her arm through his as they walked towards the gate. 'You trying to get me married off?'

'You will one day, and I think he's just right for you.'

'I'm glad you approve, but we're not making any definite plans for the future yet.'

George drove up in the truck. 'I guess from the bag you're carrying that you're going to the station. Want a lift?'

'Thanks, I'm just popping up to London for a couple of days.'

'Hop in then. It'll save you a walk.'

Hanna waved as they left, only then allowing the smile to fade from her face. Worrying times ahead again.

Two days later Jack strode into the yard waving to Hanna, a big smile on his face.

'Did you see your friends?' she asked as soon as she reached him.

He nodded, clearly excited. 'We saw the shipping owners we've been sailing for and they've got a new ship. She's doing sea trials at the moment, but she's a lovely vessel, and we've signed on for her first voyage. Every one of us from the *North Star* will be joining up again on her. It will be wonderful to see them all again.'

'Oh, you must be so pleased about that. What is your new ship called?'

'*Western Star*. All of the shipping line has a star name.'

'Nice name.' She rinsed her hands under the yard tap, shook them dry, and said, 'Let's go and see if Mildred has any tea in the pot, and then you can tell me all about it.'

Hanna hadn't asked the question she was anxious to know, but Mildred didn't hesitate when she heard about the new ship. 'And when are you leaving, young man?'

'I've got to be back in London on Friday.'

'So soon.' Mildred shook her head. 'You've hardly had time to get your strength back.'

'I'm fine,' he laughed. 'Two weeks of your cooking was all I needed.'

'Ah, well, you do have a healthy appetite. I only hope the food on your ship will be all right. Can't be easy preparing meals on a ship rolling about all over the place.'

'You don't have to worry about that. Frank's used to it and does marvels with food. Not as good as yours, of course,' he added quickly, smiling at the elderly woman.

'He got that in just in time,' she teased, winking at Hanna. 'Give him a few more years and no girl is going to be safe around him. A real charmer he's turning in to.'

Hanna listened to the banter between them, keeping a smile on her face, although she was sad to know that Jack would be leaving again in only three days. But it had been inevitable, and he was clearly happy to be going back to sea with his friends, even if it was a very hostile place at the moment.

She glanced at the clock on the kitchen wall and shot to her feet. 'Time to collect the boys. They'll be pleased to see you again, Jack.'

'I'll come with you,' Jane said, walking into the kitchen. 'Hello, Jack, did you see your friends?'

Before he could answer, Mildred said, 'He did, and he's signed on another ship.'

'Of course he has.' Jane gave Jack an understanding smile. 'These sailors can't stay on land for any length of time – as I well know.'

Pete burst into the kitchen with his grandfather right behind him. 'Did you get another ship?'

'I did, and she's a beauty.'

'Ah, tell us all about it.' George pulled out a chair and sat down. 'And how are your friends?'

As the three male heads bent together Jane touched Hanna's arm. 'We'd better leave them to it. We won't get any sense out of them while they're discussing ships.'

The twins practically ran all the way from the village in their eagerness to see Jack. When they tumbled into the kitchen he had to go through everything again for them, as they wanted to know every detail about the new ship.

'Cor, she sounds smashing!' David declared when Jack finished talking. 'And I bet she'll be fast.'

Jack nodded. 'She's faster than our other one, and she won't be as easy to catch if we can keep up a good speed. But that depends on the rest of the convoy, because we have to go at the same speed as the slowest ship.'

Hanna held her breath for a moment. This was the first time that her brother had talked about the dangers at sea, and it was a good sign.

'I want to ask you boys for a big favour.' And when they gazed up at him expectantly, he said, 'I'm sorry to say that the picture Andrew did for me went down with the ship, and I'd really love to have one from each of you to put up in my new ship. Would you do that for me?'

The boys didn't need any further encouragement, and nodding and smiling, scrambled to get their drawing paper and pencils. Then clearing a space so they had plenty of room on the table, they sat with pencils poised. 'What kind of a picture would you like?' they asked together.

'How about something to remind me of the farm, so I can think about you all while I'm at sea?'

Pursing their lips in concentration, they began on their works of art.

Seeing they were now completely absorbed, Jack stood up and beckoned to Hanna. They walked outside, and when well away from the house they leant on a fence and watched the sheep in the field.

'That was kind of you to ask the boys to draw you something, Jack. They'll be so proud to know you are taking their pictures with you. They've been so good not bombarding you with questions, although I know it's been hard for them to keep off the subject.'

'It's been hard for all of you.' Jack turned to look at her. 'You've all been very good in allowing me to recover in peace and quiet, but I'm fit again and want to go back to sea. It's absolutely essential that we keep the supplies coming. Hitler thought he could starve us into submission, and that isn't working – neither did the bombing. Captain Freeman is sure we'll get the upper hand on the U-boats eventually. They won't always have their own way. The navy will find a way to hit back.'

'I'm sure they will, and until then you make sure you stay safe.'

'Harry said that lightning never strikes twice,' Jack chuckled. 'And Frank said he hoped the Germans knew that, and perhaps Harry ought to tell them, just to make sure.'

'Your crew sound a lively crowd.' She laughed, relieved her brother was talking freely about this.

'They're good men.'

And don't forget to include yourself as one of them, she thought as she studied him carefully. The child she had cared for since she had been eight was no longer there. The person standing beside her was a man, and she was so proud of him. The kind of past they'd had could have coloured their lives and made them bitter, but that hadn't happened to them. Perhaps she hadn't done such a bad job of bringing him up. Thank goodness.

Three days later they waved Jack off at the station. The boys were there as well, having permission to miss school on this important day. They had been so pleased and excited when they'd watched Jack carefully pack their drawings.

He leant out of the carriage window, waving, and just for an instant Hanna caught a glimpse of the boy he still was – in age anyway.

'Be safe, Jack,' she said quietly to herself.

George heard her and murmured, 'Amen to that.'

Twenty-Two

A week later Alan turned up unexpectedly, and that cheered Hanna, especially when he told her that he could spend three days with her. He had intended to get a room at the village pub, but Jane insisted that he have Jack's room. He accepted gratefully, and easily settled in with everyone at the farm. He had an easy manner and the boys took to him straight away, including him in their lives as if he had always belonged.

When he saw how informal life on the farm was, he said to Hanna, 'You're all like one family here, and I would never have believed that Mrs Harcourt was your employer if I hadn't already known.'

'I know, and it's hard for me to grasp sometimes. I was given the job as nanny for the children, but from the very first moment I have been treated more like a friend or member of the family. Jack feels the same, and we bless the day Jane came to the orphanage and offered me the job. It came at just the right time when we were desperate.'

They had been talking in the quiet of the garden when Jane came up to them. 'Hanna, it's a nice day so why don't you show Alan round the village. While he is here I'll see to the boys.'

'Are you sure? I can still do my usual work. I'm sure Alan won't mind.'

'I didn't come to disrupt your routine, Mrs Harcourt,' Alan told her. 'I just want to spend some time with Hanna in her free time.'

'Of course you do, and understandably so. You go off and enjoy yourselves. It's time Hanna had a few days to herself. She works much too hard, as I keep telling her.'

'No more than anyone else on the farm,' Hanna said. 'But thank you.'

Alan added his thanks, and they left at once, looking forward to some time to themselves.

The village consisted of a pub, church, general store and post office, two schools and a police station. The police station was a converted house, and still had a pretty garden in the front.

Alan stood gazing at the small station, a smile of pleasure on his face. 'That is lovely. What a pleasure it would be to come to work at a place like this every day instead of the crowded streets of London.'

At that moment the local policeman came along, wheeling his bike. 'Hello, Hanna.'

'Hello, Ted. This is Alan and he was admiring your station house. He used to be a policeman in London before the war.'

'London, eh?' Ted shook Alan's hand. 'I'm pleased to meet you, young man. Would you like to look inside?'

'I would, very much.'

'Come on in, then, and I'll put the kettle on and we can have a nice chat. I'm the only one here now, and I should have retired some time ago, but when everyone got called up I agreed to come back for the duration.' He smiled at Alan. 'You all right to stay a while? I'll be glad to tell you all about life as a country copper.'

'Is that all right, Hanna?' Alan asked.

'We've got all day,' she said in agreement. 'I'll make the tea while you two talk.'

Walking across the field glistening with frost, Hanna pulled the knitted hat down to cover her ears, and blew on her hands to warm them up. Where had the year gone? It had been summer when Jack and Alan had been here, and now it was less than three weeks to Christmas. Jack had been back just once, and she had managed to snatch a few hours with Alan in London when he had a forty-eight-hour pass. This war was a series of brief meetings and long separations, but that made the moments together all the more precious.

'We're going to have to get the sheep in if we have an early snow fall,' George said as he trudged beside her.

She nodded. 'It's cold enough. The temperature hasn't risen enough during the day to melt the frost, and there's a feeling of snow in the air.'

George nodded as he smiled at her. 'You're turning into a real country girl, and you are so often right in your predictions about the weather. You've got a real feel for the country.'

'Grandpa! Hanna!' Pete was shouting at the top of his voice and waving for them to come to the house.

'What on earth is the matter with the boy?' George muttered. 'He's jumping up and down like a jack-in-the-box.'

'We'd better find out.' Hanna began to make her way back through the field, the ground crunching under her feet. Even when the weather was this cold it was still beautiful here, and she couldn't imagine herself living back in London.

When they walked into the kitchen everyone was there, including the boys, and they were intent on listening to the wireless. Whatever they had been listening to ended as they came in.

'Oh, you missed it!' Pete was wide-eyed. 'You'll never guess what's happened.'

'Will someone tell us what's going on?' George asked.

'The Japanese have bombed Pearl Harbor and sunk most of the American fleet. There was no declaration of war before they attacked and the Americans were taken completely by surprise.' Jane shook her head. 'The casualties must be horrendous.'

George sat down with a thump. 'That's terrible!'

Hanna was speechless with shock. How could such a thing happen? Was the world going crazy?

'Well, that's a real turn up.' Pat drew in a deep breath. 'The Americans didn't want to be dragged into the war, but they've got no choice now. The war has come to them, but to attack like that is despicable!'

The boys were looking anxiously at their mother. 'Have ships been sunk? Was Daddy there?'

'Oh, no, my darlings.' Jane sat next to her children at the table. 'The ships are American and a long way from here in a place called Hawaii. Your daddy's on convoy duty in the Atlantic at the moment.'

They looked relieved, but were still curious. 'Why were the American ships sunk?'

'We don't know the whole story yet, but I'll tell you when

we find out,' Jane told them, just as the kitchen door opened and a tall man walked in.

'Daddy!' The boys threw themselves at him, both talking excitedly at the same time.

'Whoa!' He laughed, reaching over to kiss his wife. Then he noticed the serious faces around him. 'What's happened?'

'Japan has sunk the American fleet in Pearl Harbor,' George told him. 'Took them completely by surprise.'

Sam Harcourt shook his head in disbelief and closed his eyes for a moment, then he opened them again, his expression unreadable. 'I'm going to have to make a phone call. Will the post office still be open?'

George shook his head. 'No, but you just knock on the door, Captain, and they'll open up for you. I'll take you in the truck.'

The two men left at once.

'Oh dear,' Mildred said. 'And he's only just arrived home. Let's hope he doesn't have to return to his ship at once.'

'We'd better be getting home as well; the kids will be wanting their tea.' Pat and Jean began to put on their coats.

Hanna stood up. 'I'll drive you. I think the old van has enough petrol in it.

She had to drive carefully because of the icy conditions, but she was back in less than an hour after spending a little time talking to the children about their gardens. They were quite disappointed that they couldn't do much in the winter, but had big plans for the spring. Only George and his family were in the kitchen when she arrived back.

'The captain's back and he can stay,' George told her, 'but Doris at the post office will take a message and let him know if he is recalled urgently.'

Listening to the news over the next few days they could hardly believe what was happening. Britain and her allies declared war on Japan; Hitler declared war on America, and the Americans responded by declaring war on Germany and Italy. In a few days the whole face of the war had changed. Since Dunkirk, Britain had fought at sea, in the air, and endured the bombing of their cities in a determined effort to stop the Germans invading, and they had been successful. Now with the end of 1941 fast approaching there was a glimmer of hope that the tide would at last change in Britain's favour.

Captain Harcourt stayed home for a week, and the boys were over the moon to have their father with them, but sad that he couldn't stay for Christmas. Alan was home for the festive season, but naturally spent most of the time with his parents, but he did manage to come down to see the New Year in with Hanna. She was thrilled when Jack also arrived on New Year's Eve for three days.

They had a huge party, filling the house with everyone from the farm and many from the village. At midnight they welcomed in 1942 with smiles and laughter.

'Friends!' George lifted his glass. 'We don't know what this year holds in store for us, but let us drink to the safety of all those we love, and a speedy end to the war.'

Everyone agreed, and when the glasses were empty, Alan touched Hanna's arm, nodding towards the door.

He led her into a small room used as a library and study, closing the door behind them. 'Hanna, I told myself it was foolish to make plans for the future while the war was on, but honestly, I believe it's going to be a long time before this conflict ends. I can't tell you anything, but there is a chance that I'll be shipped out soon, and I don't want to leave without knowing you will be waiting for me when I get back. I know I'm not a man who says much, but you must know how much I love you and want us to marry when we can. I still feel that should be after the war when we can do it properly and I won't have to dash away again, but in the meantime I would love us to become engaged. Would you, darling? I do love you so much.'

That was a very long speech from Alan, and Hanna threw her arms around his neck, laughing with happiness. 'Of course we can be engaged now. I've loved you from the moment we met.'

He kissed her, and then held her away so he could look into her eyes. 'You've made me very happy. We'll have a lovely

wedding when the war is over. I want to see you walking
down the aisle in a beautiful white dress, followed by brides-
maids and all the trimmings.'

'That isn't important,' she told him gently.

'Yes it is. You've been deprived of a lot of things in your
life, and I'm determined that you should have a wedding day
to remember. Hold out your left hand.' He took a small box
out of his pocket.

She watched as he slipped a diamond cluster ring on her
finger.

'That's a relief, it fits perfectly. That belonged to my grandmother, but if you don't like it we can get something else later.
I just want to know you are wearing my ring.'

'Oh, it's beautiful, Alan, and I wouldn't dream of
changing it.'

'Good, now we're engaged shall we go and tell everyone?'

It turned into a lively night of celebration, and when Hanna
saw how pleased Jack was, her happiness was complete and
the war forgotten, for a short time.

The hopes and happiness of the New Year were soon wiped
away as one piece of bad news followed another. In January
the U-boats were sinking shipping in the Atlantic at an alarming
rate, and in February Singapore fell to the Japanese and they
were advancing on many areas. Hitler was boasting that Russia
would be defeated by summer. Then a British aircraft carrier
was sunk, and the only hopeful news was that the RAF was
bombing Germany.

'What a terrible start to the year,' Jean said one day.

'It can only get better,' Pat, ever the optimist, told them.

'I do hope you're right.' Hanna grimaced, throwing a bail
of fodder into the back of the truck.

'Come on, cheer up, girls.' Pat gave a cheeky grin. 'Don't
you know the Americans are here? What are you worrying
about?'

'I haven't seen any around here yet.' Jean jumped in the back
of the truck.

'You will soon. I've been told that camps are being prepared
for them in Suffolk. They're coming in by the boatload,

evidently.' Pat got in beside Hanna. 'Off you go, girl. The animals will be getting hungry.'

Hanna couldn't help smiling broadly as she drove off. It was surprising how easily they had settled into farm work, considering they all came from the East End of London. She knew Pat and Jean were enjoying it as much as she was, and none of them wanted to go back to their former lives. A lot of decisions were going to have to be made when the men finally came home for good.

They finished their work early and Hanna had time to wash and change before going to collect the boys. Taking the engagement ring out of the box she slipped it on, admiring its beauty and what it represented – a future with Alan. It was an old ring and she loved it, but never wore it when she was working around the farm. It was far too precious for that.

George hadn't been too well for several weeks after catching a bad cold that he was having a job to shake off. But he was improving at last, much to everyone's relief. Pat, Jean and Hanna had taken on all of his work around the farm, giving him time to recover, and they didn't mind the hard work at all.

Jane had joined the WVS, and the ladies had a meeting that afternoon in the sitting room, and there was no need to disturb them, because Jane knew Hanna would go and collect the boys on time. There was a chilly March wind blowing, so she stepped out smartly and reached the school ten minutes before the bell rang.

The boys were the first out of the door, as usual, and she marvelled at how quickly they were growing. Their father was tall, over six feet, and it looked as if his sons were going to take after him. They were five now, six this year, and had moved up to the junior school. She had wondered if they would start to look slightly different as they grew, but there was no sign of that happening. They were still identical, even growing at the same rate and height. They had very different characters though, and that was the only way to tell them apart.

She always received a full report of their day as they walked through the village, and she was surprised when they both suddenly stopped talking. Looking up she saw what had caught their attention. Coming towards them were three Americans in their smart, very different uniforms.

'Hey! Look at this.' One of them was gazing intently at the boys, and then he stooped down, laughing. 'You're identical!'

'So they are!' The three men were now clustered around the twins, marvelling at the sight.

'How do you tell them apart, ma'am?' one asked.

'There are slight differences,' she answered, 'but you have to get to know them before you can see it. This is Andrew and this is David,' she told them.

'Ah, I guess you'd know by being their mother.'

'She isn't our mother.' David had found his voice at last. 'Hanna's our nanny.'

'Your nanny! My, aren't you lucky boys.'

They both nodded in agreement, smiling up at Hanna.

Andrew studied the men carefully for a few moments more, then said, 'You don't sound like us.'

'We're from America, and I'm finding it cold here. My name's Hal and I come from California, you see, and it's warm there.'

'Oh, and are you cold as well?' Andrew asked the one who had spoken to them first.

'No, I come from New York, and it can get mighty cold there. My name's Bob, by the way.'

'Jack's been there, hasn't he, Hanna?' David asked.

'Yes, and he liked it.'

'It's quite a place.' Bob dived in his pocket and brought out two small bars of chocolate. 'All right if I give the boys these, miss?'

Andrew and David had their eyes fixed on the sweets, and Hanna nodded. 'They've seen them now, so I can hardly refuse.'

Bob bent down to the boys again and handed over the chocolate bars, smiling with pleasure. 'I think I'd better give one to your nanny as well, don't you? We can't leave her out, can we?'

'Hanna likes chocolate,' David told him. 'But we don't get much now the war's on.'

'Then she deserves a treat.' He took another bar out of his pocket and handed it to Hanna.

She hesitated, not sure if she should take it, but realized they were just being kind and she didn't want to offend them. 'Thank you, but you mustn't give away all your chocolate.'

'Don't you worry about that, miss, I've got lots and I like kids. I know you don't get much here.'

She smiled at him, and then looked at the boys. 'Thank the kind gentlemen.'

'Thank you, sir.'

'What do you think of that, Bob?' One of them slapped the American with the chocolate on the back. 'Not only are you called a gentleman, but also sir. You sure have got nice manners here, miss.'

She inclined her head in acknowledgement, wanting to get away, but hesitated. Jack had been to New York quite a few times and told her that they had always been made welcome. These young men were in a strange country and probably missing their homes and families. And the twins clearly thought this was far too exciting to leave at the moment.

'Our daddy's the captain of a big ship,' David told them proudly, 'and Hanna's brother was on a ship that got sunk. But he's all right now.'

The one called Bob stooped down again. 'That sure is good news, and you must be very proud of both of them.'

'We are,' Andrew said. 'They're ever so brave, and we're going to win the war. Have you come to fight the Germans as well?'

'We sure have, sonny.'

David nodded at that reply. 'When your ships all got sunk our daddy and Jack were very upset.'

'So were we, boys. That was a terrible thing to do.'

David and Andrew nodded, their faces serious now, and when they both opened their mouths to speak again, Hanna knew it was time to go. The boys were settling in and the questions would keep pouring out. She took their hands and smiled at the Americans. 'Thank you again for the chocolate, but we must be getting back now.'

'Oh, sure, miss.' Bob stood up. 'It's been a real pleasure talking to you and these fine boys.'

When the others agreed, Hanna said, 'It was very nice to meet you, and welcome to Britain.'

The Americans watched and waved until they were out of sight, and as soon as they arrived home the boys couldn't wait to tell everyone about their meeting. After dinner the chocolate was shared out so everyone could have a piece.

Twenty-Three

There hadn't been much to cheer about as the year dragged on. Jack came home a couple of times, and apart from talking about the new ship he was on, he said nothing about what he was facing at sea. Alan was obviously abroad somewhere because Hanna hadn't seen him at all. His letters sometimes came in twos and threes, but of course gave no indication of his whereabouts. Captain Harcourt had made fleeting visits home earlier in the year, but they hadn't seen him for some time either.

'Cold and wet out there.' Pete stomped into the kitchen where they all congregated, as it was the warmest place in the house in winter, and the coolest in the summer when they opened the large doors facing the garden.

'What on earth have you been up to?' his grandmother exclaimed. 'You're filthy.'

'Been crawling through the woods,' he grinned. 'A wet November day is not the time to do that.'

Hanna had to smile. Frustrated that he was too young for the forces, Pete had joined the Home Guard as soon as they would take him, and by the look of him, he was thoroughly enjoying himself.

'Time for the news. Put the wireless on, Grandad, and see what's going on.' Pete removed his boots and jacket and then rinsed his hands under the tap before sitting down.

'Don't know that I want to hear it,' George grumbled. 'It seems to be all bad just lately.'

'That will change.' Pete nodded with confidence.

'Ah, the resilience of youth.' George switched on the wireless, tuning it carefully so they could all hear.

What they heard had them all standing on their feet, cheering and jumping around.

'That's bloody marvellous!' George beamed. 'Begging your pardon, Mrs Harcourt.'

'Swear all you like, George.'

'What's happened?' The boys were hanging on to their mother, and then they turned to Hanna, not understanding what all the fuss was about. 'What's happened?'

'The British have defeated Rommel and pushed the Germans out of North Africa. It's a big victory.'

'Is the war over then?' the boys asked.

'No, I'm afraid not, but it is something to cheer about,' Hanna explained.

When they had all calmed down, Jane said, 'Do you think that's where Alan is, Hanna?'

'I really don't know, but I wouldn't be surprised. If he is then he might be coming home soon.'

Three days later it wasn't Alan who arrived but Jack, and this was cause for more celebration. He'd walked in just as Hanna was about to go and collect the boys from school, so Jack dumped his bag and went with her. He looked well, if a little tired.

'How long have you got?' she asked as they walked to the village.

'Seven whole days.' He looked down at her and smiled. 'You're looking great, Hanna. This country life obviously suits you.'

'It does, and I'm not going to want to go back to London when the war's over, but that will depend on what Alan decides to do. He'll go back into the police force as soon as he can, and then it will depend on where he is stationed. He has suggested that he wouldn't mind being a country copper, but we'll have to wait and see about that. The boys are growing up fast, and in another couple of years they're not going to need me any more.'

'Let's hope the war is over by then, and once Alan is home for good you'll be able to plan for the future.'

'It's hard to look that far ahead because we don't know what's going to happen.' She sighed. 'Or how much longer this war will last. We've had a victory in North Africa, but we're still a long way from defeating Hitler.'

'True, but the tide could be turning in our direction at last. In the beginning we had the feeling that the Germans were invincible, but now we know they are not. We won the Battle of Britain in the air, more of their submarines are being detected and sunk, and now we've had this victory at El Alamein. I know there's no end in sight, but these are all hopeful signs.'

'Yes they are.' She slipped her hand through his arm. 'But for the next seven days we'll forget about the war and enjoy the time you are here. The boys will be excited to see you. Their father hasn't been home for months and I know they miss him very much.'

'Yes, it's hard for them. I'm looking forward to seeing them, and I've got them a couple of unusual presents from my travels.'

They didn't have time to say anything else, because as soon as they reached the school, the doors burst open and the children poured out, David and Andrew at the front as usual. They spotted Jack immediately and, yelling their welcome, they rushed towards him.

The boys were so pleased to see Jack, and had so much to tell him, that Hanna didn't get a word in all the way back to the farm.

As soon as they walked into the kitchen, Jack said, 'See my bag on that chair? There might be something in there for you. Why don't you have a look?'

Giving cries of excitement, they dived in to see what was there.

Jane shook her head as she watched her sons sorting through Jack's bag. 'Jack, I'm wasting my time telling you not to spend your money on the boys, aren't I?'

'I enjoy doing it, and it's nothing much.' Jack's expression was serious. 'You have welcomed us into your home and made us feel a part of your family. That means a great deal to both of us. More than you could ever know.'

'What are these, Jack?' David asked, staring at the thing in his hands, a puzzled expression on his face, and the same on his brother's, as he held a similar item. 'They look like dolls.'

'Ah, but they've got a secret. Can you find it?'

Eagerly setting about the task, Andrew was the first to figure it out. 'Oh, the top comes off and there's another one inside.'

'And another one inside that!' David laughed, taking out

one after the other and lining them up on the table for everyone to see.

'They're Russian!' George murmured in Hanna's ear. 'I've seen pictures of them. Your brother's been on the convoys to Russia.'

'Thank you, Uncle Jack,' the boys said together, laughing as they put the brightly coloured figures together, then took them apart again. 'Wait till we show them at school.'

Jack looked taken aback for a moment, and then grinned at Hanna. 'I seem to have been promoted.'

'That's how they think of you now, as an uncle,' Jane told him. 'And it's lovely.'

'I'm honoured.'

When she saw her brother look fondly at the boys, Hanna was thrilled for him. Jack was so good with children, and she hoped that one day he would marry and have a family of his own. But he had to get through the war first – they all had to get through the blasted war.

The next day Hanna and Jack had been feeding the animals, and all her efforts to get Jack to rest had been swept aside. After a couple of hours she had to admit that not only was her brother very fit, but unbelievably strong. When they found a fully grown sheep tangled in a wire fence, she watched him lift it free with apparent ease, and her mind went back to their father. Her memory of him wasn't all that clear because she had only been eight when he had died, but she did have a picture of a tall, strong man. Her breath caught in her throat when she realized that Jack was growing up to be just like him.

He walked back to her. 'Goodness knows how they get into such a mess. Soppy thing. I've fixed the fence so it won't happen again.'

'Good job you were here with me. I'd never have been able to free her, and now I think we are due a break and a nice cup of tea.' They got in the truck and Hanna drove them back to the house.

'You'll have to teach me how to drive while I'm here, Hanna.'

'George is the one to do that. I'm sure he'd love to teach you.' She grinned. 'I'm not allowed out on the roads yet.'

Pete and George were already sitting at the table when they arrived. 'Hanna said you might teach me to drive while I'm home?'

'We'll need more than a few days, Jack,' George told him, 'but we can make a start if you like?'

'Thanks, that would be marvellous.'

The kitchen door opened, letting in a blast of cold air as Jane arrived wearing her WVS uniform. 'Good, I'm just in time for tea. It's perishing out there.' After removing her hat and coat, she sat down. 'The Americans are throwing a big party for all the local children tomorrow afternoon at Bury St Edmonds, and everyone is invited.'

'Not me!' George held up his hands in horror.

'Nor me,' agreed his wife. 'We'll stay here in the quiet.'

'I can't come either; I'm on Home Guard duty.' Pete looked disappointed.

'Cowards,' Jane grinned, turning to Hanna. 'That leaves us, but what about you, Jack?'

'Count me in. It should be interesting.'

George drove them to the party, and after promising to come back in a couple of hours, hastily left.

The volume of sound that hit them when they stepped through the door was enough to pierce eardrums, and they stood there laughing, knowing exactly why George had driven away in such a hurry. He did love a quiet life.

The place was packed with children of all ages, and also American soldiers and airmen. It was hard to tell who was making the most noise, and Jack gazed around shaking his head in disbelief. 'They must have gathered every child for miles around. And look at the amount of food they've got,' he shouted. 'Those tables at the end of the room are about to collapse under the strain.'

'This is unbelievable!' Jane was laughing, still holding on to the boys who were taking in the chaotic scene before launching into the scrum as soon as their mother let them go. As soon as they were released they were off.

'Hey, Nanny! Glad you could make it. I'm Hal, remember?'

She nodded. 'The boys couldn't wait to come, so thank

you for inviting us. This is Mrs Harcourt and my brother, Jack.'

'And where are those boys?' Hal asked, looking around the room. 'Ah. I see them, and here they come. Swell party, isn't it?' he said, stooping down to the twins as soon as they reached them. 'Did you enjoy your chocolate?'

'Yes, thank you,' they said politely. 'We all had some.'

'Well, that's nice, and we've got lots here for you to eat. Want to come and have a look?'

When they eagerly agreed, Hal stood up, holding out his hands to each twin, and then he glanced at Mrs Harcourt. 'With your permission, ma'am?'

'Of course.'

As they walked towards the tables laden with food, Hal was shouting, 'Hey! Bob, look what I've found!'

Jack was in fits of laughter. 'Just wait until I tell the crew about this. Who is this party for? It looks as if the hosts are enjoying it as much as the kids.'

'Hello, Nanny, it's good to see you again.'

'Oh, hello. It's Bob, isn't it?' she asked, hoping she had remembered his name correctly, and when he nodded, she introduced him to Jane and her brother.

Bob shook Jack's hand vigorously. 'It's a real pleasure to meet you. I've got a brother, Greg, who is a merchant seaman. It's tough out there.'

'At times,' was all Jack said.

He nodded and smiled, clearly delighted to see them. 'Come on, folks; let's get you something to eat. You just help yourselves; we've got plenty more in the kitchen here.'

The selection of food was a rare sight and Hanna didn't know where to start, but Jack was having no trouble deciding. 'Is that real salmon?' Hanna asked Jane.

'It is, and sliced beef, chicken, ham, and a lot of things I don't know. I think I'll have a little bit of fresh salmon. It looks delicious.' Jane looked around for her sons. 'I hope they don't eat too much and make themselves sick. I've never seen so many jellies, trifles and cream cakes.'

'Nor me,' Hanna mumbled, filling her plate with the luxuries in front of her.

It was the wildest couple of hours they had ever spent, and they enjoyed every minute. So did the children. Hal and Bob had taken sole charge of the boys, making sure they had a good time, and never letting them out of their sight. Jack joined in with the fun, but Hanna and Jane were happy to watch.

Every child was given a present and a bag of goodies to take home with them at the end of the party. Hal brought the twins back to Jane with another American who said his name was Ed, and Hanna recognized him as one of those she'd met in the village. Bob was still talking earnestly with Jack, obviously having taken a liking to him.

'Thank you for a lovely party.' Jane smiled at her sons. 'Have you said thank you to Hal, Bob and Ed for taking care of you?'

'Yes, we have.' Their faces were glowing with pleasure. 'We've had fun.'

'So I noticed.' The level of noise had subsided now and Jane was able to talk without shouting. She shook hands with the three Americans. 'This has been very kind of you. We live at Harcourt Farm, just outside the village, and you would be welcome there if you would like to visit us.'

'Oh, ma'am.' They all looked quite overcome. 'We'd sure love to do that.' Hal turned to his friends. 'Wouldn't we?'

They all nodded. 'Thank you. When can we come?'

'Any time. Mildred, our cook, always has a pot of tea on the go.'

'Ah.' Ed couldn't quite hide the grimace. 'We can't get used to your tea, so could we bring our coffee with us?'

'Of course,' Jane laughed. 'Tea is an acquired taste.'

At that moment George arrived and tooted to let them know he was there.

On the way home the boys were too tired to talk much, and too full of food to stay awake.

'What an afternoon!' Jack prodded his sister playfully. 'And why do they call you Nanny?'

She grinned. 'When we met them they thought I was the twins' mother, but the boys quickly told them I was their nanny, and it seems to have stuck.'

'It was kind of you to invite them to the farm, Mrs Harcourt,'

Jack said. 'They're a long way from home and missing their families.'

'I got that feeling as well. This blasted war has torn families apart all over the world.'

Twenty-Four

Two days later Jack was walking across the yard, heading for the house, when he saw Bob the American waving frantically at him. He had a man with him whom Jack hadn't seen before. He went over to them, smiling. 'Hello, Bob, have you recovered from the party yet?'

'Sure, that was great. The kids had fun, and so did we.'

'So I noticed,' Jack laughed.

Bob grinned and then turned to the man standing beside him. 'My brother turned up out of the blue, and I had to bring him over to meet you. Greg, this is Jack. I told you about him.'

They were obviously brothers, but Greg was a few years older, taller, and had an easy smile. Jack took to him at once as they shook hands. 'I'm pleased to meet you. Come into the house where it's warmer.'

Hanna was there with Mildred and George, and after introductions were made, Mildred put the kettle on to boil. 'We'll have a nice cup of tea to warm us up.'

The Americans hesitated, glancing at each other, then Bob said, 'I hope you won't be offended, ma'am, but we brought this with us.'

They all stared at the packet Bob placed on the table. 'Ground coffee?' Mildred gasped. 'My goodness, it's an age since I've seen any of that!'

'I'm afraid we can't get on with your tea. I've tried since I've been here,' Bob told them. 'I really have.'

They were all laughing at the apologetic expression on his face.

'Don't worry about it,' George said. 'We do love our cup of tea, and it's helped us through some tough times. First sign of trouble in this country and on goes the kettle.'

Both Bob and Greg smiled and relaxed. 'Do you have a coffee pot, ma'am?' Greg stood up.

'Somewhere.' Mildred began to rummage in the back of a cupboard and came out triumphant. 'Found it! I'll wash it out first because it hasn't been used for quite a while.'

Greg soon had the kitchen filled with the wonderful smell of freshly brewed coffee. At that moment Jane walked in and stopped, and a look of delight crossed her face. 'Oh my, is that real coffee I can smell?'

'It certainly is, ma'am.' Bob had scrambled to his feet. 'I've brought my brother to meet you all. Greg, this is Mrs Harcourt.'

He inclined his head. 'Pleased to meet you, ma'am. I hope you don't mind us just turning up like this?'

'Not at all. I told Bob and his friends that they can come any time.'

Hanna was busy putting out the cups, and then handing them round as Greg filled each one with coffee.

'Oh, what a treat.' Jane drew in the smell before taking a sip, then sighed. 'That's just heaven!'

Bob, Greg and Jack drank it black, but the others added a little milk.

'Would you like to stay for lunch?' Jane asked them.

'Oh no.' The Americans were both shaking their heads. 'That's very kind of you, but we can't eat your food. We've been told we mustn't because you hardly get enough to feed yourselves. We came to see if Jack would come and have a drink with us at the village pub?'

'I'd like that.' Jack drained his cup and stood up. 'They'll be open now.'

'It's been nice to see you again, Bob, and to meet you, Greg.' Hanna smiled at them and then at her brother. 'Enjoy your drink. I'm sure you've got a lot to talk about.'

'We sure have, Nanny.'

'My name is Hanna,' she laughed. 'Not even the boys call me Nanny.'

As the men began to walk out of the kitchen, Mildred caught them and held up the opened packet of coffee. 'You forgot this.'

'No, you keep it. We've got plenty back at the base.'

'Nice folks,' Greg remarked, as they walked towards the village.

'They've been wonderful to Hanna and me. This is the first time we've ever had anything like a real home. We were brought up in an orphanage. We went there when Hanna was eight and I was five.'

'Gee, that's tough.' Greg shook his head sadly. 'We're lucky. We've got great folks.'

'Er . . . Hanna wears a ring on her left hand. Is she spoken for, Jack?' Bob asked.

'Yes, she's engaged to a fine man. He's in the army and hasn't been home for some time, so we believe he might be in North Africa.'

Greg whistled through his teeth. 'That's been a real hot spot, but then so have many places. I came through London on my way here, and the bombers have made a mess of parts. I wouldn't like to be there during a raid.'

'You'd rather be in a convoy being shot to pieces by U-boats, would you?' Jack asked dryly.

'As a matter of fact, I would.'

The two sailors burst into amused laughter, understanding each other.

'I don't know how you two can joke about it. I'd be terrified.'

Jack glanced at Bob, his expression serious. 'Who says we're not scared? We spend night after night fully clothed in case a torpedo hits and we have to jump overboard – again,' he added. 'Is it the same for you, Greg?'

'Just the same, but I've been lucky so far, and hope my luck holds. Have you been to the States?' Greg asked, changing the subject as they went into the pub and settled at a corner table.

'Several times to New York, but my last couple of trips have been to Russia. Winter there is so cold that everything gets iced up on the ship.'

'Yeah, so I've heard. I'd rather be in warmer waters. If you go overboard in those conditions you don't stand any chance of surviving.' Greg began to write in a little book, then tore out the page and handed it to Jack. 'Our folks live in New York, so if you go there again we'd be real grateful if you'd drop in and see them for us. It's tough on them with us both being away, and it would mean a lot to them to talk to someone who has seen us.'

Jack took the address from Greg and tucked it safely into his wallet. 'I'll certainly visit them the next time we dock in New York.'

'Thanks, pal, they would be delighted to see you.'

They spent the next hour talking about many things without touching on the war again, and Jack thoroughly enjoyed their company. When they parted he wondered if he would ever see Greg again. He hoped so, and he would keep his promise to see their family at the first opportunity.

The end of the week's leave came all too soon, and Jack was once again back on his ship, heading out to join up with another convoy. 'Anyone know where we're going?' he asked.

'Not yet, but I hope it's not Russia again.' Frank blew on his hands. 'I never knew it could be that cold.'

'Nor me!' Bill looked out to sea. 'Ah, there's the rest of the convoy. We'll soon be on our way now.'

Jack borrowed Bill's binoculars and scanned the ocean. 'Phew! Big convoy this time. There are at least three Royal Navy ships as escort. If they're all coming with us then they must be expecting trouble.'

Frank snorted. 'There's always trouble!'

'Let's have a look. I only saw three.' Bill took the glasses and said nothing for a while, then pointed over to their left. 'There's another one. That makes four, and I'd say you're right. Wherever we're going they could be expecting trouble.'

Harry joined them. 'With a convoy this big the U-boats will be after us like a pack of wolves. Where the hell are we going? Not Russia again, I hope. That was a massacre.'

'I wouldn't mind New York,' Jack said. 'I met a couple of Americans and they asked me to go and see their parents.'

'Not this trip.'

The men turned to find the petty officer behind them. 'Canada is our destination, and we've just received orders to take our place in the convoy.'

They all split up to carry out their allotted duties. Because of Jack's excellent distance sight, he now did regular watches,

some at night and others during the day. When they were
under attack he was always called upon, and often spent long
hours scanning the sea for any sign of submarines or survivors
if ships had been hit. No one had any sleep during those times,
and Jack was much happier being kept busy. There was less
time to think about what was happening.

They'd had air cover for a while, but now that was gone
the atmosphere was tense.

'Anything?' an officer asked.

Jack shook his head. 'Not so far, sir, but they're there. I can
feel it.'

'Me too. Keep your eyes peeled. They're probably waiting
for others to join them.'

Two hours later and the first ship was hit, quickly followed
by two more. Then the escorts began to sweep the ocean to
the rear of the convoy, dropping depth charges.

'At least that should make them dive deep, giving us a respite,'
Harry said, standing by ready to give aid to any wounded. He
was their first-aid man and usually kept busy on these convoys.

'Or seek refuge right underneath us,' Jack pointed out.

'That too.' Harry grimaced.

One of the support ships was off their port side when there
was a terrific explosion. They watched as the vessel listed badly,
and men began to jump overboard.

'Oh, hell! She's going down fast. They haven't had time to
launch lifeboats.' Jack trained the glasses on the scene and felt
their ship change course.

'Get those men out of the sea!' the officer was yelling.
'Scramble nets over the side!'

Some men were able to climb aboard on their own, but
others needed help. Jack and the crew worked frantically to
pull as many as possible to safety, knowing that every moment
they stayed there put them at great risk.

'Thanks, mate,' one man gasped, as Jack dragged him on to
the deck.

'Who's your captain?' he asked urgently.

'Johnson. Don't know if he made it though.'

Jack let out a pent-up breath. He had been afraid he would
hear the names of Harcourt or Freeman.

They stayed as long as they could – too long really – but had been determined to pick up as many from the water as they could find. The engines sprang into life and Jack scanned the sea anxiously for survivors, and finding none they got under way again. It was a blessing their ship was quite fast because they had to put on as much speed as possible to catch up with the rest of the convoy.

When it came in sight and they took their position again, Frank joined Jack on the deck. 'Phew! That was risky, but we couldn't leave those men behind, and we were the nearest ship to them. We managed to find a lot of men, and we're now packed tight. Hope to God those subs don't strike us now.'

Jack nodded. 'It doesn't bear thinking about. Still, you know what Harry said, lightning doesn't strike twice.'

'Don't say that, Jack!' Frank held up his hands in horror. 'We don't want to tempt fate.'

'I didn't know you were superstitious.'

'I never used to be, but I am now.' Frank pulled a face. 'Daft, isn't it? As if any kind of superstition is going to stop a torpedo heading our way. Ah, well, I'd better go and get some food and tea for these poor devils. You're not going to get much more than sandwiches today, Jack. Sorry, but I've got far too many mouths to feed.'

'Don't worry, that will do fine. Just make them thick slices of bread.'

Frank chuckled. 'I'll see you don't go hungry.'

They lost another two ships before they reached their destination, and by then they were all exhausted.

'Doesn't get any easier, does it?' Bill remarked.

'It will.' One of the Royal Navy sailors joined them as they manoeuvred into the dock. 'We're sinking more subs now. We've got them on the run.'

Jack and the others looked at him in disbelief. 'We haven't noticed.'

'You will. Take my word for it. Now, I'd better go and check on my mates.' He went to walk away and then turned back. 'I expect you'll be glad to get rid of us, but thanks. We're missing three men, but without your help it would have been a lot more.'

'No thanks needed,' Bill told him. 'We know what it's like to have a ship blown out from under you.'

'Ah.' The sailor nodded. 'Thanks, anyway.'

They watched him walk away, and Bill gave a wry smile. 'Poor bloke's still suffering from shock if he thinks we've got the submarines on the run.'

'Must be.' Frank gave a grim kind of smile. 'We haven't got much in the way of food left. Wonder how long we'll be here?'

'Not long. I've just been told we'll be loading almost at once because there's a convoy already gathering, and we are to join her.'

'That's a shame.' Jack studied the activity on the docks. 'This is my first time in Canada.'

'Never mind, lad, we'll be here again, and let's hope it's in summer. I'm tired of being cold.'

'I'll ask Hanna to knit you a woolly hat.'

'Hey! Don't forget me.' Frank blew on his hands. 'And a pair of gloves, please.'

'All right. Two hats and two pairs of gloves.' Jack grinned at his friends. They all had dark circles under their eyes, were looking dishevelled and none too clean, but just relieved to have reached their destination in one piece. It was a shame they couldn't stay for a couple of days. The break would have done them all good, but that was how it went sometimes, and they just accepted it. Perhaps the journey back would be easier.

In less than twenty-four hours they were taking their place in the convoy, and Jack was in his usual position, surveying the lines of ships.

'What have we got?' Bill asked as he joined him.

'They look like troop ships right in the middle, and British and Canadian escorts. That was obviously the reason we had to load so quickly. Let's hope we have a trouble-free crossing.'

Their hopes were realized when they reached Liverpool without the loss of even one ship.

'That's one to write about in your diary,' Bill told Jack. 'We all made it for once, so perhaps that sailor was talking sense after all.'

Jack nodded. 'Feels good, doesn't it? This was one of the

best-protected convoys we've been on. Not only plenty of escorts, but air cover for part of the way. They were determined to get those troops here safely.'

'They're going to be needed when we make our final push to finish off Hitler.' Frank signed. 'And that can't be soon enough for me. Oh, to get back to the days when all we had to worry about was the weather, and not what was lurking underneath the sea. Do you remember your first voyage with us, Jack? All that sun, all those exotic places.'

'Seems like a dream now,' Jack laughed at the blissful expression on Frank's face. 'But those days will return.'

'Of course they will. Now, back to the present. We've got two days, and that isn't enough time to get home, so what are we going to do?'

'Find somewhere comfortable and warm to relax. We're all tired out.'

'I know just the place.' Bill ushered them off the ship and took them to a small lodging house where they spent the next two days sleeping and eating.

Feeling refreshed and ready to face another trip, they returned to the ship. They were all busy until they were well under way, and then Bill came into the mess and sat next to Jack. 'We're back on the Atlantic run, lad, and unless we have a quick turnaround we won't be home in time for Christmas.'

'Perhaps we can spend it in New York.' Frank checked the ovens to see how the shepherd's pie was getting on. 'Might even get turkey there.'

'Wouldn't mind that,' Jack agreed. 'But I'm hoping we at least get enough time ashore so I can keep my promise to visit Greg and Bob's parents.'

'Oh, yes, they're the Americans you met.'

Jack nodded. 'I liked them, especially Greg. He's a merchant seaman, just like us.'

'Have you got the address handy?'

Taking the piece of paper out of his wallet, he handed it to Bill, who studied it. 'Hmm, I don't know where that is, but we'll find it.' He looked pointedly at Jack. 'You are taking us with you, aren't you?'

'You know I never go anywhere without you.' He shook

his head when they both grinned. 'But you've got to promise to behave yourselves.'

'We'll be good boys,' Frank said, with mock humility, and then the three men roared with laughter.

They were only two days out when the alarm sounded and they were running to their stations. Jack immediately had the binoculars trained on the sea. 'Torpedo! Port side – stern!'

The message was shouted through the ship and they just had time to change course enough for it to miss them by the smallest of margins.

'Phew! That was close.' The officer with Jack slapped him on the back. 'Well spotted. I didn't see it.'

'Here comes another one! That's way off and going to miss us as well.'

They watched as it went harmlessly by, and as they were at the rear of the convoy there was nothing else for it to hit.

'The navy's after it,' someone shouted.

An hour later they were still watching the navy ship searching, searching. Then depth charges began to explode in the water. 'They might have found it!'

'It must be hell down there.' Bill arrived to get a better view of the battle area. 'I'd rather be up here.'

The explosions continued one after another. 'They're determined to get her . . . And I think they have!' Jack pointed excitedly. 'Look, is that debris out there?'

'Yes,' the officer remarked. 'And more than debris . . . it looks as if they've blown her to bits. There won't be any survivors from that.'

'Poor devils,' Bill said quietly. 'I know they've been sinking our ships in large numbers, and we've got to get them, but when you think about it, they're just men like us.'

Jack had to agree. War, and the killing that went with it, was cruel and senseless, but there would be a lot more of it before the end finally came.

Twenty-Five

The view of New York as they approached never ceased to thrill Jack. He had travelled quite a lot now and this city was unlike any other place in the world.

'Looks like we'll be spending a while here this time, lad, so you'll have time to go and see the family you told us about. There's some delay in assembling the return convoy.'

Jack nodded, never taking his eyes off the scene. 'Good, that means I can go and see Bob and Greg's parents as soon as we get ashore – just in case we are recalled suddenly.'

'Best to, as you never can be sure about these things. Let's hope they don't get that convoy assembled for a few days.'

It was another twenty-four hours before they had permission to leave the ship and they made their way ashore as soon as they could.

'The best way to find this place will be to take a cab.' Frank pointed to a line of them waiting outside the docks. They had been to the city several times, and it hadn't taken them long to start calling them cabs instead of taxis.

When they reached one, Jack showed the driver the address. 'Can you take us to this place?'

'Sure, buddy, hop in.'

The cab roared off as soon as they were in, and Bill grimaced. 'Hey, mate, we've been dodging torpedoes on the way here, and we'd like to reach our destination unhurt.'

'No worries,' the driver laughed, taking the next corner at high speed. 'I'm the safest driver in New York.'

'Ah, thanks for telling us that.' Bill grabbed the handle on the door to steady himself as they swung on to a main road. 'That's comforting to know.'

Something suddenly occurred to Jack. 'Do you think I should take a present with me? Perhaps some flowers and say they are from their sons?'

'Good idea.' Bill tapped the driver on the shoulder. 'Could you stop at a florist's if you see one?'

'Know just the place.'

The cab took another sudden swerve and then screeched to a halt in front of a shop. Jack jumped out at once and ran into the shop. The assistant smiled at him and he smiled back, noting how pretty she was. 'I'd like some flowers, please, done up really nice and a card to go with them.'

'You English?'

'How did you guess?' he laughed. 'I came in on the last convoy.'

'And you want flowers for your girl?'

'No,' he shook his head. 'I met two Americans when I was last home, and they've asked me to visit their parents. I want these for the mother.'

'That's lovely. I'm sure they'll be very pleased. What would you like?'

'I'll leave that to you.' He watched her as she prepared a large arrangement of roses and other flowers he didn't know the names of. She really was very pretty. He hadn't had much time to think about girlfriends, as the only thing on his mind was getting through the war in one piece. This was a difficult time for relationships, and being a merchant seaman made it even more difficult when they were home for a few days, and then off again. Bill and Frank seemed to manage it all right though, so it must be possible, but the girl would have to be very understanding.

After writing the card, he paid for the flowers and dashed back to the cab.

'Took you long enough. Pretty, was she?'

'Very.' Jack held firmly on to the flowers as the cab shot forward once again.

'Do you want me to wait?' the driver asked, pulling up outside a pleasant-looking house.

'No, thanks,' Bill said as he paid him.

'OK, enjoy your visit.' Then he was tearing up the street.

'Nice place.' Frank was gazing around the quiet, tree-lined street. 'We'll wait here for you and make our way back if they ask you to stay awhile.'

Feeling very awkward holding an enormous bunch of flowers, Jack walked up to the front door, knocked, and when a woman answered, he said, 'Mrs Lucknor?'

'That's me.' She glanced from Jack to the flowers, looking slightly puzzled.

'I met your sons, Bob and Greg, in England, and they asked me to call.' He held out the flowers. 'These are for you.'

'Oh, my.' Tears filled her eyes when she took the bouquet and read the card. 'Warren! Warren! Come here!'

A man came rushing to the door. 'What's the matter, Babs?'

'Look!' She held out the flowers. 'This young man has brought me these from Bob and Greg. He met them in England.'

'That's good of you.' He pumped Jack's hand. 'Come in, and tell us how they are.'

'Are those your friends?' Mrs Lucknor asked, seeing Bill and Frank standing by the road.

'Yes, we're on the same ship. We're British merchant seamen and arrived recently.'

'Bring them in, Warren.' She gave her husband a push. 'It's cold out there.'

They were soon sitting in a comfortable lounge, in front of a brightly burning log fire, drinking coffee and being plied with things to eat.

Mrs Lucknor had arranged the flowers in a vase and placed them on a small table by the window. Then she sat down, her hands clasped tightly together. 'Are our boys all right?' There was a slight tremble in her voice. 'From what we've heard, England's a dangerous place to be.'

'They are fine, and Bob is quite safe where he is. I met Greg when he was visiting Bob. It's a quiet village, and my sister is there, having moved out of London with her employer. Hanna is looking after two young boys, twins, and they moved to the farm to get away from the bombing.'

Warren Lucknor leant forward. 'We've got no idea what conditions are like over there, or exactly where Bob is stationed. Tell us all about it.'

For the next hour Jack told them about the farm and the people living there, and described the pretty little village for them in detail. He explained how he had met their sons, and had

them roaring with laughter about the party the Americans had
given for the local children. The Lucknors were smiling happily
by the time he finished.

'Thank you, Jack,' Warren said. 'You've put our mind at rest
about Bob, at least. I'm afraid Greg is in the same dangerous
business as you. Did you have much trouble coming over?'

'No more than usual,' Jack said dismissively.

Knowing that was all he was going to get, Warren smiled
at them. 'Do you know how long you'll be here?'

'We're not sure,' Bill told him, 'but it might be for a while.'

'Wonderful! You must all stay with us until your ship leaves,
and we'll show you the sights.'

'Oh, but we couldn't put you to all that trouble,' Jack
protested. 'We can sleep on the ship, but we'll come and see
you again before we leave.'

'Jack's right.' Bill shook his head. 'You can't put us all up.
We only came with Jack to help him find your house. You've
been very kind inviting us in, but we mustn't impose on your
hospitality.'

'You would be doing us a very big favour by staying,' Babs
Lucknor told them earnestly. 'This is a big house and far too
empty since our boys left.'

'But we haven't got any overnight clothes with us, and we
would have to let the ship know if we're not going back there
every night.'

'I'll drive you back to your ship so you can collect your
gear, and let them know where you'll be.' Warren stood up,
clearly determined not to let them refuse. 'By the time we get
back, Babs will have dinner ready.'

'Warren, we've got room for two more as well.' Babs' smile
was excited. 'Might as well fill the house up. These poor boys
deserve a little comfort.'

'They sure do.' Warren looked at Jack. 'You'll find two more
of your pals for us?'

Jack glanced quickly at Bill, who shrugged. Frank was grinning and said, 'We'll see what we can do for you, Mrs Lucknor.'

While Warren went to get the car out of the garage and
his wife had already disappeared upstairs to see about the
arrangements, Jack asked his friends, 'What are we going

to do? We can't let them feed and house all of us, but they're determined.'

'They'll be upset if we refuse, Jack. Didn't you see their faces when you told them about their sons? You've made them very happy, lad, so let's accept gratefully, and just make sure we don't overstay our welcome.'

Warren tooted the car horn to let them know he was ready, and they all filed out of the house and got in the very large car. After a much smoother journey than the one they'd had coming, Warren waited outside the dock gates for them.

'Who else are we going to ask?' Frank pursed his lips. 'The first two we see?'

'Might as well, but most of them will be ashore already.' Bill strode on to the ship. 'What about those two over there? They look as if they don't know what to do with themselves.'

'Harry and Jim?' Jack laughed. 'They'll jump at the chance.' And they did.

'Right, that's settled. You go and get your gear while I tell them where they can find us, and see if they know how long it will be before we sail.' Bill strode away, and the rest of them made for the crew's quarters.

Bill soon joined them. 'We've got permission to stay ashore. It seems there's little chance of the convoy assembling within the next few days, but if it does then they'll send someone for us.'

They were all in high spirits when they met Warren at the gates, and looking forward to a few days in the comfort of a real home. When they reached the house it was full of friends and neighbours, all anxious to meet the British sailors.

'This is Jack.' Babs dragged him forward as soon as he stepped inside the house, and he was immediately surrounded by smiling people wanting to talk to him. He found the situation hard to cope with, for although he had left the orphanage some time ago now, life had not equipped him for anything like this. While he tried to answer their questions, he thought how fortunate Bob and Greg had been to grow up in a family like this. He really hoped they both came through the war and returned safely to their home.

Feeling quite overwhelmed by the eagerness of the people

around him to make them feel welcome, he was relieved when he sensed Bill come and stand beside him, resting his hand on Jack's shoulder, and joining in with the conversation. He took a deep breath and gave his friend a grateful glance.

Babs clapped her hands for silence. 'OK everyone, the food is ready, so let the boys eat in peace. They'll be here for a while so you'll have time to talk to them later.'

Amid much laughter, they all began to file out, and Jack took another deep breath.

'All right, lad?'

He shook his head and grimaced. 'I'm not used to anything like that, and it was hard. I felt quite overwhelmed by the people crowding around me. Most of them have sons or husbands away, many in England, and they naturally want news of what it's like for them.'

'Something smells good, Mrs Lucknor.' Frank was drawn towards the food. 'Can I help you serve? I'm the cook on our ship.'

'Why, thank you, Frank.' Babs beamed, clearly happy to have young men filling the house again. 'It's lovely to be cooking for a crowd again. Our boys were always bringing friends home.'

They spent a quiet evening sitting around the fire and talking, and the next day Jack and Bill went with Warren to get a Christmas tree for the house. The festive season was only two days away, and the Lucknors were clearly delighted that they could all stay. And so were they. It was going to be a lavish Christmas by the look of things, and it would be a real treat for all of them.

There was a constant stream of people in and out of the house, and the neighbours in the street quickly adopted one of the sailors each, and everyone was going out of their way to see that they all had a good time.

Harry came back late from his adopted house, grinning. 'This is great, a real family Christmas. That convoy can take its time.'

Much to everyone's relief, by Boxing Day no one had come for them, and the house was full again. They were all sitting around with drinks in their hands, talking, when the front door opened, making Babs and Warren jump to their feet, yelling with delight. They threw their arms around the tall man standing in the doorway.

'Who's that?' Bill asked Jack.

'It's Greg!' Jack was also on his feet. 'You'll like him.'

Disentangling himself from his parents, Greg's eyes immediately rested on Jack, laughing as he gave him a great bear hug. 'Jack! It's great to see you. I saw the British ships and wondered if you were here. What luck!'

'We arrived some days ago and can't leave yet. Your parents have kindly taken a crowd of us in. I'm glad you could get home.'

'Me too.' He glanced around. 'Hey, Mom, have you taken in the entire crew?'

'No,' she laughed, wiping away a tear. 'Only five, and the neighbours have adopted most of them, but we've managed to hang on to Jack and Bill – just about.'

Harry looked concerned. 'Mrs Lucknor, I believe I'm in Greg's room.'

The next-door neighbours who had taken a liking to Harry jumped to their feet. 'Don't worry about that, Harry; you can sleep at our house. We've got plenty of room.'

'Oh, thanks. I'll move my gear now.' Harry smiled at Greg. 'Can't have you sleeping on the floor in your own home.'

'Good, that's settled then. You'll be very comfortable there, Harry.' Warren smiled and then turned to his son. 'How long are you here for?'

'Don't know. The weather was foul and we were late arriving, so it might be a quick turnaround. The convoy is already gathering, but let's forget about that for the time being. Jack, his sister, and everyone at the farm made us real welcome, and Bob can go there anytime he wants, so I'd like to show him and his friends some of the countryside around here. Now, introduce me to your shipmates, Jack. And I'm starving, Mom.'

Fortunately they had three more days for Greg to drive Jack and Bill around, showing them places of interest away from the city. The others were with their adopted families being royally entertained. When the recall came it was for Greg as well. After tearful goodbyes, Babs made Jack promise that he would ask Hanna to write to them regularly. They all arrived back at the docks after having had a marvellous Christmas.

'Looks like we're on the same convoy.' Greg clasped Jack's hand. 'See you back in Liverpool.'

They boarded their ships, knowing that they would be seeing in 1944 at sea.

Twenty-Six

The New Year had arrived during a violent storm, and with the ship pitching and rolling so badly, a celebration of any kind had been impossible. But by some miracle they didn't lose one ship on the return journey, and were jubilant as the entire convoy approached England.

Jack scanned the sea filled with ships and grinned at Bill. 'What a lovely sight. Do you think the bad weather kept the subs away?'

'Might have helped.' Bill pursed his lips thoughtfully. 'But the air cover we're now getting for part of the way is also helping. Those planes can see the subs better than we can, and they're sinking a few.'

Nodding in agreement, Jack said, 'I wonder if we'll have enough time to get home?'

'Won't know until we dock. If we can, and Greg's free, will you take him home with you?'

'Oh, yes. His brother would be pleased to see him, and I'm sure Greg could stay at the farm with us. Mrs Harcourt's good like that.'

'That would be nice, because his family were certainly kind to us. It made being away from home at that time easier to take. They're good people.'

With so many ships arriving it was some time before they were docked and unloaded. Then they heard the good news that they had five days' leave before sailing again.

'Terrific!' Jack was pleased. 'That means three days at home. Now I must see if I can find Greg. Hope they haven't been sent somewhere else to unload.'

'Off you go then, lad.' Bill slapped him on the shoulder. 'We'll see you in five days. Have a good leave.'

'And you.' Jack grabbed his bag and practically ran off the ship. 'Do you know if there are any American ships here?' he called to a group of dock workers.

'Think there's a couple further down,' one man pointed.

'Thanks.' Jack was off running. If he couldn't find Greg he would have to go without him, but he didn't want to do that. He had really enjoyed spending time with Greg and his parents in America, and he wanted to repay that kindness in some way, if he could. He stopped for a moment to look around him, and then through the milling crowd of activity he caught sight of a tall figure striding towards him. He waved, breaking into a broad smile. There he was.

'Hi, Jack, I've been looking for you. I've got five days before I sail again. How much time have you got?'

'The same. That's marvellous; you can come home with me and stay at the farm. Bob and everyone will be so pleased to see you.'

'That would be great. Thanks, Jack.'

It was eight o'clock in the evening when they reached the farm. And when Jack opened the kitchen door and looked in, everyone was there, including the boys, who launched themselves at him.

It was chaos for a while as they all greeted the returning sailors, and then Jack pulled Greg forward. 'Mrs Harcourt, could Greg stay here? It will only be for three days, and then we have to return to our ships.'

'Of course he can. Welcome, Greg.'

'Are you sure, ma'am? I could get somewhere in the village.'

'I wouldn't hear of it. We have plenty of room and you are very welcome. Your brother comes here whenever he can get away. And please call me Jane. That goes for you as well, Jack, as I've told you time and time again. We don't stand on formality in this household.'

'Thank you,' they both said.

Mildred was already at the stove, and glanced over her shoulder. 'You boys must be hungry. I've got a hearty stew here and some fresh bread, and it won't take more than a few minutes to heat through. So sit you down now.'

'We're starving, actually,' Jack laughed.

'Of course you are.'

★   ★   ★

The three days flew by and Hanna had never seen Jack so happy. She had gained the impression that Bill had become a father figure to her brother, but in Greg it looked as if he'd found a friend. They laughed and joked together, enjoying the same things. They came from different countries, but had such a lot in common, and it delighted her to see them together.

They were still smiling as she waved goodbye to them at the station. Bob was standing beside her and was quite upset to see his brother go, so she slipped her arm through his. 'Come back to the farm, Bob. The boys aren't at school today and they'll cheer you up.'

His gloom lifted and he nodded. 'I'd like that. You will write to our folks, won't you, Hanna? They would love to have letters from you.'

'Of course I will.' She smiled up at him. 'It sounds as if Jack and his friends had a lovely Christmas with your family. That was so kind of them, and I'll write tonight thanking them.'

'Oh, we always had a house full. Mom loves that.' He looked down at her, a puzzled frown on his face. 'How do you do it, Hanna?'

'Do what?'

'Keep seeing your brother off, knowing the dangers he is facing at sea, and going back to your life, still smiling. You all do it. How?'

'Because we have to, Bob. Jack made his choice to stay in the merchant navy when the war broke out, and I respect that. He's doing what he has to, and I'm supporting him by being here to welcome him back with a smile on my face. The same goes for when he leaves again. It would disturb him to see me breaking my heart every time he goes back to sea. But because we keep our worries and fears hidden it doesn't mean we are unfeeling. I've looked after my brother since he was five years old and tried to protect him, but now I can't. I've had to let him go. He is his own person now, and I'm proud of him, but it's still hard – very hard. Do you understand?'

'I think so.' Bob squeezed her hand. 'Thank you for talking to me like this, Hanna. You're a real lovely girl, and if you weren't wearing that ring on your left hand I would be trying to win you for myself.'

'I don't believe that. I bet you have a string of girls back home,' she teased.

'Ah, you've found me out.' He winked at her. 'But they're a long way away. How big is this man of yours?'

They were both laughing when they reached the farm, heading straight for the warmth of the kitchen. Hal and Ed were already there, regular visitors now as well, and making coffee. The smell of fresh coffee filled the room. The Americans wouldn't let anyone else make it, and that was understandable. They knew just how they liked it, and it was too precious to be wasted. They were all very aware that everything had to be brought in by ship.

The three Americans loved the twins, and the feeling was mutual. The boys even managed to coax them into doing a bit of digging in the garden when the weather was good enough, though Hanna wasn't sure much work got done. They spent more time playing and messing about than actually working.

'Could have some snow before long.' George walked into the kitchen rubbing his hands together. 'We'll bring the sheep in if it gets too bad, Hanna. I've already alerted Jean and Pat.'

'Want coffee, George?' Ed asked.

'Rather have a cup of tea, but don't you try to make it.' George winked at his wife. 'These boys tried to make some tea once, and it was so weak it could hardly crawl out of the pot.'

There were roars of laughter, as this was a standing joke among them. The English couldn't make a drinkable cup of coffee, and the Americans couldn't make a decent cup of tea. Greg was the only one of them who seemed to enjoy tea now and again.

Hanna suppressed a sigh as she thought of Jack and Greg – two young men constantly facing unknown dangers at sea. *Be safe*, she silently prayed, and sighed again. Her list of people to worry about was growing all the time.

It was July before Alan returned from North Africa, and when she saw him walk into the yard, it was a moment of sheer joy. It had been such a long time since she had seen him. She rushed to meet him and was lifted off the ground and swung round. 'Oh, it's wonderful to see you. I've missed you so much.'

'And you're as beautiful as ever,' he laughed, putting her down and stepping back to take a good look at her. 'No, I'll correct that – you're even more beautiful, if a bit dirty.'

'I've been cleaning out the pigs,' she laughed. 'Can you stay? Please say you can stay.'

'I've got seven days, but I must spend some of that time with my parents.'

'Of course you must. Have you been home first?'

He nodded. 'Just overnight, but I couldn't wait to see you, and they understand. They send their love, by the way, and thank you for all your letters.'

The boys, always eager for visitors, had come up beside them and were eyeing Alan with interest. She urged them forward. 'This is Alan. You've met him before, but you might not remember.'

'We do,' David said. 'You were a policeman.'

'My goodness! What memories you've got.'

'You haven't been here for a long, long time,' Andrew told him.

'No, I've been away.' Alan glanced across the yard and saw the three Americans, so he stooped down to David and Andrew. 'Are you going to introduce me to your friends?'

Andrew caught hold of Alan's hand and towed him across the yard to them. 'They come from ever such a long way away.'

'This is Alan,' David declared. 'He belongs to Hanna, and he's been away.'

Bob chuckled. 'And he's a lucky man. I'm Bob, and this is Hal and Ed. We're sure pleased to meet you, Alan.'

They all shook hands, and Ed was studying Alan's badges. 'You look as if you've been somewhere hot. Like the desert?'

Alan gave a slight nod of his head, but said nothing.

'Fine job you did out there,' Hal said quietly, then changed the subject. 'We've got some real coffee in the house if you fancy a cup?'

'Real coffee? I'd love one.'

An hour later when everyone had had a chance to greet

Alan, and he was settled in a room, the Americans returned to their camp. The boys were asleep for their nap so Alan and Hanna were able to slip away on their own.

'Let's walk to the village, darling. I'd like to see the English countryside again. It's so green here,' he sighed, 'and very beautiful.'

'Worth fighting for?'

He nodded. 'Even if the cost is high. Now, tell me what you've been doing, how Jack is, and about those Americans.'

Hanna talked, sensing that Alan only wanted to listen and not say much. It was a lovely day and after walking right through the village and into the open countryside, they found an old fallen tree and sat on it, enjoying the sunshine and being together again. She could see the change in Alan, just as Jack had been changed by his experiences. Her brother had needed time to come to terms with what had happened to him, and so did Alan. The only sound was birdsong, and she saw him close his eyes, listening and absorbing the peace.

After a few moments he opened his eyes again and smiled at her. 'Do you know I used to dream of something like this, and often wondered if I would ever see it again – or you.'

'I can understand that.'

'Are you happy here, darling? Do you ever yearn to go back to London?'

'To be honest, I love it here and it wouldn't worry me if I never saw London again.'

'Good, because I was thinking that it would be nice to be a village copper.'

'That's a lovely idea, but do you think it would be possible?'

'Might be.' He shrugged. 'But we've got a long way to go before we can make definite plans for the future. Troops and equipment are building up in the country, Hanna. There are British, Canadian, Australians, Americans, Free French, and others. The last big effort to beat Hitler is being planned, and I don't think it's too far away.'

'And you'll be a part of it.'

'That's what we're all here for.' He hugged her tightly. 'But that means we've got to hang on a bit longer before we can decide our future – a future at peace.'

'How much longer do you think before we're able to put an end to this madness?'

'It will be a huge undertaking and take time to organize, so I'm only guessing, but perhaps by the end of next year.'

'Let's hope so.' She smiled at a small rabbit who had come quite close, and then bounded away.

Alan laughed. 'He'd better not let anyone else see him or he'll end up in some stew pot. Come on, we'll walk back through the village so I can have another look at the police house.'

'Still a policeman at heart,' she teased.

'Always, and if I can find somewhere more peaceful than London, then that will be fine.'

'For me too.' Hanna clasped Alan's hand tightly. 'When Jack was about to board his first ship, we watched the sun rise on a new day — a new life for both of us — and when the war is finally over we'll be able to welcome in a new day for all of us.'

'That will be something to look forward to.'

Hanna nodded as they walked hand in hand back to the village.

Twenty-Seven

Hanna thought a lot about those precious moments she had spent with Alan when he had talked about the possibility of the war ending, and what he wanted to do once he was out of the army. He would make an excellent village policeman, she thought, as she planted out neat rows of lettuce. The last of the frosts had gone and there was a great deal to do on the farm. She was kept busy and quite happy about that because the boys would be eight this year and didn't need her so much. They had always been independent, but were even more so now. Jane was talking about going back to London now the danger of raids had diminished, but Hanna loved it on the farm and would ask if she could stay. If Jane and the boys weren't here she wouldn't be able to stay at the house, of course, so she would try to find somewhere to live until Alan came back for good. She had promised Jack that he would have a home to come back to, and she would make sure he did.

'Another convoy of lorries has just rumbled through the village,' George said, as he came up to Hanna. 'More Americans arriving. Troops are pouring in from everywhere, and it looks as if 1944 is going to be the year we finally put an end to this damned war.'

Hanna straightened up. 'When do you think it will be, George?'

'Early summer's the best time to cross the Channel, so I'd guess in the next couple of months.' He pursed his lips. 'We don't see so much of the American boys now their training has been stepped up. No . . . it won't be long now.'

Like everyone else, Hanna longed for the end of the war, but she went cold when she thought of the cost in young lives, including the danger to some very dear to her.

George smiled down at her. 'Alan's bound to get home for a few days, so you can expect him to walk through these gates any time soon. And Captain Harcourt's just arrived on seven days' leave.'

'Oh, that's wonderful! He hasn't been home for such a long time. Jane and the boys will be so delighted.'

'They are,' he laughed. 'It's bedlam in there, and those kids are looking more like their father every day.'

'I know.' Hanna shook her head. 'They were only three when I first saw them, and look at them now. Where have the years gone, George?'

'Not been easy, have they? We were glad Pete was too young to get caught up in this mess. Our daughter died a couple of months after he was born, and we've had him since he was a baby. Means the world to us, he does.'

'I didn't know that, George. I'm so sorry.'

'We don't talk about it, and Pete's never known anything else.'

'What about his father?'

'Oh, him! He walked out before the baby was born. Never seen him since, and don't want to.'

'Pete was very lucky to have you.' Hanna couldn't help thinking of their years in the orphanage, and was glad that Pete had escaped that kind of life.

'Oh, we've been the lucky ones, Hanna. Anyway, mustn't forget what I came here for. Mildred said could you find her a few more onions and potatoes for dinner?'

'Of course. We've got plenty in the store shed. I'll bring a few carrots as well, just in case she needs them.'

Although the captain was home, the Harcourts still insisted on eating in the kitchen with the rest of them. It was a lively affair, with the twins in high spirits, keeping them all entertained, and Hanna watched the captain begin to relax. She recognized the signs of strain, having seen it so often in Jack, and again in Alan when he had returned from North Africa.

'Daddy, Mummy wants to go back to London.' Andrew didn't look too pleased about the prospect.

'She told me, but I've persuaded her to wait a little longer.'

'Oh, good.' Andrew beamed. 'We like it here.'

And Hanna was as pleased as the boys, because it meant she could carry on as usual for a while longer.

The next morning the three Americans turned up and they met the captain for the first time. Somehow their paths had never crossed on his brief visits home. The boys were at school, and Jane had popped to the village to see someone. Noting that the four men were already deep in conversation, Hanna just waved to them and went back to work in the garden. Pete was out with his Home Guard unit, so she was quite alone, working behind a row of raspberry bushes.

After a while she heard the gate open and the sound of men's voices drifted over to her, but she moved so they could see she was there, and kept on working. There had been a lot of rain recently, and it was surprising how quickly the weeds shot up. This was a lovely tranquil spot away from the bustle of the other farm work, and she knew the men probably wanted somewhere peaceful to talk.

' . . . looks like we'll be moving out soon.'

Hanna recognized Hal's voice as the men walked slowly around the garden.

'We've been told the beaches will be bombarded before we land.'

The captain's voice was too deep for Hanna to hear his reply, but they were coming closer and she moved out further so they could see her clearly, looked up and gave a little wave, then returned to her weeding. They knew she was there now and could move away if they didn't want her to hear what they were saying. But they smiled at her and kept on walking and talking.

'What chance do you have of knocking out the enemy before we go in, sir?' Ed asked.

'That we can't be sure of, but you can be certain that we will do our very best to protect you as much as we can.'

'Can't ask for more than that, sir,' Bob said. 'Would you join us for a drink at the pub?'

'That's an excellent idea. Hanna,' the captain called, 'tell Jane I've gone to the pub for a drink.'

'I will.' When the gate closed behind them, Hanna rested on the hoe, deep in thought. From the little snatches of conversation she had caught, it was clear that George had been right. The invasion of France was close – very close.

An hour later Jane looked in the garden. 'Have you seen Sam, Hanna?'

'He went to the village with the Americans for a drink.'

'Ah, he might be some time then. I'll go and collect the boys later, so you can carry on with what you're doing.'

Pete arrived back just then and the two of them spent the rest of the day working in the garden.

It was dinner time before the captain arrived home, and Mildred nodded. 'You're just in time. I'm about to dish up.'

'I hear you met our regular visitors,' Jane said, smiling at her husband. 'What do you think of them?'

'They're interesting and easy to get on with. After we'd had a drink at the pub they insisted on taking me back to their base to meet some of their other colleagues. I've been plied with food and drink all afternoon,' Sam laughed.

'I expect they were pleased to have someone they could talk about the war with, and what is going to happen soon,' George said.

'They wanted to talk, and that is understandable. They're a long way from home and naturally apprehensive, as are we all.'

Jane nodded. 'We've been happy to let them come here whenever they wanted to, and I think they've enjoyed the farm, and the company.'

'They have, and they said that one day they would bring their families here to meet everyone who has been so kind to them.'

'They're nice boys and it's been a pleasure to have them around the place.' Mildred put more vegetables on the table. 'But we're not going to see much more of them, are we?'

'I really can't say how much longer they will be here, Mildred.'

The boys had been quietly eating their dinner, but now looked concerned. 'Are they going away, Daddy?'

'They will be leaving at some time, David. They are only stationed here for a while.'

'That's a shame. We like them, they're fun.'

'We all like them, Andrew.' Jane smiled at both of her sons. 'But they'll still be here for a while yet, I expect.'

The boys nodded and went back to eating. Hanna watched their faces and realized that they were used to people coming for a while and then leaving. All their lives their father had arrived home for a few days, and then left again. Whereas other young children might be upset, they accepted this as normal.

Later that evening when Hanna was alone in the kitchen writing her letters to Alan, Jack and Bob's parents in America, Sam Harcourt came in and sat at the table with her.

'Am I disturbing you?'

'Not at all.' She put down her pen.

'How's Jack?'

'He's doing fine. I understand that they're not losing quite so many ships now.'

'We've been sinking quite a few U-boats and they no longer have it all their own way. But they are still at risk, though not as much as before, and that's an improvement.' The captain studied Hanna. 'At least you have the comfort of knowing that your brother won't be involved in the invasion, when it comes.'

'Yes, but I expect Alan will, and the Americans we've got to know.' Hanna took a deep breath before saying, 'I know you'll think this is a daft question, but what are the chances that the invasion will be successful and bring an end to the war?'

He was silent for a while, and then looked up. 'It will be a success because it has to be. We can't have another Dunkirk, Hanna. But that won't happen again because this time we're not facing this alone. I don't believe for one moment it's going to be easy, but we will succeed.' Then he stood up. 'I've disturbed you long enough. Remember me to Jack when you write to him.'

'I will.'

He paused at the door. 'I know you must be feeling unsettled now the boys are older and Jane is talking about returning to London, but I would appreciate it if you stayed at the farm for the time being. It's a great comfort to know you are here with my family, and have been through this long conflict.' When she nodded, he smiled and said, 'Thank you. Goodnight, Hanna.'

Her smile turned to a frown as the door closed behind him.

He obviously knew what was coming, and that it was going to be a hard fight for all concerned.

Hanna had never been a regular churchgoer, but the boys said their prayers every night before going to sleep, and from now on she would pray for a rapid end to this terrible war, and the safety of all those dear to them.

The next morning Hanna was walking across the yard on her way to the garden, when a car drew up outside the house.

'Hello, Hanna!' Rose called, as soon as she stepped out of the car. 'How are you?'

'I'm fine, thank you, Mrs Freeman.' She waited while a man also got out of the car and began to walk towards her. Her breath caught in her throat. Bill Freeman had been impressive enough the first time she had seen him, but towering over her in his officer's uniform he was something else.

'How is your brother?' he asked in his quiet way.

'Very well, sir. And thank you so much for bringing him home after his ship had been sunk.'

He merely inclined his head in acknowledgement. 'Is he at sea now?'

'Yes, sir.'

'I believe I asked you to call me Bill.'

She couldn't do that! She heard Rose laugh at the look of horror there must be on her face.

'Bill,' Rose admonished, 'stop teasing Hanna. You'll frighten her.'

'Me? I couldn't frighten anyone. I've never frightened you.' There was a look of pure devilment in his eyes.

'Ah well, I'm different. I can just imagine you on that ship. You never raise your voice, but I'll bet the crew trip over themselves to carry out your orders.'

A slight smile crossed his face as he looked at Hanna. 'Don't take any notice of what Rose says. Everyone runs for cover when they see her coming. She'd have my crew jumping overboard to get away from her.'

Hanna couldn't help laughing at the teasing going on between them. They obviously cared for and respected each other a great deal.

'Rose, Bill!' Jane rushed out of the house with her husband. 'What a lovely surprise! Did you bring Kate with you?'

'No, she's with her grandfather in Wales. This is just a flying visit.'

'But you must stay for lunch,' Jane insisted. 'You can't come all this way, say hello, and then disappear again.'

After kissing Rose on the cheek, Sam Harcourt shook Bill's hand, smiling broadly with pleasure. 'It's good to see you.'

'And you, Sam. Have you got a decent pub in the village?'

'Of course. What time is lunch, Jane?' he asked his wife.

'One o'clock.'

'Make it two. Come on, Bill, let's leave the women to it.'

Before walking away, Bill smiled at Hanna. 'Remember me to Jack when you see him again.'

'I will, s—' The look on his face stopped her, and she shook with laughter. 'I will, Bill.'

'Thank you. That wasn't so hard, was it?'

She shook her head and watched the two impressive men walk out of the gate. Jane and Rose had already gone back into the house, so Hanna made her way to the garden, still laughing to herself.

Twenty-Eight

'Ah, there you are.' George walked into the storage shed, shaking the rain out of his thinning hair. 'I've just been told that troops are moving out. The roads are full of lorries and tanks, so it looks as if the big push might be on.'

Hanna looked through the open door at the lashing rain, and her insides tightened. 'But the weather is terrible. Surely they can't cross the Channel in this?'

'Perhaps not, but I expect they want to be ready to move as soon as it clears. It will take some time to get everyone in place. The Americans left yesterday evidently.'

'Oh, and we never got a chance to wish them well.' Hanna shook her head sadly. 'I must write a long, cheerful letter to Bob's parents because they'll be worried when they hear the news.'

'They'll appreciate that, but no mention of this. It's got to be kept a secret, if that is at all possible.' George patted Hanna's shoulder. 'This had to come, and the sooner it starts the better. If all goes well this war could be over by Christmas. At least you know Jack won't be involved.'

'I'm relieved about that, of course, but Alan will be and so will many others we know as well.'

George nodded. 'Mildred was making an apple pie so let's go and see if we can cadge a piece, and then we'll see if there is anything on the news. Though I doubt it. Until we actually land in France I don't think there will even be a whisper from official sources. They won't want the Germans to know we're coming, though how an operation of this size can be kept a secret is a mystery to me. Come on, I'm hungry and gasping for a cuppa.'

That brought a smile to Hanna's face. 'Tea, the cure for all ills.'

'Don't mock it,' George grinned. 'There's a lot of truth in these old wives' tales.'

★　★　★

It was nearly a week later before they heard that the landings had taken place on 6 June, and that troops were already moving into France. While that news brought a feeling of hope, there was also anxiety for those taking part.

They all listened intently to the news every evening and Hanna kept herself busy on the farm, and spent time with the boys when they wanted her to. They were so insistent on doing everything for themselves now, so she wasn't needed quite so much, but there was enough work to keep her busy around the farm. Pat and Jean were also concerned about their husbands, and Hanna spent a couple of evenings a week playing cards with them. It helped them all to take their minds off the war for a short time, and she always had a good laugh with the two women from London.

A week after the landings they were all dismayed to hear that flying bombs were falling on London, making George swear. 'He's going to have one last go at us, isn't he!'

'I'm afraid so.' Jane sat back, a look of disgust on her face. 'I was thinking of going back to London, but I can't now. Sam was right to urge me to stay here a while longer.'

The boys smiled at each other, and Hanna thought that at least someone was happy about it. She could understand Jane wanting to go back to her home and friends, but the boys were settled in school, had made lots of friends, and really enjoyed living on the farm. It would be hard to uproot them now.

While they were discussing the new threat, the kitchen door opened and Jack walked in. As usual the boys reached him before Hanna could. When she finally managed to give him a welcome hug, she asked, 'Isn't Greg with you?'

'Not this time.'

'Sit down, Jack.' Mildred always made a fuss of him whenever he appeared. 'You must be hungry.'

'How did you guess?' He grinned.

It had been some months since she had seen her brother, and she studied him carefully, rather shocked by what she saw. The young boy she had watched sail away that first time no longer existed. He would be twenty-one in November, and the person sitting at the table was a man who had seen terrible things, and suffered a great deal of hardship. But it had moulded him into the brother she loved and had the greatest admiration for. How proud their parents would have been of him.

'Don't look so sad, Hanna,' Jack told her. 'The war could be over in a few months, and then Alan will be home for good and you can get married.'

'I'm not sad. I was just thinking.'

'About what?'

'Oh, all sorts of things. How long will you be home for?' she asked, changing the subject.

'A whole week this time.'

'Wonderful!' Hanna smiled. 'They've got a dance at the village hall tomorrow night. How about being my partner? We're short of men now the Americans have left, and you'll be in big demand.'

Jack tipped his head back and laughed. 'I'll be all right as long as they keep playing a waltz. I haven't progressed beyond that.'

'Now is your chance to learn.' She gave him a teasing smile. 'There are some pretty girls in the village, and they'll be queuing up to be with you. You wait until you see Pat and Jean jive. They're really good.'

'I'll look forward to it.' He sniffed appreciatively at the shepherd's pie Mildred placed in front of him. 'That smells delicious, and it's just what I need.'

The boys waited patiently while he finished his meal, gazing over at his bag in the corner of the room from time to time. Jack winked at Hanna once, fully aware of the twins' eagerness to look in his bag, but knowing they mustn't until Jack said they could. Her brother was building up their excitement by making them wait.

When he had finished eating and had a cup of tea in front of him, he nodded to the twins. 'You'd better see what you can find, hadn't you?'

Scrambling off their chairs they pounced on the bag, experts now at getting it open. As usual there were two packets in there, and they sat on the floor to open them, gasping with delight at the beautiful trains each of them held.

'Wow!' Two faces turned towards him wreathed in identical smiles. 'Thank you. They're wonderful!'

'I'll bring you a piece each time I go to America until you have a full set.'

'Jack.' Jane sighed. 'You really are too good to the boys.'

'I know you've told me often enough not to bring them presents, but it gives them such pleasure, and I love to see their expressions. We didn't have much at the orphanage, and although Hanna was wonderful and did everything she could to see I had as happy a childhood as possible, we never had much to smile about.' He cast Hanna an affectionate glance. 'And I don't think Hanna even had a childhood, and that wasn't right. It makes me happy to see what it should have been like.'

'Of course.' Jane nodded, sadness in her eyes. 'I never realized.'

Taking a deep breath, Hanna fought to stop the tears from falling. This was the first time she had ever heard her brother talk so frankly about their years in the orphanage. She had told herself many times that it was all behind them and could be forgotten, but now she knew that it would never quite leave them. They had moved on with their lives, but their childhood experiences had moulded them into what they were today. When she saw her brother now she knew they had come out of it well, but a part of the past would always be with them.

When they were alone later in the evening, she said, 'I've never heard you talk about the orphanage before, Jack.'

He gave one of his easy smiles and shrugged. 'I don't mind talking about it now, Hanna. I'm not ashamed that we came from there; it wasn't our fault, and we've turned out all right. We could have ended up all bitter inside, but we didn't, and that's quite an achievement. And the way we've come through that is all down to you. You remained cheerful, sensible and strong, and that rubbed off on me. You sacrificed your childhood to become my protector, and that's something I'll never forget.'

'Oh, Jack, I only did what I thought was best for us, and if you had been the oldest you would have done the same for me.' She tipped her head to one side, studying him carefully. 'I only have a vague recollection of our father, but I have watched you grow more and more like him over the last few years.'

'Do you think so?' He looked pleased. 'I've tried and tried to remember what they looked like, but I can't picture them at all.'

'You definitely take after our father, tall and well built, but I'm smaller and much more like our mother.'

'It's nice to know that we've both got something of them in us.' He stood up and held out his arms. 'If I'm going to this dance then you had better teach me a quickstep or I'll be stepping on my poor partner's toes all the time.'

They spent the next hour dancing around the kitchen and laughing. It was lovely to be carefree, even if it was only for a short time. They might now have hope that the war would be over in the not too distant future, but until then there was still danger at sea for Jack.

The village hall was crowded, and everyone was in high spirits, buoyed up by the news of troops liberating parts of France. Pat and Jean waved when they came in, so they joined them.

'Oh good, you've brought a man with you.' Pat slipped her hand through Jack's arm. 'I bags the first dance with our sailor.'

Jack chuckled. 'I must warn you, Pat, that I'm not much of a dancer.'

'You'll do fine. You're so tall and handsome the girls won't worry what your feet are doing.'

Shaking his head in amusement, Jack allowed himself to be dragged on to the dance floor. It was a quickstep and Hanna watched to see if he had remembered any of the steps. He had and was managing quite well. 'Pat's happy tonight,' Hanna remarked.

'Don't be fooled. Underneath that smile she's just like the rest of us – worried sick about our men. But we can't help them, or change what might happen, so we keep smiling, praying for a speedy end to the war, and their safe return.' Jean took hold of Hanna. 'Come on, let's dance. I'll lead because we're not going to get many partners tonight now the Americans have moved out.'

Jack danced with the three of them a couple of times, and although he said he wasn't much of a dancer, Hanna quickly realized that wasn't so. He had good rhythm, was light on his feet, and picked up the steps quickly.

They had just finished a waltz when her brother whispered in her ear, 'Who is that girl over there? The one in the blue frock?'

'You mean the blonde?' Hanna asked.

He nodded, never taking his eyes off the girl.

'That's Beth Grafton. She works in the local shop.' When she saw how interested Jack was she gave him a little push. 'Go and ask her to dance.'

He hesitated for a moment, and when the band began to play again, he strode over to her. Hanna watched and smiled when Beth stood up to dance with Jack.

'Ah,' said Pat, 'he's had his eyes on her ever since he arrived. Glad he's finally asked her to dance. But that means we've lost our partner.'

Pat was right about that because they didn't see much of Jack for the rest of the evening when he got in with Beth's friends, and it did Hanna good to see him so relaxed and happy.

After the last dance Jack rushed over. 'Hanna, are you going back with Jean and Pat? Only I'd like to walk Beth home.'

'Yes, you go ahead. Have you enjoyed yourself?'

He nodded and grinned. 'I'm glad I came.'

'Good, now don't keep Beth waiting. I'll see you in the morning.'

During the rest of his leave Jack took Beth out a couple of times, and seemed quite taken with her. And, as always, Hanna, George and the boys went to the station to see him off.

'Beth said she'll write to me,' Jack told Hanna, as they waited for the train to arrive. 'I hope she does.'

'I'm sure she will. You like her.'

'We get on well together.' Jack shrugged. 'But it's early days. We've got to get to know each other, and that isn't going to be easy when I have to keep leaving, but it's the life I've chosen for myself. She seems quite happy with that, but we'll see.'

'When you meet the right girl, she will accept that you're away a lot. If she loves you and knows that the sea means a great deal to you, then she will make that her life as well. Look at Jane. The captain is away more than he's home, and yet they are very happy together.'

'You're right, of course. It's a case of finding the right one to spend the rest of your life with.' He smiled down at her. 'Just like you have in Alan.'

The train rumbled into the station and Jack jumped on, waving all the time until it was out of sight.

As always, Hanna said quietly, 'Be safe, Jack.'

Twenty-Nine

It wasn't until after Paris was liberated on August the twenty-fifth that Hanna received three letters at once from Alan, and she read them with relief. He had survived the landings without injury and appeared to be in good spirits. Then in early September rockets began to fall on London, causing more death and destruction, and their joy at the news from Europe took a dip.

'He won't give up, will he?' Pat slammed her fork into the ground to dig out some potatoes.

'That damned man can't last much longer, surely?' Jean tossed the vegetables into a sack and tied it up. 'But it's taking longer than expected to reach Germany, and with winter just round the corner, that will slow things up even more. This waiting is all the more frustrating because we know the end must now be near. The only problem is, that man in Germany doesn't seem to have received the message yet.'

'Well, hang on a bit until we've cleared this field and then I'll nip over and tell him, shall I?' Pat joked.

Hanna laughed. 'Good idea, Pat, but I can't see the war being over by Christmas, as everyone was predicting, can you?'

'I doubt it.' Pat grimaced. 'Still, there's no point fretting about it. We've got plenty to keep us busy.'

They worked silently for another hour. It was back-breaking work, but it had to be done, and Hanna was quite pleased when it was time to go and collect the boys. 'I've got to go, girls,' she called.

They waved and Hanna hurried off to make herself present-able before going to the village.

When she reached the school it was still ten minutes to go before they all came out so she looked in at the store to say hello to Beth. Since Jack had met Beth at the dance, Hanna had taken every chance to speak to her, and the more she came to know her, the more she liked her. She seemed a sensible, level-headed girl, and appeared to understand the kind of life Jack had chosen for himself.

'Hello, Beth.' The shop wasn't busy and Hanna stepped inside for a moment. 'Heard from Jack lately?'

Beth came over to her, smiling happily. 'I had a long letter two days ago. Have you any idea when he might be home again?'

'Sorry.' Hanna shook her head. 'In peace time I always had some idea when his ship would be returning, but I'm afraid that all through the war I've never even known where he is. We'll only know when he turns up.'

'Oh well, that's something to look forward to. What about your Alan? Any news from him?'

'I've heard from him at last, and he's all right.'

'My dad says that the war can't last much longer, and he reckons that the end of this year is now out of the question, but it should be over by the spring of next year.'

'Hope he's right. It seems to have been going on for ever, and I can hardly remember what it was like to be at peace.' Hanna glanced at the clock. 'Oh, I must go, or the boys will be out of school and tearing off on their own. They're always the first through the door.'

'You coming to the dance on Saturday?' Beth called as Hanna hurried towards the door.

'Yes, see you there.' Hanna ran the few yards to the school and got there just in time. She didn't have the chance to say much on the walk to the farm because the boys never stopped talking for one moment as they told her every detail of their day.

The next morning Hanna received a letter from Bob's parents, and as she read it the tears trickled down her face.

'Whatever is the matter?' Mildred's face was anxious as she sat next to Hanna. 'Nothing's happened to Jack or Alan, has it?'

'No, it's from Bob's parents. Ed was killed in the landings, but Bob and Hal have survived and are all right.'

'Oh, I'm sorry about Ed. Such nice boys, and I particularly liked Ed.' Mildred sighed and gave a sad smile. 'Do you remember how they wouldn't let us make their coffee, and couldn't stand the taste of tea?'

Hanna nodded and wiped away the tears. 'I was praying that they would all survive the war. There's been so much suffering and destruction, and all because of one man. I'll be glad when it's all over.'

'So will we all!'

The winter dragged by and they listened avidly to the news bulletins, waiting, hoping, that the end wasn't far off now. When spring finally arrived they were shocked by the news that President Roosevelt had died on April twelfth, and sad that he hadn't lived long enough to see the victory that was surely about to come.

Then on April thirtieth the news came that Hitler had committed suicide, and they knew that now it could only be a matter of days before this awful conflict finally came to an end.

'Hanna! Hanna!' The boys ran into the garden waving little flags. 'It's over! The war's over!'

Right behind them were Jane, George, Mildred and Pete, quickly followed by Pat and Jean.

'Germany has surrendered!' George was rubbing his hands together in excitement. 'May the seventh will go down in history as a great day!'

'We're going to have a big party tomorrow.' The boys' faces were glowing, picking up on everyone else's joy.

'We certainly are.' Pat took hold of the boys' hands and danced them round and round. 'We're going to line the village street with tables, and decorate everywhere.'

'We're going to need everyone's help,' Jean told them, 'and any food you can supply.'

'That will be my job.' Mildred appeared delighted at the prospect of providing food for a party.

That evening everyone from the farm gathered in the sitting room to celebrate the end of the war in Europe, their thoughts going out to those who weren't able to be with them. The boys were now old enough to understand, and were allowed to stay up for a while so they could join in. They were far too excited to sleep, anyway.

Pat raised her glass. 'Here's to all our men, and may they come home soon safe and sound.'

'Soon!' Jean couldn't stop smiling. 'And we can start to live our normal lives again.'

'What are you both going to do now?' George asked the two Londoners. 'You've been a great help around the farm and I'll miss you if you go.'

'Ah . . . well.' Pat looked at Jane. 'We was going to have a word with you about that. We've grown fond of our homes here, and the kids are happy at the village school. Our homes in London are just a great damned hole in the ground, and none of us fancy going back to that. We like living in the country, so do our kids. They've got room to run and play in green fields instead of grey concrete. Our blokes like it here as well, so . . .'

'Then you must stay,' Jane said, before Pat had time to finish what she was going to say. 'The cottages are yours for as long as you want them. Wait until your men come home for good and then decide what you would all like to do, but as far as I'm concerned, I will be happy to have you stay in the cottages.'

'Oh, thank you!' Both women smiled with obvious relief, and Jean said, 'That's taken a load off our minds. We know you've said before that we could stay, but we wasn't sure. Can we both still help George on the farm? Part time, of course.'

'Yes, if that's what you want. Arrange it with George, and I know he will be glad of your help.'

'I certainly will. You're a couple of very good workers.' George smiled, pleased.

By nine o'clock all the children were having a job to keep their eyes open, so Hanna put the boys to bed, and then found somewhere for the other children to sleep until their parents left the party. Her thoughts naturally rested on Jack and Alan, wondering where they had been when the news of Germany's surrender had come through.

'What's going on?' Jack rushed up on deck when he heard the ship's sirens blasting away. They were only a couple of hours from reaching Liverpool, but this was a hell of a racket to be making. The deck was crowded and just as he arrived a Spitfire roared overhead and executed a beautiful victory roll, one of the escort ships steamed past sounding a horn, and men were cheering.

Jack stood there, mouth open as it dawned on him – the war must be over! There was no way the ships would be making all this noise otherwise, even if they were nearing the coast. Someone spun him round and he looked into Frank's beaming face, and Bill was thumping him on the back.

'We made it, lad! The war is over at last.' Bill had to shout to make himself heard. 'We've been saving a little keg of rum for just this occasion. We're going to have one hell of a celebration.'

Frank was busy handing round mugs with a small tot of rum in them, and there was much laughter as the mugs were swiftly emptied. Then a voice came over the speakers, 'Let's get this ship into dock.'

They all rushed to their stations, and as they made their way into the docks, Jack knew that this moment was something he would never forget. Everyone was cheering and smiling, joy and relief on each face.

'I know we've been expecting this, but it still came as a bit of a shock. How do you feel now the war for us is really over?' Bill asked, when they were safely docked.

'Stunned,' Jack admitted. 'It's hard to grasp it's all over, and not only that, but we are still in one piece. I can hardly believe we have survived.'

Bill shook his head. 'That's nothing short of a miracle, lad. Thousands of merchant seamen didn't live to see this day. And we mustn't forget that.'

'We won't.' Frank sighed deeply. 'Now we can get back to being sailors again, instead of targets for the U-boats.'

'And you had better get around to marrying that girl of yours, Frank. You've got no excuse now, and she's waited long enough.'

'First thing I'm going to do when I get home, Bill.'

After a wild night of partying, and the prospect of two weeks' leave in front of him, Jack made his way to the farm. On his way he saw that the entire country was celebrating; flags were flying everywhere, and the streets were crowded. He was looking forward to seeing Hanna again, and Beth. They had been writing regularly and now he would have the time to get to know her better. He also wanted to find out if Alan was all right, and he really hoped so. Alan would make Hanna a good husband, and she deserved a happy home and family of her own. Those years in the orphanage would have been unbearable if it hadn't been for her. He'd had someone to turn to, but she had shouldered all the responsibility and stood alone. It was only after they had both left the orphanage that he had fully recognized what she had done for him. She had only been a child herself, and in her quiet way had shown great strength of character. And that strength had shone through when he had boarded his first ship. It must have torn her apart, but there had been no fuss or tears; she had let him go with her blessing and a smile on her face. His sister really was something special, and he hoped Alan knew that.

When he walked into the farm there wasn't a soul around, and remembering the street parties he'd seen on his way here, he dumped his bag and walked to the village.

The party was in full swing, and he just stood there for a while, taking in the scene. There was a long table down the middle of the road, full of sandwiches and cakes, obviously provided by the entire village. It took a few moments to locate Hanna, and he smiled when he saw her with Beth. They were both laughing and trying to control some of the excited children.

Suddenly Hanna turned as if sensing him there, and started waving, grabbing hold of Beth's arm. Both of them came towards him and he hugged Hanna and then Beth, delighted to be home with them and able to celebrate the end of the war in Europe. 'Ah, it's good to see you both, and enjoying yourselves.'

'Welcome home, Jack,' Hanna laughed. 'You're just in time to give us a hand. This party is turning out to be hard work.'

'Jack!' The boys had spotted him at last and came tearing towards him, broad grins on their faces, and hands covered in jam.

He dodged behind his sister and Beth, pretending that he needed their protection from the onslaught. 'Hold it, boys!'

he cried in mock terror. 'You're too big now for me to take you both on at once.'

'No we're not!' Screaming with laughter they began to try and get to him, causing everyone in the street to stop and watch to see what all the fun was about.

Jack took off, dodging round the tables, with the twins in hot pursuit.

Hanna watched and felt a tear of pure relief running down her cheek. She swiped it away. This was no time for tears, but it was such a relief to know that at last Jack would be safe in the profession he had chosen for himself. The next time he sailed away there wouldn't be U-boats stalking his ship any more.

'It's been a worrying time for you, hasn't it?' Beth said, noticing the moisture in Hanna's eyes.

She nodded. 'I was terrified for him, and struggled all through the war not to show it. We could so easily have lost him, and nearly did at least once. I expect there were many other times he never mentioned, but when war came he was determined to stay in the merchant navy, and I respected that. Over these desperate years I've watched him grow into a fine man.'

'Yes, he has.' Beth smiled at Hanna. 'But I think we had better go and rescue him. He's got at least a dozen kids after him now.'

The village celebration had been a huge success and enjoyed by all, and later that evening they sat around the kitchen table, exhausted.

Beth had come back with them, and Hanna felt a wonderful sense of contentment, thinking that all she needed now was Alan here as well, and her happiness would be complete.

Thirty

'Nothing for you again, Hanna.' The elderly postman smiled apologetically. 'Your young man is probably on his way home and hasn't had time to write. There are thousands of troops all over the place, and it will take some time to get them all home.'

'Of course.' She nodded as she took a letter for Jane from him, knowing he was trying to be comforting. 'Thanks, Fred.'

Hanna found Jane in the kitchen talking to Mildred. All through the war they had all lived together at the farm as one family, supporting each other through the rough times of the long war. Now, four weeks on, they were each looking to the future. Hanna knew that Jane wanted to go back to London, but was reluctant to take the boys out of their school where they were happy. Jack's future was clear to him: the merchant navy. Even after all he had gone through over the last few years, his enthusiasm and love of the sea had not diminished one little bit. In fact he was now going to start studying, and hopefully work his way up to becoming an officer one day. He had also found a lovely girl, who seemed to understand that the sea was his life, and he was obviously more than fond of her. It looked as if Beth felt the same about Jack, and Hanna couldn't be more pleased for both of them. Her future was with Alan, but this long delay in hearing from him was unsettling. It just wasn't like him, and she knew letters were coming through from Germany because Pat and Jean were getting them without much delay. So why hadn't she heard from Alan?

'Letter for you.' She handed it to Jane and sat down at the kitchen table, checking there was hot tea in the pot, and pouring herself a cup.

'Thanks.' Jane noted Hanna's empty hands after she took the letter from her. 'Wasn't there anything for you?'

'Not today.' Hanna smiled and stood up, not wanting to

show her concern. She was probably worrying over nothing. It must be chaotic in Europe at this time, and it wouldn't be surprising if Alan didn't have the time to write at the moment. 'I'll go and see if Pat and Jean need any help.'

'Sit down, Hanna,' Jane ordered gently. 'I've come to know you quite well over the years, and I count you as a friend, so won't you tell me what's bothering you? And don't try to tell me that nothing is, because I won't believe you. I know you well enough to understand that you try to keep your feelings to yourself, but you have a very expressive face.'

Hanna sighed and sat down again. 'I haven't heard from Alan, or his parents, for some time, and that isn't like any of them. Mr and Mrs Rogers have written every week without fail, and you know I get loads of letters from Alan. Sometimes two or three at once, but I've had nothing for ages. I don't like this silence, and I do admit that it is worrying me.'

'It does seem strange, but give it a while longer, and if you don't hear within the next couple of weeks then you had better go to London and see Alan's parents.' Jane smiled. 'Try not to worry too much, Hanna. It's probably just a glitch in the postal system.'

'You're right, of course, and I'm just being silly.'

'You are never silly, Hanna.'

She gave a dry laugh. 'I wish that were true. Now I'd better get on with some work.'

She found Pat on her own checking on the lambs. 'Growing fast, aren't they?' she said, joining Pat in the field. 'Where's Jean?'

Pat beamed. 'Her Bert came home last night so George told her she wouldn't be needed today. He just walked in, and we didn't even know he was on his way home.'

'That's wonderful news!' Hanna felt a sense of relief sweep through her. That's what Alan would do. She was worrying over nothing. 'Your Charlie won't be far behind then.'

'Hope not.' Pat sighed. 'It will be so good to have them back. Any idea where Alan is?'

'None at all,' was all she said. 'Will your husbands be happy to stay here?'

'We talked it over with Bert last night, and he was all for

us staying. There's nothing in London for us and we love the cottages. We've never had such a nice place to live in before, and our kids think it's paradise. Bert and Charlie are good mates and both lorry drivers, so Bert said they might get a couple of old lorries and do them up. He reckons there will be plenty of them for sale, and they should be able to find loads of work around here.' Pat shoved her hands in her pockets and gazed at the field of sheep. 'Bert and Charlie often talked about how they'd like to work for themselves. This could be their chance.'

'That sounds exciting, Pat. I do hope it all works out for you.'

Pat nodded, her expression serious now. 'You too, Hanna. We've all got to start picking up the pieces and look to the future. Been afraid to do that, haven't we, not knowing if our men were going to survive. We've been lucky, when so many haven't. It's been a terrible waste of young lives.'

'It certainly has, but we've got a lot to be grateful for,' Hanna said in agreement. 'Now, what's your next job?'

'Greenhouse, nipping out shoots on the tomato plants.'

'Not my favourite job,' Hanna grimaced. 'But come on, it will get done quicker with the two of us.'

'I was hoping you'd say that.' Pat grinned, as they made their way towards the greenhouse.

Another two weeks went by and there was still no word from Alan or his parents. Now she was getting not only worried, but frightened as well. Something was going on and no one was telling her, and when she thought about that, anger began to mingle with her other emotions. All manner of reasons were running through her mind, and she didn't like any of them.

'What is it, Hanna?' Pat sat beside her on the garden seat. 'You look so unhappy, and that isn't like you.'

'I still haven't heard from Alan or his parents,' she blurted out. 'I don't understand it. If something has happened to him Mr and Mrs Rogers would surely have let me know straight away. And if he's changed his mind about wanting to marry me, then he should have the decency to tell me, not leave me like this wondering what the hell is going on. I can't go on like this, Pat. One minute I'm worried in case something has happened to him, and the next I'm angry he hasn't had the courage to tell me he's changed his mind about us. I'm not a weakling, Pat. I've had to deal with plenty of hard knocks in the past, and I'm sure there will be many more in the future.'

'I'm sure Alan hasn't changed his mind,' Pat said firmly. 'There must be another reason for this silence.'

'I'm not so sure. The more I think about it, the more certain I feel that he might have met someone else.' Hanna shook her head. 'Such a lot has happened since we met, and the war has changed everyone. He could feel quite different about us now.' She looked at Pat, her expression anguished. 'It would break my heart, but I would understand. Whatever is going on, I've got to know!'

'There's only one way to find out, Hanna. Go to London and see Alan's parents. You can't keep torturing yourself like this.'

Hanna stood up quickly. 'You're right, and Jane has told me the same thing. I've been waiting and hoping it wouldn't be necessary, but I've had enough. I'll leave first thing in the morning.'

With Jane's permission to stay in London for as long as necessary, Hanna caught an early train and went straight to Mr and Mrs Rogers' house. Mr Rogers opened the door, and for a moment he just stared at her as if he didn't know what to say. Her insides churned, he looked pale and had dark smudges under his eyes. Something was definitely wrong, and she wasn't going to leave until she found out what it was.

When he didn't speak, she said, 'Hello, Mr Rogers, can I come in, please?'

'Oh, yes.' He stood back and let her step inside. 'I wasn't expecting you.'

Obviously, she thought, walking straight into the front room. Mrs Rogers was there, and when her husband went and stood beside his wife, Hanna faced them. 'I've come because I want to know why I haven't heard from Alan or you since the war ended six weeks ago. If Alan has changed his mind about us then I expect him to tell me.'

'Oh no, Hanna!' Mrs Rogers stepped forward. 'Alan's loved you from the moment he saw you in Mrs Harcourt's. That hasn't changed.'

Hanna frowned at Mrs Rogers' distress. 'Then what is going on?'

'Tell her,' Alan's mother said to her husband. 'We shouldn't have kept this from her. She has a right to know.'

He nodded and took hold of Hanna's hands. 'We didn't want to worry you unnecessarily, and we – I – decided to wait until we had more definite news. I'm sorry, my dear, we should have told you as soon as the notification came through, but we kept waiting and hoping that it wouldn't be necessary.'

Alan's father was rambling and not telling her anything, so she said firmly, 'Is Alan all right? I want to know now!'

'We don't know.' Mr Rogers sighed deeply. 'Three days after the war officially ended we received a telegram saying that Alan was missing. A couple of days after that we received a letter from his commanding officer. It seems that Alan went on a patrol with three other men the day the Germans surrendered, and none of them have been seen since. We were hoping desperately that he would turn up quite quickly.'

'But he hasn't.' Hanna's voice was shaking with unshed tears. 'You should have told me.'

'I know, and I'm sorry, my dear, but you've had such a lot of worry with your brother. Your life hasn't been easy and I didn't want to add to your concerns if we didn't have to.'

'And you think leaving me to imagine all sorts of things was a better idea?' She shook her head in disbelief, anger burning through her grief. 'The fact that I grew up without a family has nothing to do with this! Thousands of people in this war have had to deal with distressing losses, some more than others, and like them, I deal with what life throws at me in the best way I can. I would much rather have the facts, and then I know what I'm facing. I've learnt to swing with the blows, and so has Jack. You had no right to leave me floundering like this!'

'We know that now, and I do believe you are stronger than we are.' Mrs Rogers came and hugged her. 'Please don't be angry with us, Hanna. We were only trying to protect you, and that was wrong of us. The war is over and our boy is missing, and we just haven't been thinking straight.'

As the anger drained away, Hanna took a deep breath, all too aware that this was their only child they were talking about. They must also be devastated that this had happened, and right at the end of the fighting too. 'I'm not angry with you now,' she said quietly. 'I understand that you were only doing what you thought was right.'

'But it wasn't, was it?' Mr Rogers looked contrite.

'No.' Hanna shook her head, struggling to keep her grief at bay. 'But what's done is done. We can't change that so let's put it behind us. I've already forgotten it.'

'Thank you, Hanna,' Alan's parents said together.

'Sit down, my dear, and I'll make us a nice cup of tea. I'm sure we all need one, and a bite to eat, because you must be hungry after your journey.' Mrs Rogers took Hanna's hand for a moment, tears in her eyes. 'We're so glad you're here.' Then she hurried out to the kitchen.

Mr Rogers sat down and took a deep shuddering breath, running his hand through his still abundant hair. 'This is damned hard to take. Another day and Alan would have been safe. Can you stay for a while, my dear? It would be a great comfort to both of us. We feel lost and helpless.'

'I don't have to rush back. Jane – Mrs Harcourt – has told me to stay as long as I need to.' Hanna stood up to help with the tray of tea and sandwiches.

'That would be lovely, Hanna. Mrs Harcourt seems to be a kind woman.' Mrs Rogers handed round the cups. 'It would be a blessing to have you with us. The waiting is so hard.'

'I know. When Jack was missing I never gave up hope that he was alive. He turned up eventually, battered and weak, but he came back to me. I'm going to believe that Alan will also come home, and until we hear anything else that's what I'll hold to again. Waiting is hard and distressing, but that's what we must do – that is all we can do. Wait.'

Thirty-One

Three days later there was still no news of Alan, and Hanna was working in the Rogers' small back garden in an effort to keep busy. She felt stifled being back in London, and longed for the open countryside once again where she could go out into the field with the sheep and let her grief come to the surface. She didn't dare do that here because it would only distress Alan's parents even more. She needed to be strong for them, but keeping her feelings bottled up inside was making her feel ill. The thought that she might never see Alan again was unbearable, and when those thoughts came into her head she fought hard to banish them. Keeping hope alive was her one aim.

'Hanna, we've never had such a tidy garden, but this isn't necessary.'

She glanced up at Mr Rogers. 'I like to keep busy.'

'I can see that, and I can also see that you are missing the farm. You must go back, my dear. We've been grateful for your company, but there isn't anything more you can do for us, and we're being selfish keeping you here. Go home, dear, and I'll come and see you the moment we have any news. I promise,' Alan's father added.

'Well, if you're sure? I admit that I am missing the country-side. I really wouldn't want to come back to London to live.'

He nodded. 'And I know Alan feels the same. He told us he wants to become a country copper.'

When Hanna saw the pain flood his expression, she clasped his arm. 'I know this seems to be going on and on, but we mustn't give up. Alan could have been taken prisoner at the last minute, or something like that. There's still hope, and we must believe that there is.'

He bent and kissed her cheek. 'You're a brave and sensible girl, and our Alan is lucky to have found you.'

'I've always thought I was the lucky one. You know, when

he came to the Harcourts' that day with Talbot, I was so frightened, but Alan was kind and he dealt firmly with Talbot. I've loved him from that first meeting, and always will.'

'And he feels the same about you, and I'm sure if he's still alive out there, he will do everything in his power to get home again.' Mrs Rogers joined them and gave a tired smile. 'Go home, Hanna, and thank you for spending this time with us. It has meant a great deal to us.'

Seeing they meant it, she accepted gratefully, yearning to get back to the place she now called home, and the comfort of having her friends around her.

There wasn't a train until three that afternoon, so Hanna stayed and had lunch with the Rogers and then made her way to the station. On the journey back she sat quietly on a corner seat, gazing out of the window, and concentrated on the passing scenery, not wanting to let her thoughts dwell too much on what might have happened to Alan. To think that his young life could have been taken from him, and their chance of happiness together snatched from them, hurt so much it made her want to double up in pain.

It was quite late when she arrived back at the farm, but Mildred insisted she have a proper meal, although she didn't feel like eating. They all wanted to know how she had got on in London, and when she told them that Alan had been posted as missing, they were all very upset. Understanding how distressing this was for her, they didn't press for details of her visit, leaving her to go to bed and get some rest.

Alone in her room that night she allowed the tears to flow for the first time since she'd heard the awful news about Alan. And it was a relief to let her grief come to the surface.

The next morning she was out in her beloved garden, working hard. She had only been away a short time, but there was plenty to do. The weeds sprang up as soon as you took your eyes off them.

'Hanna.'

Feeling a hand on her shoulder she looked up, and then scrambled to her feet, hugging her brother. 'Jack! Oh I'm so glad to see you!'

He rocked her gently. 'I've just heard about Alan. You mustn't give up hope.'

'I won't.' She stood back to gaze up at her brother. 'I swear you grow taller every time you come home.'

'I hope not. I already top six feet.' He studied her face intently. 'Alan will come back, Hanna.'

'Of course he will, but the waiting for news is hard, Jack. Every time things seem to be going well for us life throws another brick at us. But do you know?' There was a determined glint in her eyes. 'I'm going ahead with our plans. The boys will be going to a private school next year, and Jane will be returning to her home in London. George said I can work at the farm for a wage, and a small cottage in the village will be up for rent after Christmas. I'd already said I'd have it before the news about Alan arrived. He said he wants to live here as well, so that's how it's going to be. All of us are going to make our home here, no matter what happens.'

'Good.' He smiled down at her. 'You can show me the cottage while I'm here. I've got two weeks.'

'Oh, that's wonderful! We'll see the cottage tomorrow, and Beth will be so pleased to see you.'

'I can't wait.' He took hold of her hand. 'But Mildred told me dinner will be ready in thirty minutes, so I'll eat first and then go to the village and see Beth.'

'Have you seen Greg?' she asked, as they walked towards the house.

'We met a couple of weeks ago and were able to spend an evening together. We don't see each other very often, but we keep in touch. Bob's back home, evidently, and so is Hal. Do you know if Bill Freeman survived the war?'

'Yes, and he'll be out of the navy by the end of the year, Jane told me. He was only in for the duration of the war.'

'That's good news. He's a fine man. Saved our lives, and then went out of his way to see we were treated well.'

The next afternoon Jack surveyed the cottage Hanna would be renting, and nodded his approval. 'Very nice, Hanna. There's only one thing, there aren't any roses around the door,' he joked. 'You've got to put roses round the door, just like we always dreamed of having.'

'That will be my first job. It looks small but it has two bedrooms and a small box room upstairs, so there will be plenty of room for all of us.'

'That's fine, and I'll have the box room because I'm only home for a short time after each trip.'

Hanna looked at her brother in horror. 'I'm not putting you in a box room! You'll have a proper bedroom, and no arguments about it. This will be the home we've always promised ourselves. I've already talked this over with Alan, and he agrees.'

When her voice broke slightly, Jack folded her in his arms. 'Easy, Hanna, this will make a lovely home for all three of us.'

She gulped, and managed to smile. 'It will. We can't go inside at the moment because it's still occupied, but I'll show it to you properly as soon as it's empty. Now, I've got to get back. Are you coming or staying in the village?'

'Beth isn't free until after six o'clock, so I'll walk back with you.'

They had just reached the yard when Hanna stopped suddenly and gripped her brother's arm. 'That's Alan's father talking to George and Jane. There must be news! Oh, please God, let it be good!'

'Let's find out.' Jack took hold of her arm and urged her forward.

The moment Alan's father saw her he waved, a broad smile on his face, and Hanna had a job to keep her shaking legs moving.

'My dear,' he said, coming to meet her. 'News arrived this morning. Alan's safe and on his way home. He should be here some time within the next couple of days.'

'Oh, thank God!' If it hadn't been for Jack's supporting arm she would have collapsed with relief. 'Is he all right? Where has he been?'

'We haven't any details yet. We'll have to wait for Alan to tell us because all we've had so far is a brief note saying he's safe and will be home soon. Will you come back to London with me? He'll want to see you as soon as he arrives.'

'Go and pack your bag, Hanna,' Jane said. 'You must stay

for as long as you want to.' She turned to Mr Rogers, smiling. 'If Alan needs a peaceful place to rest, then he is welcome here, and perhaps you and your wife would also like to come and stay for a while.'

'Oh, that's very kind of you, Mrs Harcourt. We'll see how Alan is when he gets home, and I'm sure a holiday here would do all of us good.'

'That's settled then. I'll leave it up to you.'

'I'll come with you, Hanna.'

She smiled up at her brother and shook her head. 'I'll be all right now I know Alan is safe. You spend some time with Beth, and I'll be back before you leave again.'

'I need to go to the house,' Jane told them, 'so I'll travel up with you. Mildred will look after the boys for a couple of days.'

Once all arrangements were made they caught the next train to London.

They went straight to check that Alan hadn't come home yet, and when he hadn't, Jane asked, 'Would you mind if I take Hanna to my house for a couple of hours? She won't be long, I promise.'

Alan's parents didn't mind, and Hanna was curious. 'What do you want me to do?'

'Nothing.' Jane smiled as she opened the door. 'I just want to show you something.'

The housekeeper was out when they walked in and Hanna followed Jane up the stairs to the master bedroom, watching as she took something out of the huge wardrobe and laid it on the bed.

Jane looked quite excited. 'Take the wrappings off, Hanna.'

Wondering what all this could be about, Hanna removed the dust sheet and loads of tissue paper to reveal what was underneath. She gasped when she saw the exquisite creation. 'Oh, that's beautiful!'

'It was my wedding dress. Try it on, Hanna. It should fit you as we're about the same height, and I was as slim as you are before I had the twins.'

'But . . . but . . .' Hanna was lost for words.

Seeing her confusion, Jane began to undo the buttons.

'With everything still rationed you are not going to be able to buy a really good dress for your wedding, and this one is here doing nothing. Try it, and if you don't like it you don't have to wear it.'

'How could I not like it?' Hanna shook her head, not being able to believe this was happening. The dress on the bed must have cost a fortune.

'Come on, my dear, at least try it on,' Jane urged, holding it up.

Quickly slipping out of her frock, Hanna let Jane help her into the lace and satin gown, sighing with pleasure as it slipped into place and the buttons all down the back were fastened.

'That's a perfect fit. We won't have to alter a thing. You look so beautiful, but let us add the finishing touch.' Jane wiped a bit of moisture away from her eyes as she opened another box containing a flowing veil and tiara. She fussed getting everything in place, and then stepped back, head on one side as she studied Hanna. 'Perfect – just perfect. Take a look.'

Hanna stood in front of the long mirror, hardly able to believe that the reflection was of her. 'Can I really wear this?' she whispered.

'You've become like a daughter to us, Hanna, and we would be very proud to see you walking down the aisle in the dress I wore on my wedding day.'

'And I would be proud to wear it.' Hanna gulped back the emotion. 'I don't know what to say. Thank you seems so inadequate.'

'It will do just fine.' Jane began to remove the veil. 'Alan wants the wedding day to be special for you, and so do Sam and I. Now, are you going to be married from here or the farm?'

'I don't know yet. We've never discussed any details.'

'Well, if you decide on the farm, then Alan's parents can stay with us, and I'll see that the dress is safely delivered there. Once you've decided on a date, Sam will do everything he can to be there.'

'Do you think Mr and Mrs Freeman will come? That would mean so much to Jack and myself.'

'I know they would be delighted. Now, you had better get back. I promised Alan's parents that I wouldn't keep you long.'

It was another two days before Alan finally arrived home, and Hanna stood back while his parents joyfully greeted him. Then he saw her and held out his arms.

She rushed to him and was engulfed in a bear hug. 'Oh, darling, where have you been?'

'Playing hide and seek with a bunch of young German soldiers.' He laughed, standing back to take a good look at her. 'But I'll tell you about it later. We've got a wedding to plan first. We've waited long enough, and we mustn't waste another moment.'

They talked well into the night, and when Hanna told Alan about the cottage he was delighted. After much discussion, it was agreed that the wedding should be in the village church, if it could be arranged.

Hanna was pleased about that because the farm felt like her home, and everyone there her family. Alan had been determined to have all the arrangements for the wedding settled, not wanting to wait any longer before they were married, and hadn't said a word about what had happened to him. Hanna wouldn't ask, as she was all too aware that he might not be ready to talk about it yet.

However, his father wanted to know, and finally asked, 'Are you going to tell us what happened to you?'

Alan lit another cigarette and sat back. 'We were on patrol the day of the official announcement that the war was over. There were two isolated houses and they looked empty, but we decided to check them out. When we went round the back German soldiers suddenly surrounded us. We told them the war was over, but they didn't believe us. Fortunately they weren't battle-hardened soldiers, but a group of very young men. A couple of them spoke quite good English and we eventually managed to convince them that the fighting was over. They had a big discussion amongst themselves, and then told us that they would only surrender to the Americans, and we were to be their hostages. We spent our time looking for the American lines. When we eventually found them the

Germans sent me out to talk to them. I explained our situation and two came back with me. One spoke good German, and the youngsters surrendered without any fuss. It seems they were terrified of being captured, and thought they would have more chance of surviving with the Americans.' Alan shook his head. 'I'm sorry you had the worry, but we were never in danger. Those young men just wanted to surrender and go home safely, just like all of us.'

After all the talking, Alan could hardly keep his eyes open, and was looking drained. He had made light of his experiences, but Hanna could see the strain. She clasped his hand. 'I think it's time we all had some sleep, and tomorrow you can decide if you would like to come to the farm for a rest, or stay here. Jane said your mother and father can come as well.'

'Did she? Oh, I'd like that. We could go and see the vicar at the church, and get some of the arrangements in place.' Alan turned to his parents. 'What about it? Do you fancy a few days in the country?'

'We'd love to come,' they both agreed, smiling happily.

With that settled, they all slept soundly that night.

Thirty-Two

Early the next morning Hanna went to see if Jane had returned to the farm. Mrs Potter was there and told her that Mrs Harcourt had only stayed for a day, and she wouldn't let Hanna go until she heard all the news. After staying to talk to the elderly housekeeper for an hour, she returned to the Rogers house and found them all ready and waiting to catch the train.

When they reached the farm everyone was overjoyed to see them, and excited that the wedding was going to take place there. Mildred was immediately making plans for the food, and insisted on making the wedding cake herself with some ingredients she had saved for a special occasion. 'I've even got some icing,' she told them proudly. 'So you'll have a proper wedding cake.'

Jack brought Beth back after she had finished work, and when Hanna asked her to be her bridesmaid, she was thrilled. Then Jack, Alan and Jane spent some time trying to fix a date when they would all be home. It wasn't easy with the captain and Jack so often at sea, but they finally managed to settle on a date in six weeks' time. After dinner they went to the village pub for a celebration, leaving the twins in the capable care of Mildred.

The next morning Hanna and Alan went to see the vicar, and as Hanna had lived in the village for five years he was quite happy to marry them. He understood about them wanting the sailors in the family to be present, and gave them the date they asked for, saying that they could change it if any problems arose.

Jack was waiting to see how they got on when they came out of the church, and as Hanna wanted her brother to take their father's place and give her away, she was still concerned in case he was unable to get home.

'I'll be here,' he told her, when she voiced her worry to him again. 'Nothing will keep me away.'

There was such certainty in his voice that Hanna knew he meant what he said and smiled in relief. 'Beth will make a lovely bridesmaid, so I'll have to talk to her about her dress, and what colour she would like. I'll only have the one. I don't think the twins would care to be pageboys.'

This produced roars of laughter, and Alan mopped his brow in mock horror. 'I can just imagine the chaos they could cause.'

'The boys aren't that bad!' she protested, trying to keep a straight face. 'But we must find a role for them or they'll be upset to be left out.'

'Hmm.' Alan murmured thoughtfully. 'They could stand at the door and hand out buttonhole flowers to anyone who hasn't got one.'

'That should do,' Jack nodded. 'But we'll need someone to keep an eye on them. Can I invite Bill and Frank from the ship, with their families, of course? Bill will keep them in line.'

'Of course you can. It would be lovely if they could come, wouldn't it, Alan?'

'Absolutely. We'd all love to meet your friends, Jack.'

The time flew by, and by the end of the week everything was in place for the wedding. Once that was done Alan started to think about his future. 'I'm just going to the village police station to have a word with them.'

Hanna wished him luck, praying that this would be possible for him, because she knew how much he wanted to live and work in the village.

He was only gone about an hour, and when he came into the garden to see her, he was smiling. 'There will soon be a vacancy, because the constable stayed on beyond retirement to help out during the war, as you already know, and will be leaving within the next month. I've got to put in for the position, of course, but with my record in the London police force there shouldn't be any problems. They are going to keep the job open for me.'

'That's wonderful! I've got more good news. Jane said that we can live here until the cottage is ready.'

'That's good of her.' They sat on the garden seat in the sunshine, and he nodded with satisfaction. 'Well, I'd say everything is set. Now all I've got to do is get out of this khaki uniform and back into my navy blue.'

Two days later Alan left to report back and get demobbed. Jack would also be leaving early the next morning, and Hanna was up before dawn to see her brother had a good breakfast before he left.

They walked outside and stood in the tranquil garden, drinking in the peace of the moment. Jack draped an arm around Hanna's shoulder, and gazed up at the sky just beginning to show a touch of light. 'I remember when we did this at the docks before I boarded my first ship.'

Hanna nodded. 'We welcomed that dawn as a new day and a new life ahead of us.'

'Little did we know,' Jack sighed, 'just what a long and perilous day it was going to be. But we made it through, Hanna.'

'Yes we did, and it has been a hard road to travel, but we are in a very different position now. Then we had nothing – no home, no family, and only the clothes we stood up in. Now I have Alan, you have Beth and a way of life you love, and friends surround us. It has been a long hard day, as you said, but I couldn't ask for more, Jack.'

'Neither could I. Look, there's the sun coming to shine on another new day for us.' He smiled down at his sister. 'It won't be perfect; in with the good times we'll still have problems to face in the future, but I think we're up to it, don't you?'

'Without a doubt.' She lifted her face to catch the first rays of the sun, and said softly, 'Welcome to our new day, and a new beginning.'